PRAISE FOR
THE *NEW YORK TIMES* BESTSELLING
SECOND CHANCE CAT MYSTERIES

"A surefire winner."
—Miranda James, *New York Times* bestselling author

"An affirmation of friendship as well as a tantalizing whodunit, *The Whole Cat and Caboodle* marks a promising start to a series sure to appeal to anyone who loves a combination of felonies and felines."
—*Richmond Times-Dispatch*

"Ryan kicks off the new Second Chance Cat Mystery series with a lot of excitement. Her small Maine town is filled with unique characters . . . This tale is enjoyable from beginning to end; readers will look forward to more."
—*RT Book Reviews*

"Cozy readers will enjoy the new Second Chance Cat series."
—*Gumshoe Review*

"If you enjoy a cozy mystery featuring a lovable protagonist with a bevy of staunch friends, a shop you'd love to explore, plenty of suspects, and a super smart cat, you'll love *The Whole Cat and Caboodle*."

—MyShelf.com

"Enjoyable . . . Remember, everyone has a secret, even the cat."
—*Kings River Life Magazine*

"I am absolutely crazy about this series . . . The cast of characters is phenomenal . . . I loved every minute of this book."
—Melissa's Mochas, Mysteries & Meows

Titles by Sofie Ryan

THE FAST AND THE FURRIEST

A SECOND CHANCE CAT MYSTERY

Sofie Ryan

BERKLEY PRIME CRIME
New York

BERKLEY PRIME CRIME
Published by Berkley
An imprint of Penguin Random House LLC
375 Hudson Street, New York, New York 10014

Copyright © 2018 by Darlene Ryan
Excerpt from *A Whisker of Trouble* copyright © 2016 by Darlene Ryan
Penguin Random House supports copyright. Copyright fuels creativity, encourages
diverse voices, promotes free speech, and creates a vibrant culture. Thank you for buying
an authorized edition of this book and for complying with copyright laws by not
reproducing, scanning, or distributing any part of it in any form without permission.
You are supporting writers and allowing Penguin Random House to continue to
publish books for every reader.

BERKLEY is a registered trademark and BERKLEY PRIME CRIME and the B colophon
are trademarks of Penguin Random House LLC.

ISBN: 9781101991220

First Edition: February 2018

Printed in the United States of America
1 3 5 7 9 10 8 6 4 2

Cover art by Mary Ann Lasher
Cover design by Katie Anderson

Acknowledgments

As always, I appreciate the support and encouragement of my friends, both online and off. Special thanks go to my editor, Jessica Wade, as well as Miranda Hill and Tara O'Connor. My agent, Kim Lionetti dons many hats on my behalf: advisor; manager; hand-holder; and cheerleader, and wears them all well. A huge thank-you goes to my readers. Thank you for embracing Sarah, Elvis, and the Angels. I've gotten to know so many of you from your e-mails and notes and it's been wonderful to meet so many fellow cat people. And last but never least, thank you to Patrick and Lauren for always being on my team.

Chapter 1

I set the sandwich on top of the dresser. I could tell right away that Elvis was not sold on my idea of supper. He gave the blue bubble glass plate a suspicious look and his eyes narrowed, but he didn't say a word. He was exceedingly polite, for the most part.

Not to mention he was a cat.

"What? You don't like it?" I asked. "It's peanut butter, dill pickle and bacon."

His whiskers twitched at the last word. In Elvis's world everything went better with bacon, except maybe peanut butter and dill pickles.

I picked up half the sandwich and took a bite. "It's good. I swear," I mumbled around a mouthful of creamy, salty, crispy goodness. Elvis may have been polite, but he wasn't a stickler with respect to table manners. "You know, this isn't that different from the real Elvis's favorite sandwich," I told him. "Peanut butter, banana and bacon."

The cat made a huffy sound through his nose at me. As far as he was concerned he was the "real" Elvis, a sleek black cat with a rakish scar across his nose. I reached over and stroked his fur. The top of his head was warm from the early-evening August sun. He closed his green eyes and began to purr.

I set my food down and reached for the mug that held my coffee. It was one of twelve I'd bought when a diner up in Belfast had closed and auctioned off its contents back in the spring. The mugs had replaced the mismatched yard sale collection we'd had in the staff room. I'd also bought a mint green Hamilton Beach milk shake maker and a box of 45s from the diner's jukebox to sell in the shop.

My shop, Second Chance, was a repurpose store, offering everything from furniture to housewares to musical instruments—most of it from the '50s through the '70s. It was part secondhand shop, part thrift store. Some items even got new lives, like the tub chair that in its previous incarnation had actually been a bathtub, or the china cups and saucers that were now tiny planters.

The store was located in an eighteen hundreds red-brick house, just where Mill Street began to climb uphill, in the town of North Harbor, Maine. We were on the edge of the downtown, about a fifteen-minute walk from the harbor front and close to a highway off-ramp, which made it easy for tour buses to find us.

Elvis and I had stayed late to work on my latest project: turning a small metal table with a glass top and a glass shelf into a bar cart. I'd brought the sandwich makings with me for supper, along with a bit of dry cat food for Elvis so we didn't have to go home and come back again. Second Chance had been busy all day. We'd been open for more than a year now and I was tickled to see that some of the same tourists who had discovered us just a few months after we'd opened were coming back again. I was happy the repurpose shop was still busy as summer began to wind down, and I was hoping that would continue into the fall, but so many customers meant that I didn't get a lot of time to work on new items to add to our dwindling inventory.

Right now we were replenishing our stock with things we were selling on consignment for Clayton McNamara. Clayton had lived in North Harbor all his life. In fact he'd been romantically involved with my grandmother—when they were both in the first grade. Their short-lived romance had ended when she kissed another man. In Gram's defense he did have two peanut butter cookies in his lunchbox.

At the urging of his daughter and his nephew, my friend Glenn, the old man was trying to make some space in his small house and clear out several outbuildings on the property. I'd bought some pieces of furniture and kitchen items from one of those buildings. They were projects I hoped to get to in the fall. The rest, most of which had belonged to Clayton's father, was being sold in the shop. We were getting ready to tackle the house next and we were also planning a yard sale for September. Work was pretty much all I'd been focusing on for the last couple of weeks and that was fine with me.

I took another bite of my sandwich. Elvis was the only guy in my life at the moment. "Which is also fine by me," I said aloud.

He turned to look at me and he almost looked a bit puzzled. "It's okay with me that you're the only guy in my life," I said by way of explanation, in case his confusion was from what I'd said. "You know what Liz says: 'A woman without a man is like a fish without a bicycle.'"

It was hard not to miss the irony in hearing Liz say those words. Elizabeth Emmerson Kiley French had been married and widowed twice, and everyone who met her was charmed by her—unless they made the mistake of getting on her bad side. She was smart, beautiful and tart tongued. Men, even those a lot younger than she was, tended to lose their ability to think straight around her.

Liz was one of my grandmother's oldest friends. She, along with Charlotte Elliot and Rose Jackson, were sort of my fairy godmothers. They spoiled me a lot, nagged me on occasion and weren't shy about sharing their opinion on whatever was happening in my life. I'd suggested once that Liz should learn the words to "Bibbidi-Bobbidi-Boo," the fairy godmother's song from the Disney version of *Cinderella*. Liz hadn't been shy about telling me what she thought of *that* idea.

Rose and Charlotte both worked part-time for me at Second Chance. The rest of their time was spent working at their detective agency, Charlotte's Angels, along with Rose's gentleman friend, Alfred Peterson, quite likely the world's oldest computer hacker. Mr. P. had met all the requirements for becoming a licensed private investigator set out by the state of Maine. For the past several months Rose had been working as his apprentice.

Cases just seemed to fall into their lap. Their first investigation had started when their friend Maddie Hamilton was arrested for murder. The Angels' most recent case had begun to unwind after Rose had gone to make a very unauthorized delivery to a customer and seen a body that subsequently disappeared.

The Angels didn't have a case at the moment and I was hoping it stayed that way for a while. Because when

Rose and her cohorts were investigating I always ended up getting pulled into things, no matter how vehemently I swore it wasn't going to happen this time. It had been nice to have nothing more pressing to worry about than what color to paint a trash-picked rocking chair. The only lump in the gravy was that a reality TV crew had been shooting in our neighborhood for the past three days. They were filming a pilot for some kind of treasure hunt show and the street had been clogged from early in the morning until after dark.

Thankfully, they had moved elsewhere in town right before lunch. Just that morning Rose and Elvis and I had arrived at the shop to find the parking lot more than half-full of the crew's vehicles—without my permission—and a dusty half-ton truck blocking the entrance to the space. The driver was behind the wheel, intently watching the camera crew doing something in the middle of the street several buildings away. He wore a backward Yankees ball cap and I could see several days of scruff on his face. The hat alone was enough to get him the stink eye in North Harbor, where everyone bled Sox red.

Before I could do anything, Rose had marched over to the truck and smacked the hood with the flat of her hand. The sound had echoed down the street. The driver had jumped, slopping coffee, or whatever he'd been drinking from the take-out cup he was holding, onto his shirt. As he turned toward the driver's side window I saw that the front of his green T-shirt said *Kale Yeah!*

I'd watched Rose talk to the man. He had wide shoulders and wiry arms under smooth brown skin and he seemed to be shrinking back into his seat. Although I couldn't hear Rose's words, I knew her body language.

It had struck fear in the hearts of more than one middle school student back when she was still teaching.

After a couple of minutes she came back to my SUV, a satisfied look on her face and her ubiquitous tote bag over one arm. The truck pulled away.

"What did you say to him?" I'd asked.

"I simply reminded that young man of the importance of manners and respect for other people's property," she'd said. "And I may have mentioned how many of the nice young men and women on the town's police force are former students of mine." She'd given me an innocent look that could rival any of Elvis's. "Then he remembered a previous engagement so everything worked out just fine."

"Okay," I'd said slowly, looking down the street in the direction of the camera crew. "Do you think he's involved in the production somehow?"

Rose had shaken her head. "I think he's just another looky-loo. If he were working then why wasn't he actually doing something other than blocking our parking lot?"

"Good point," I'd said. "At least I can pull in now. Thank you."

She'd smiled. "You're welcome, dear."

She'd started for the back door and I pulled into the lot. After I'd let Rose and Elvis into the shop I'd gone in search of the person in charge of the treasure hunt project. Half an hour later the crew's vehicles were still in the parking area but I had a check in my hand large enough to take the edge off my annoyance.

I ate the last bite of my supper now—fishing out a bit of bacon for Elvis—and finished my coffee. I pulled my hair up into a ponytail and then I got to work, using a

screwdriver and a thin-bladed putty knife to remove
the glass top and the shelf below it from the cart. I was
the only one still around. Rose and Mr. P. had gone to
watch *Rear Window* at the library as part of their week-
long Hitchcock film festival. Liz's teenage granddaughter, Avery, who lived with her and worked part-time for
me, had gone home for a short visit with her parents.

Liz and Charlotte were having dinner with Maddie.
The three of them had been sorting books for the upcoming library book sale. Charlotte had called earlier
to tell me that she had set aside several books she
thought might be valuable to get a second opinion from
me. I knew a little bit about old books from my mother,
who had a small collection of first editions of some classic children's books.

"Bring them with you tomorrow," I'd told Charlotte.
"I can always take photos and e-mail them to Mom if I
need to."

Mac, my right-hand man and jack-of-all-trades, was
out sailing. And my best friend, Jess, was at her shop
down on the waterfront, working on a gorgeous gold
dress for one of her customers who was planning a fall-
themed second wedding. Since everyone else was busy,
it had seemed like a good night to get some work done.

It had been a beautiful day, with the sky an endless,
cloudless blue overhead, but now heavy clouds were
rolling in from the water and I wondered if we'd get
some rain later.

For now I was happy to be outside working. Elvis
seemed content to stay just inside the garage door,
stretched out on the top of the dresser that Mac had
finished sanding and cleaning earlier in the day, watch-

ing me and making little murping comments from time to time.

Owning a repurpose shop hadn't been my plan when I graduated. I'd worked in radio after college, eventually hosting a popular evening program playing classic rock and interviewing some of the genre's best musicians. Then one day I was replaced by a syndicated music feed out of Los Angeles and a nineteen-year-old who read the weather twice an hour and called everyone "dude."

Growing up I'd spent my summers in North Harbor with my grandmother. It was where my father had been born and raised. I'd even bought a house that I'd reno-vated and rented. When my job vanished, I'd landed at Gram's planning to hide under the covers and eat grilled cheese sandwiches. I'd ended up opening Second Chance instead.

I'd been working for about half an hour, sanding the metal frame of the cart, when a white Audi roadster pulled into the parking lot. The driver, in strappy flat sandals, easily had a couple of inches on my five-foot-six height. She was in her early thirties, I guessed, and the sleeveless blue and white sundress she wore showed off her dark skin.

Her hair was a mass of gorgeous, caramel-colored ringlets, worn chin length. Like a lot of women with straight hair, I'd always secretly wanted curls like that.

This woman could easily be a model, I thought, and not just because she was so striking. She had perfect posture and she seemed to glide, not walk, as she made her way over to me. I felt grubby and sweaty in com-parison.

I pulled the sanding mask off my face and wiped the

dust from my hands with a rag. "Hi," I said, smiling at her.

She gave me a polite smile back. "I'm looking for Mac McKenzie," she said, glancing around. "Is he here?"

I shook my head. "I'm sorry. He won't be back for a while." Mac was crewing on the boat of a friend who wanted to get in some practice time before an upcoming race.

The woman exhaled softly, giving her head a little shake. "Do you by any chance know where I could find him?"

I explained about Mac being out on the water, sailing. "It'll probably be a couple of hours before they come back in. Is there anything I could help you with?"

She shook her head. "Thank you, but I need to talk to him. It's, uh, personal." She was holding what looked to be a tiny carved wooden bird and she turned it over in her fingers. Some kind of talisman or good luck charm? I wondered.

Mac had worked with me for over a year and this was the first time anyone had shown up looking for him. I couldn't help wondering why this woman I'd never seen before wanted him now. He was intensely private, so even though we worked together every day, I knew very little about his life both now, and before he'd arrived in North Harbor about eighteen months ago.

I did know that Mac had been a financial planner in Boston, but he had walked away from that life to live in Maine full-time and sail, which was his real passion. There were eight windjammer schooners based in North Harbor, along with dozens of other sailing vessels. In his free time Mac crewed for pretty much anyone who needed him. Eventually he wanted to build his own boat. He'd taken the job at Second Chance because he said he liked working with his hands.

The woman put the little carving in her pocket and offered her hand then. "I'm sorry," she said. "I should have introduced myself. I'm Erin Fellowes."

"I'm Sarah Grayson," I said, wiping my hand on my shorts before I took hers. "Mac works here with me."

She nodded. "It's nice to meet you. I'm a friend of Mac's wife, Leila."

For a moment I froze. I'm not even sure I took a breath.

Wife?

Mac had a *wife*?

Just then Elvis knocked a small recipe box off the top of the dresser. I swung around automatically and the cat gave me his best *Oh, did I do that?* look.

"Oh, I'm sorry," Erin said as though she'd been the one to nudge the turquoise plastic box onto the floor.

"It's all right," I said. "Elvis is pretty good at interrupting the conversation when he thinks he's being left out." I bent down to pick up the box and the recipe cards that had spilled out, which gave me a chance to collect myself.

Mac was married? Why didn't I know that?

"His name is Elvis?" Erin asked. She smiled at the cat—the first genuine smile I'd seen since she pulled into the lot—and extended her hand so he could sniff it.

"After the King of Rock and Roll," I said, straightening up.

Elvis was his usual charming self, tipping his head to show off the scar that cut diagonally across his nose and blinking his green eyes at her. Erin was clearly enchanted by him and started to stroke his fur.

She glanced at me and the smile faded from her face. "It's really important that I talk to Mac as soon as possible," she said.

Watching Elvis from the corner of my eye, I knew she was telling the truth. There was no change in the cat's blissful expression as she scratched behind his left ear.

I wasn't exactly sure how, but Elvis could somehow tell when a person was lying. His green eyes would narrow and one ear would turn to the side as his expression soured. It had happened enough times that I'd come to believe the behavior wasn't a coincidence. And I wasn't the only one who had noticed how Elvis reacted in response to a lie. Both Jess and Mac thought the cat was reading the same sort of physical reactions a polygraph did, which was as good an explanation as any.

"I'm staying at the Rosemont Inn," Erin said. She pulled a small spiral-bound notebook and a pen from her multicolored, cross-body bag, wrote something on one of the pages, then tore it out and handed it to me. "That's my cell number."

"I'll give it to Mac as soon as he comes back." I folded the piece of paper in half and tucked it in the pocket of my shorts.

"Thank you," she said. She hesitated for a moment. Something flashed across her face. Regret? Sadness? I wasn't sure. "Please, tell him . . . tell him I believe him."

I watched her walk across the lot, climb into the white sports car and drive away.

I turned around to find Elvis watching me.

"Mac has a wife."

"Mrr," he said, wrinkling his whiskers. It seemed that was news to him as well.

"Why didn't I know? Why didn't he tell me?" I pulled a hand over my neck. "It's not that he had any kind of obligation to tell me," I said. "But why didn't he want to?"

I closed my eyes for a moment and exhaled slowly. This was a reminder of how little of himself Mac shared—with anyone. I didn't like how shut out it made me feel. I thought of Mac as a friend—a close one. Was I wrong?

I opened my eyes and looked at Elvis, who stared back at me, his green eyes unblinking. "Enough," I said. "Mac is allowed to keep things to himself. I'm not getting crazy about this." I pulled the sanding mask back up onto my face. Elvis very wisely kept whatever he was thinking to himself.

It was about an hour and a half later that I looked up and saw Mac walking toward me across the parking lot, his backpack over one shoulder, the hood of his gray sweatshirt over his head. A week ago he'd bought a truck from Clayton McNamara. There were three vehicles on the old man's property. The half-ton wasn't pretty, but it ran well and Mac still walked a lot of places so it seemed like it would serve his purposes.

The clouds had closed ranks and it was beginning to spit rain. I'd just gotten everything moved inside the old garage. Elvis had taken refuge on the seat of a wooden rocking chair, his expression cranky at the imminent rain. I set down the rag I'd been using to clean dust off the metal table and stood up.

Mac was tall and strong with light brown skin and close-cropped black hair. He smiled and raised a hand in hello. "Looks good," he said as he ducked inside the building.

"Thanks," I said. I suddenly felt awkward and I didn't like the feeling. Mac and I were friends. Erin Fellowes showing up hadn't changed that as far as I was concerned. I fished the piece of paper with her phone number out of my pocket and held it out to him.

"The guys from the B and B?" he asked, taking the paper and frowning as he unfolded it.

I shook my head. "Erin Fellowes is looking for you."

For a moment Mac said nothing, his body went rigid and his dark eyes stayed locked on my face. Finally he spoke. "She was here." It wasn't a question.

"She said it was very important that she talks to you." I cleared my throat. "She asked me to tell you that she believes you." I stopped talking then, mostly because I really didn't know what else to say.

I watched emotions play across Mac's face—fear, surprise, embarrassment.

"I owe you an explanation," he began.

I shook my head again. "No you don't. You've always made it clear that your personal life was private and I can respect that." In the last hour and a half I'd decided that truly was how I felt.

Mac set his backpack at his feet. His movements were tight and controlled. "There are things I *want* to tell you," he said. He glanced at the slip of paper. "I'm sorry. I need to call Erin first. She wouldn't be here if it wasn't important."

I brushed bits of paint off my shirt. "I'll give you some privacy."

"Please stay," he said. He pulled out his cell phone.

I watched silently as he punched the number into the phone, wrapping my arms around my midsection almost as though I was hugging myself. After a moment he shook his head. He waited a moment and then said, "Erin, it's Mac. Please call me back." He recited his cell number and ended the call.

"She's staying at the Rosemont."

"I need to go talk to her." He put the phone in his pocket. "Can I stop by the house after?"

Behind me Elvis made a low mrr.

"Yes," I said.

He nodded. "Okay, then. I'll see you in a little while." He pulled his keys out of his pocket and started over to the truck.

I didn't move until Mac pulled onto the street. What did Erin Fellowes want to talk to him about? Why was she here?

Elvis cocked his head to one side and meowed. It seemed he had questions, too.

I shrugged. "I don't know, either," I said.

I put the rest of my supplies away and locked the garage. Then I picked up Elvis and got in my SUV. We headed for home, Elvis backseat driving the way he always did.

Mac had all the answers and I was going to have to wait until he showed up to get them.

"I hate waiting," I said, glancing over at Elvis beside me on the passenger seat. His green eyes were fixed on the road ahead of us.

"Mrr," he said, mostly as an afterthought, it seemed to me. I was fairly sure it was the cat version of "whatever."

Chapter 2

Close to two hours had passed and it was dark outside and raining before Mac knocked on my door. I was curled up on the sofa with Elvis and a bowl of buttered popcorn, watching a repeat of the last episode of *Restless Days* before the new episode of the campy nighttime soap aired in another day.

My house was an 1860s, two-story Victorian, divided into three apartments. I lived in the front unit. My grandmother lived in the upstairs apartment, or at least she had until she'd gone off on a very extended honeymoon with her new husband, John. Rose had moved into the third apartment at the back the previous winter, after her lease hadn't been renewed at Legacy Place, the senior apartment complex where she'd lived for the previous two years. Rose derisively referred to the building as Shady Pines and hadn't exactly been unhappy about being asked to leave.

I muted the TV and put the popcorn on the counter as I went to answer the door, which really wouldn't dissuade Elvis if he decided he wanted some. He craned his neck to look at the red glass bowl and then yawned and stretched out across half the sofa, rolling onto his back. Licking butter and salt from the inside of the bowl wasn't worth the effort of getting up and jumping onto the counter.

"Hi," Mac said. "I'm sorry it took so long." He looked tired. There were lines pulling at the corners of his mouth and his eyes.

"C'mon in," I said.

He followed me inside, pulling off his damp sweat-shirt. I took it from him, draping it over one of the stools at the counter. Then I grabbed the remote and turned off the TV. Elvis, who had been watching the screen upside down, rolled over and turned his attention to Mac. I sat down next to the cat, curling one leg underneath me.

Mac took the nearby chair. He leaned forward, elbows on his knees. "Sarah, did Erin say anything about why she wanted to talk to me? Or how she even knew I was here in North Harbor?"

I shook my head. "The only thing she said was that it was important that she talk to you and that she believed you." I paused. "And that she was a friend of your wife."

His gaze flicked away from mine for a moment.

"You didn't find her, did you?" I said.

He shook his head. "I went to the inn but Erin wasn't there. I checked all the nearby restaurants. I left two more messages on her phone. I drove around downtown but I couldn't find her. I even went back to the shop in case she'd decided to go back and wait for me there." He smoothed a hand back over his damp hair and turned all his attention to me. "I don't want to talk about

Erin right now, Sarah." His mouth moved as though he needed to try out what he wanted to say before he actually said the words. "You know now that I was—and still am—married."

I nodded.

He took out his wallet, pulled out a photo and handed it to me. Most people carried their photos on their phone but Mac wasn't most people.

The photograph was of a woman, in her early thirties I was guessing. It looked to have been taken on the deck of a sailboat. She had a thick mass of dark curly hair, worn loose to her shoulders, dark eyes and dark skin. But it was her smile that was so striking. Even in the small photo it lit up her face. I wondered what it was like to have that smile turned on you in person.

"This is Leila," I said, handing the picture back to him.

He nodded.

"You're still married. Where is she?"

He swallowed, then took a deep breath and let it out slowly. "She's in a long-term care facility in Providence. She's been in a coma ever since a carbon monoxide leak in our house two years ago.

It was the last thing I'd expected him to say. "I don't understand. Why . . . why aren't you there?"

It was impossible to miss the pain etched into every line on his face. "At first the police believed the leak was an accident," he said. "There were renovations going on in the house and we'd been having problems with the gas water heater, but then there were some things that made them suspect that what happened to Leila was deliberate. I was their main suspect."

I folded my arms over my chest, hugging myself against the unbelievability of what Mac was telling me. "I don't understand. What things?"

"First of all, there was nothing to suggest anyone had broken into the house. And no one had been working on the water heater that day." He cleared his throat. "The police thought it was . . . suspicious that there were no fingerprints on one section of vent pipe, but we'd had the water heater looked at twice that month. A repairman could have wiped it with a rag."

"Were you charged with anything?" I asked.

"I was never arrested, and the police finally concluded what happened was just a horrible accident, but Leila's parents filed a civil suit and went to court to get temporary guardianship of her. Eventually, I agreed to let them have control of her care." He sat stiff and unmoving on the edge of the chair, the only movement the clenching and flexing of his left hand.

"The doctors said she would never wake up. Her brain had been without oxygen for too long. It was . . . it was very hard for everyone to accept." He cleared his throat. "The only reason I agreed to let her parents have guardianship of Leila was because I knew if I didn't they would bankrupt me and there wouldn't be enough money for top-quality care for her. They kept putting up roadblocks to me seeing her. I'd put everything we had into a trust for her care and finally I left."

"I'm so sorry," I said. "I can't . . . I can't even imagine what you've been through." I couldn't. The thought of my brother, Liam, or my grandmother, or anyone else I loved being in a coma and not being able to see them was somewhere my mind wouldn't go.

Mac looked down at his feet. "I'm sorry, Sarah. I should have told you."

I shook my head. "Don't apologize. You don't owe anyone—not me, not anyone—an explanation."

His dark eyes met mine again. "At first I just didn't want to talk about it and I was still fighting with Leila's parents to at least be kept updated on how she was. And then the more time that went by, the harder it was to talk about everything."

Elvis nudged my hand with his head and I began to stroke his fur. "You think Erin being here has something to do with Leila?"

Mac nodded. "She sided with Leila's parents. I haven't spoken to her in close to two years. Why else would she be here?"

"Why now?" I asked. Elvis stretched his two front paws across my lap.

"I don't know. Something must have happened. You said she told you to tell me she believed me."

"She did," I said. "She seemed—I'm not sure—sad, sorry maybe."

"I don't know what else it could be." He pulled out his phone. "I'm going to try the hospital and see if maybe I can at least make sure Leila is all right. I get updates according to a schedule the lawyers set up so I don't know if they'll tell me anything, but it's worth a try."

There was a knock then at the door.

"I'll get that," I said. I moved the cat off my lap and got to my feet. Elvis stretched and moved into my place.

Michelle Andrews was at the door. "Hi," I said.

I was surprised to see her standing there. Michelle had been my summertime best friend when we were kids. Every year we'd just picked up where we'd left off the summer before. But we'd had a falling-out as teenagers and had just reconnected a year ago. We were slowly rebuilding our friendship and I was happy to have her back in my life. Things were complicated a little—sometimes a lot—by the fact that Michelle was a detective on the North Harbor police force, and the Angels had gotten involved in more than one of her cases, which meant I'd ended up involved, too.

Michelle rarely just stopped by. Even as I was wondering what she was doing at my door, the fact that she was dressed in her work clothes—gray trousers, a fitted, pale blue shirt with three-quarter-length sleeves and a police-issue navy blue rain jacket—was also registering.

"I'm sorry to bother you this late, Sarah," she said. "But I'm looking for Mac. Do you have any idea where he is?" Her auburn hair was pulled back in a ponytail and she wore her father's heavy gold watch on her left arm.

The popcorn I'd eaten suddenly felt like a lump of lead in my stomach. "Why are you looking for him?" I didn't mean to sound suspicious but I could hear it in my voice.

"I'm right here," Mac said behind me.

"I just need to talk to you for a minute," Michelle said. "Could we step outside?"

"No," I said, putting my hand on the doorframe. "What do you want to talk to Mac about?"

"I just have some questions." She made an offhand gesture with one hand as though this was no big deal. Some sort of internal radar told me it was.

Mac put a hand on my shoulder. "It's okay, Sarah."

I glanced back at him.

"It's fine," he said softly.

I knew it wasn't fine.

Two weekends ago it had rained all day Sunday and Elvis and I had indulged in a marathon session of *Star Trek: The Next Generation*. Whenever something went wrong on the bridge of the Starship *Enterprise* Commander William T. Riker, played by the yummy Jonathan Frakes, would call out, "Red alert!" Right now my internal warning system was doing the same thing.

"Questions about what?" I asked. I kept my hand on the doorframe. I didn't have any illusions that I could actually keep Michelle out or Mac in but the symbolism felt important.

Michelle looked at Mac. "Do you know a woman named Erin Fellowes?"

Mac's dark eyes narrowed. "Has something happened? Is Erin all right?"

"Why don't we go over to the station and get out of Sarah's way?" Michelle said. She hadn't answered Mac's questions.

"Something's wrong," he said. "Where's Erin? Has she been hurt?"

"Mac, you should call a lawyer," I said, feeling tension coil in my shoulders.

Michelle turned her attention to me. "Why does Mac need a lawyer?" she asked, once more not answering Mac's question.

"I *don't* need one," he said, an edge of aggravation in his voice.

"Because you're here asking questions," I told Michelle, ignoring what Mac had just said. "It's late. You're not checking out a reference or playing matchmaker. This has to do with a case."

I pulled my phone out of my pocket with my free hand and brought up Josh Evans's number. It said something that I had the lawyer's office and cell number on speed dial. Luckily he answered on the third ring. I explained that Michelle was at the door with questions for Mac and unlike the two of them I thought it was a bad idea for Mac to talk to her without Josh here.

"Let me talk to him," Josh said without preamble.

Wordlessly I handed the phone to Mac. He turned away and lowered his voice.

"This isn't personal," I said to Michelle. "And it doesn't mean I don't trust you."

Her expression was somber. "You're putting yourself in the middle of something you'd be better staying out of, Sarah."

"It's not the first time," I said, giving her a small smile, which I hoped could somehow lighten the mood.

I got a hint of a smile in return. "No, it's not," she agreed.

Mac touched my arm and handed the phone back. "Josh will be here in a few minutes," he said to Michelle, with what seemed to me to be a note of apology in his voice. "I told him I'd wait to talk to you until he arrived. Could you just tell me whether Erin's all right?"

Josh had obviously been more persuasive than I'd been.

Michelle's expression tightened. I probably wouldn't have noticed if I hadn't known her so well. She gestured toward the driveway. "I think it would be best if I waited outside."

I nodded. She turned away and I closed the door and made my way into the kitchen, where I started the coffeemaker. I had a feeling I was going to need a cup. Probably more than one.

"How did Josh convince you to wait for him?" I said over my shoulder to Mac.

"He said—and this is a direct quote—'Don't be such a guy. Listen to Sarah.'"

I swung all the way around to look at him. "You're making that up."

He held up both hands in a gesture of acquiescence. "I'm not. I swear."

I shrugged. "It does sound like Josh."

Mac glanced at the front door then his eyes came back to me, and the start of a smile I'd seen on his face had disappeared. "You think something happened to Erin. You think she was mugged or roughed up in some way. That's why you didn't want me to talk to Michelle without Josh."

"I think it's possible. Why else would Michelle be looking for you?" I got three mugs down from the cupboard.

His eyes darted to the door again.

I knew what he was thinking. "Don't," I said softly. "Josh will be here in five minutes, tops. He drives faster than I do. If Erin was seriously hurt or in the hospital I think Michelle would have said so."

When the coffee was ready I poured a cup for Mac and handed it to him. "There are no cookies," I said. "But I do have soda crackers and"—I did a quick mental inventory of the cupboards and the fridge—"and that's it."

Elvis had made his way to the top of his cat tower.

He lifted his head and meowed. "And Elvis seems to be willing to share his fish crackers with you."

I poured another cup and added cream and two generous spoons of sugar. "I'll be right back," I said to Mac.

"Where are you going?" he said.

"I'm taking Michelle a cup of coffee."

He reached out and caught my arm. "She's right, Sarah," he said. "You shouldn't be mixed up in this whatever this is."

"Question," I said. "What would Rose do?"

Mac rolled his eyes, letting go of my arm. "Exactly what you're about to do. Although she'd have cookies."

"You can call her a bad influence, then, because I'm taking Michelle a cup of coffee. I'll be right back."

Michelle's car was parked in front of the house. The rain had let up and she was leaning against the front passenger door, arms folded across her midsection, an expression I couldn't read on her face.

I handed her the mug without comment.

"Thank you," she said. She took a drink. "Umm, that's good."

"You're welcome," I said, stuffing my hands in my pockets. "So far, when it comes to cooking, coffee and gravy are my specialties."

"You can go a long way in life with coffee and gravy," she said. I was pretty sure I saw the corners of her mouth curve up. "Did you come out to try to wheedle some information from me?"

I shook my head. "Nah, I would have gone into Rose's apartment and gotten a couple of cookies if I wanted to do that. I just wanted to say I'm sorry. I meant what I said—calling Josh had nothing to do with me not trusting you."

For a moment she didn't say anything. She took another sip of her coffee. "I know," she finally said. Her eyes met mine and I knew she was telling the truth.

"We're good, then?" Our past estrangement had happened because I'd said something cruel in anger about Michelle's father after he'd been convicted of embezzlement, something I hadn't meant for her to hear and for a long time didn't know that she had. My words had cut her deeply and I didn't want to do that to her ever again.

"We're good." She did smile then. Just as quickly as it came, it disappeared again. "Sarah, how well do you know Mac?" she asked. She watched me over the top of her mug.

My heart started to thump in my chest and my stomach took a nervous dip. "I probably know him as well as anyone does here in town," I said, trying to keep my tone light. "And I trust him as much as I trust anyone— Jess or Rose. Or you."

She nodded but she didn't say anything else and neither did I.

Josh arrived a few minutes later. I'd known him most of my life and in a lot of ways the adult Josh wasn't that different from the kid. He wore his sandy hair in the same short, spiky style he'd sported when he was twelve, except now I was fairly certain he wasn't getting it styled at Supercuts. Thanks to a late growth spurt he was almost six feet tall and time had smoothed away a lot, but thankfully not all, of his endearing geekiness. He was wearing khaki shorts, a blue plaid shirt and deck shoes.

He looked more like the kid who had gotten five of us free chocolate-dip cones at Hawthorne's ice cream stand, arguing that their sign was deceptive, than the busy lawyer he was today.

Josh and Michelle followed me back inside, exchanging pleasantries about the weather. I knew Josh would say no to coffee, but I had two bottles of root beer in the refrigerator. I opened one, poured it over a glass of ice and handed it to him.

"Thanks, Sarah," he said. He took a long drink and then looked at Michelle. "I need a minute to talk to my client."

She nodded. "I'll wait in the hallway."

"So will I," I said.

Mac frowned. "Sarah, you don't have to go."

"Yes, she does," Josh said. He looked at me. "Thanks."

Out in the hallway I slouched against the doorframe while Michelle leaned on the wall opposite the apartment door. She checked her phone; I studied the baseboard wondering if it needed a coat of paint.

Finally I gave her a sheepish smile. "Do you want to make awkward chitchat or just go for uncomfortable silence?"

"Let's try awkward chitchat."

My mind went blank. "Uh, nice weather we've been having lately," I finally said.

Michelle laughed. "Uncomfortable silence is good, too," she said.

Luckily Josh called us back in then. "You have some questions for Mac," he said to Michelle, getting right to the point.

Her body language was all business—shoulders

squared, feet planted slightly apart, face unreadable. "Do you know a woman named Erin Fellowes?" she asked Mac again.

Mac glanced at Josh, who gave an almost imperceptible nod. "Yes. Erin is—was—friends with my wife."

Michelle knew Mac had a wife, I realized immediately. She had an excellent poker face but she wasn't so good that there wouldn't have been at least a small change of expression, a flash in her eyes, a tightening of the muscles in her jaw, if she hadn't been aware of the information.

How long had she known? I couldn't help wondering.

"Why are the police interested in Ms. Fellowes?" Josh asked. "Is she in some kind of trouble? Have you arrested her?" He adjusted the corner of his glasses with one finger. He still wore the same style of black-framed eyewear he'd worn as a kid, except now the frames were a designer brand and I doubted he'd repair them with duct tape or a length of picture frame wire if they broke.

Michelle's sharp gaze went from Josh to Mac and back to the lawyer. This time I did see the muscles in her jaw clench, and all at once I knew what she was going to say. I knew why she was here to talk to Mac. Still, I waited to hear the words, hoping I would somehow be wrong.

"I'm sorry to have to tell you this," she said. "Erin Fellowes is dead."

Chapter 3

"Are you sure?" Mac said. He'd gone pale.

Michelle nodded. "Yes."

He closed his eyes for a brief moment. My heart ached for him.

"What happened?" Josh asked.

"You know I can't give you any details," Michelle said. She was in police officer mode now.

"So why do you want to talk to my client?" I noted his choice of words: "my client," not Mac. Josh was all business as well.

"Erin Fellowes had directions for Second Chance on her phone and three messages from Mac."

"I've got directions for half a dozen places on my phone at any given time," Josh said with a shrug of his shoulders. "And messages from all sorts of people. That doesn't prove anything. What else do you have?"

Michelle didn't answer. She pulled her phone out of her pocket, glanced at it and then put it away again.

"I know you have something," he said. "You wouldn't

have shown up here and then waited for me if you didn't." He raised an eyebrow.

In return Michelle gave him a grudging smile. "Fine. Erin Fellowes was seen arguing with a man who matches Mac's description down on the waterfront."

Josh immediately shot Mac a warning look. Mac gritted his teeth but he didn't speak.

"You know how unreliable these things are," Josh said with a shrug. "Not to mention, this ID had to have happened once it started to rain and likely after it started to get dark. If that's all you have, I think we're done."

"I didn't do anything to Erin," Mac said. "I didn't see her. And I didn't talk to her."

"Are you charging Mac with something?" Josh asked, sending Mac a look that I knew meant *Stop talking.*

Michelle shook her head. "No. Not now I'm not."

"Well, then, if you don't have anything else to share, this conversation is over."

"For now," she said.

"If you need to talk to Mac again, please call my office," Josh said in the same conversational tone of voice he might have used to comment on the weather. "I think you have my number." He moved to show her out.

Michelle looked at me for a long moment. "Good night, Sarah," she said, and then she left.

Josh stood in the hallway watching through the glass panel in the front door until Michelle pulled away from the curb. Then he came back inside. Mac was still standing in the middle of the room, arms folded on the top of his head. I had dropped down onto one of the stools at the counter. Josh picked up the glass of root beer he'd set on my coffee table and took a long drink.

"So what happens now?" Mac asked. He was restlessly shifting his weight from one foot to the other.

"What happens now is you're in my office at nine thirty tomorrow morning," Josh said, gesturing at him with the almost-empty glass, "because I want to hear about your entire day today, every tiny detail from the moment you got out of bed until right now."

Mac nodded. "I'll be there."

"And for future reference, when I tell you not to talk, don't talk." There was a warning in his gaze.

"I didn't hurt Erin. I didn't even see her."

Josh held up a hand to stop Mac from saying anything more. "I believe you," he said, reaching over to set the glass on the counter. "It doesn't change anything. Don't volunteer any information unless I tell you to."

"Thank you for coming, Josh," I said, sliding off the stool.

He smiled and once again I saw the kid who had climbed trees with me in my grandmother's backyard and who had worn a Darkwing Duck cape every day for one entire summer. "You and your friends keep my life interesting, Sarah," he said. He glanced at Mac. "Nine thirty," he repeated. And then he left.

I went into the kitchen. I'd remembered that I had half a pan of white chocolate bark that Rose had made and given me that morning. I took the lid off the container, took out a triangle of the candy studded with dried cranberries and pistachios, popped it in my mouth and set the tin on the coffee table. I knew I wouldn't be stopping at just one piece. I sat on the sofa, pulling up my legs and wrapping one arm around my knees.

Mac sat down in the chair again. "I'm sorry for getting you involved in all of this," he said. His right hand was pulled into a fist and he kept smacking it absently with the palm of his other hand.

"I'm sorry Erin is dead," I said.

"I don't understand what she was doing here. I told you, she sided with Leila's parents in everything. I haven't spoken to her in a long time." He closed his eyes for a moment and sighed softly. "I still have to find out if anything has changed with Leila." He stood up and I got to my feet as well. "I have to go," he said, reaching for his sweatshirt.

"I'll be there early to open the shop," I said. I rubbed a dab of white chocolate off the end of my finger. "You can take the SUV to Josh's office."

He almost smiled. "I have the truck now, remember? And my feet work, too. But thank you. Thank you for the offer. Thank you for listening. Thank you for calling Josh."

"Anytime," I said. "Whatever you need." For a moment we just stood there, looking at each other, and I had the sense that we were moving toward each other, so slowly the motion couldn't be seen.

Then Elvis jumped down from the top of his tower. Whatever had been happening or about to happen between Mac and me passed.

"I'll see you in the morning," he said. "Sleep well."

I nodded. "You, too." I closed the door behind him and then bent down and picked up Elvis, who was at my feet now. "You have lousy timing," I told him. He nuzzled my hand, found another dab of chocolate on the edge of my thumb and began to lick it away. Clearly he didn't care about his timing at all.

I was just finishing breakfast the next morning—a scrambled egg with spinach, tiny tomatoes and mushrooms over an English muffin, plus lots of coffee—when I heard a knock at the door. "That's probably Rose," I said to Elvis, who was sitting on a stool next to me at the counter, mooching bits of egg.

But it wasn't Rose. It was Nick.

"Hi," he said. Nick Elliot filled the doorway. He was over six feet tall with the wide shoulders of an NFL lineman, although hockey was actually his sport. Nick was clean-shaven but his sandy hair was due for a trim. He was dressed in a blue golf shirt and black pants with a multitude of pockets—his work clothes, I knew.

"You have two minutes," I said, turning and heading back over to the kitchen counter. I knew what was coming and I wanted my coffee.

"Two minutes for what?" he asked as he followed me, closing the door behind us.

I picked up my cup and sat down on the stool again, back to the counter this time. Elvis turned around and studied Nick, his furry black head cocked to one side.

"For your speech, the one in which you tell me to be careful and to not get involved in Michelle's case." I took a sip of coffee and smiled at him over the rim of the cup. "Oh, and how Rose and the Angels shouldn't get involved, either, because that's gone so well every other time you've made that suggestion."

He had the good grace to blush. "Am I really that predictable?"

"You're that pigheaded," I said.

Ever since they'd taken on their first case Nick had been butting heads with Rose, Liz, Mr. P. and Charlotte—who was his mother. He thought detective work was too dangerous and the four of them didn't have a clue what they were doing, despite the fact that Mr. P. had met all the requirements of the state to be a licensed private investigator and Rose was about to. Not to mention that they all had lots of life experience.

Nick was a former paramedic who was now an investigator for the state medical examiner's office. He was a smart, well-educated man, but he had blinders when it came to his mother and her friends. I think what he really wanted was for them to just bake cookies and organize walkathons for new playground equipment for the elementary school, not ferret out clues and chase down suspects.

"You know Mac has a connection to the woman that was killed last night," I continued.

"I wasn't going to give you a speech," he said, a note of defensiveness in his voice. "And I wasn't going to say anything about Rose and my mother and their cohorts. I know that ship has sailed."

"I'm glad you get that," I said. The amusement I felt at his discomfort had to be showing on my face.

"I just want you to be careful."

There was something stuck in his hair, just above his left ear. I slipped off the stool, reached up and grabbed a Cheerio. "Why do you have breakfast cereal in your hair?" I asked.

Nick leaned his head forward and gave it a shake. "Crap! I thought I got it all."

"Some new styling product I don't know about?" I teased.

He laughed. "No. It's actually Liam's fault."

I folded my arms over my chest, happy to talk about something other than investigations and dead bodies. "Oh, this is going to be good, I can tell. Elaborate."

"It's just that your brother has arms like a spider monkey."

"Liam has feet like a monkey, too," I said. "He can pick up things with his toes." There was only a month between my brother—who was technically my stepbrother—and me. We had been alternately torturing each other and covering for each other from the day his father married my mother. And Liam and Nick had been fast friends from the moment they met when they were seven years old.

"Well, as far as I know, he was using his abnormally long arms when he put the cereal at the back of the very top cupboard in my kitchen—which isn't where it goes, by the way."

"And you did that thing he does when things are out of reach of his monkey arms. You kept jumping until you got a couple of fingers on the edge of the box."

"And it kind of fell on my head," Nick finished, looking a little shamefaced.

I tipped my head back to look up at him. "Why can't either one of you ever just get something to stand on?"

"We're guys," he said with a grin. "We like a challenge."

"I think you just like making a mess." I reached up to straighten his collar.

He caught my hand and gave it a squeeze. "Seriously, Sarah, just please be careful," he said. "You don't know that much about Mac's past. You didn't know he had a wife, did you?"

I pulled my hand away. "My conversations with Mac are private. And you can't think Mac had anything to do with what happened to Erin Fellowes. C'mon, Nick, you know him."

"All I'm saying is—" He stopped abruptly and shook his head. "No. I'm not doing this."

"Doing what?" I countered.

"Apologizing for caring about you."

"How about apologizing for jumping to conclusions about Mac without any basis for them? How many times has Mac been on your side?"

"I'm not jumping to any conclusions about Mac, Sarah, so I don't need to apologize. I will say that it does feel that I keep saying the same thing to you because it doesn't seem to get through. I care about you. I don't want you to get hurt."

I struggled to keep my frustration in check and my voice down. "Why can't you just have faith in people and support them without treating them like they're stupid?"

He pressed his lips together for a moment before he answered, and when he did speak his voice was tight. "I don't think you're stupid and I have never treated you that way. Why do you have a different standard of behavior when it comes to me?"

"I don't," I snapped, anger sharpening my voice.

His dark eyes narrowed. "Really? Why is it, then, that when my mother or Rose worries about you or Liam, it's because they care, but when I do it's because I'm pigheaded and condescending?"

Before I could answer, a stern voice said, "Stop it!"

Nick and I both turned toward the door. Rose was standing there all five-foot-maybe in sensible shoes. She looked at Nick. "It would be best for now if you left."

He started to object but she held up one hand. "Now is not the time, Nicolas." She made her way over to him, a tiny woman with short, white hair, warm gray eyes and a stubborn streak that made a mule look easygoing. She reached up and poked his shoulder with one finger. "Get," she said.

Nick shot a quick look in my direction, mouthed the word "later" and left.

Rose smiled at me. "I know it's not my morning to work, dear," she said. "But I have some things to take care of in the office so I'm going to ride in with you if that's all right." She reached over and gave Elvis a scratch on the top of his head. "I just need to get my bag and change my shoes and I'm ready." She started for the door. "Don't forget to turn off the coffeepot," she added over her shoulder.

I put my dishes in the dishwasher, turned off the coffeepot and went to brush my teeth. When I came out with my briefcase Elvis was waiting by the front door. Rose came out of her apartment as I was locking my front door.

We walked out to the car. It was another beautiful

late August day. Winters in Maine could be challenging but the summer weather more than made up for the dark, snowy January days.

North Harbor sits on the midcoast of Maine, stretching from the Atlantic Ocean in the south up to the Swift Hills in the north. "Where the hills touch the sea" is the way the town's been described for the past 250 years. It's full of beautiful, old buildings, acclaimed restaurants and intriguing little shops. North Harbor was settled by Alexander Swift back in the late 1760s. It has a year-round population of about thirteen thousand but that number can more than triple in the summer with tourists and summer residents.

I opened the passenger door and Elvis jumped up on the seat. Rose got in beside him.

"Are we picking up Mr. P.?" I asked.

She shook her head. "Thank you, dear, but no. Alfred has to take his glasses to be adjusted. One of the arms is a bit too high. It makes him look a little cockeyed."

I backed out onto the street. I was still waiting for Rose to ask why Nick and I had been arguing. "You missed a very thought-provoking discussion after the movie last night," she said.

Okay, so apparently we weren't going to talk about Nick.

"Ann asked if anyone thought Mr. Hitchcock was sexist. Alfred said yes."

I shot a quick glance in her direction. "And you didn't?"

She folded her hands primly in her lap. "I said if anything, he had mother issues. Look how he portrayed them in his movies. That led to a discussion with a young man with green hair about the causes of an Oedipus complex and what kind of a relationship Hitchcock had with his own mother. It was fascinating."

"Sounds like it," I said. Elvis murped his agreement.

"How do you feel about a man bun?" Rose asked.

Talking to Rose often led to things veering off into the conversational bushes. "Is Mr. P. thinking about a new hairstyle?" I asked.

She started to laugh. "Oh my word, I just got a mental picture of that." She pressed the back of her hand to her mouth for a moment, shoulders shaking. "Please don't tell Alfred I laughed."

"Your secret's safe with me," I said with a smile.

"The young man with the green hair had a man bun. I'm still trying to decide how I feel about them."

Out of the corner of my eye I could see she was frowning. "I've never really thought much about them," I said. Or talked about them, for that matter, although it was better than arguing with Nick. "I guess I don't really have an opinion."

I stopped at the corner, put on my blinker and turned left. Elvis scanned the road the way he always did.

"Well, on the one hand they're very tidy," Rose said.

I nodded. "That's true."

"But on the other hand they're not exactly sexy. Speaking just for myself, they don't make me think, *Hmmm, I'd like to get some of that.*"

I tried to stop the laugh that bubbled up and failed, so I turned it into a cough instead.

"Are you all right, dear?" Rose said.

"Just something in the back of my throat," I managed to choke out.

She reached over and patted my arm. "I think the ragweed is early this year. We should get you a neti pot."

I had no idea what a neti pot was but I had a feeling I was probably going to find out.

When we got to Second Chance I parked and turned to get my briefcase from the backseat. Rose had already gotten out and was reaching for Elvis. "He can walk, Rose," I said.

"The pavement is too hot for his feet." She picked the cat up and Elvis meowed and wrinkled his whiskers at me, cat for "nyah, nyah, nyah."

We found Mac inside at the workbench with the mechanism of a wooden music box spread out in front of him. There was a mug of coffee at his elbow and I wondered how much sleep he'd gotten last night.

"Good morning," he said.

"Good morning," Rose replied. She set Elvis on the bench. Her blue and white canvas tote was over her arm and I hoped she had cookies inside because I needed some sugar. I caught a whiff of Mac's coffee. And more caffeine.

"How are you connected to the woman who was found last night down by the waterfront?" she asked.

I frowned at her. "How did you know?"

Elvis walked over to Mac and poked his furry nose in the top of Mac's coffee cup. I made a shooing gesture at him and he made a face back at me before sitting down and starting to wash his front paws.

Rose was looking at me. "I pay attention. And you and Nicolas aren't exactly quiet when you're talking." She gave me a pointed look when she said "talking."

Mac turned to me. "Nick showed up last night?"

"This morning."

I waited for him to say something in response, but he didn't. He set down the tiny screwdriver he'd been holding and turned all his attention to Rose. "The woman's name is Erin Fellowes. She is—she was—my wife's best friend. My wife's name is Leila. She's in a rehab facility in a coma. Erin came here to talk to me but I didn't get a chance to talk to her before she died." He paused. "And for the record, I didn't kill her."

Rose made a dismissive gesture with her free hand. "Well, of course I know that," she said. "We'll all meet at my apartment tonight at seven. I'll make cheesecake brownies. You can explain everything to all of us at once." She started for the shop. "I'm going to put the kettle on," she called over her shoulder.

We watched her go. I realized that Rose had to have heard pretty much all of my conversation with Nick. She always said she had ears like a wolf. And the conversation on the ride over—Hitchcock, sexism and man buns—had all been a way to distract me.

Mac picked up the screwdriver again, turning it over in his fingers. He looked up at me. "I can't let them get involved in the investigation into Erin's death," he said. "You know how much trouble it's going to make. With Michelle and with Nick."

I couldn't help it. Maybe it was all the stress of the last twelve hours, but I started to laugh. "You're not going to get a vote on that," I said. "Give it up, Mac. Like it or not, the Angels are on the case."

Chapter 4

Mac knocked on my apartment door just before seven. "I'm not so sure this is a good idea," he said. He was wearing jeans and a gray Red Sox T-shirt and he'd shaved.

"Would you like me to repeat everything you've said to me about the Angels investigating a case?" I asked.

He smiled. "Okay, I get your point."

I smiled back at him. "All the things you said to me were true. Rose, Mr. P. and the rest of the crew are good investigators." Even as I said the words I realized how much I meant them.

I locked the door and we headed down the hall to Rose's apartment. "Where's Elvis?" Mac asked. "Shouldn't he be sitting outside Rose's front door waiting for us already?"

Rose was one of Elvis's favorite people. She talked to him like he was a person and she always seemed to have a bit of chicken or a chopped sardine for him.

"He went early to help her get set up."

"You're not joking," he said.

I shook my head. "No, I'm not. We got home and he followed Rose down the hallway. When I called him she turned around and said, 'Elvis is going to help me get things set up.' That was pretty much that. I didn't get a vote."

Everyone was seated around the table in Rose's small kitchen—even Elvis had a chair. Rose got everyone settled with tea and brownies, then she turned to Mac, gave him an encouraging smile and said, "Go ahead."

Mac's forearms were propped on the edge of the table, his hands wrapped around the cup Rose had set in front of him. I could see the muscles tense in his arms. He looked around the table before he spoke. "I have a wife," he said. He let the words sink in for a moment. Mr. P. didn't look surprised, which told me Rose had shared what she'd learned that morning with him, but everyone else did.

I saw Rose shoot Liz a look. Liz glared back but said nothing—which was actually a bit of a surprise.

"Her name is Leila," Mac continued. "A couple of years ago we bought a house, an old one, and we were working on renovating it on the weekends and paying to have some things done, too." I saw a brief smile flash across his face at the memory. "We'd been having problems with the old furnace and the water heater and we'd decided it made more sense to just have the whole HVAC system replaced."

His voice was calm and steady but his hands were squeezing his cup so hard the skin was stretched tightly across his knuckles.

"I was out of town on business and Leila was sleeping in a room downstairs that we were eventually going to turn into a den. She'd made a makeshift bed on the sofa that was in the room, because of the smell of varnish on the hardwood floors on the second floor. And it was colder up there, too, because of the issues with the furnace." He glanced down at his cup and swallowed. "I wasn't supposed to be back until the next morning but my meetings finished early and . . . and I wanted to get home. It was just after two a.m. when I got there. I didn't want to wake her up because she'd had a cold and she'd been having trouble sleeping. So I went to sleep in our bedroom upstairs. I opened the window a crack and I kept the door shut against the odor. I didn't mind the cold." He stopped, raised his head and looked around the table again. I could see the pain in his eyes and the tight lines around his mouth. "I found her unconscious when I got up about five o'clock. Carbon monoxide. She's been in a coma ever since."

Liz pressed her lips together. Charlotte reached over and gave Mac's arm a gentle squeeze.

"The police suspected you," Mr. P. said. I could see the concern in his eyes. He was a bald and bespectacled little man, whip-smart, with a generous heart and the computer skills of a dark Webmaster.

Mac nodded. "Yes. The hot water heater turned out to be the source of the carbon monoxide. It was old, like everything else in the house, and it was leaking just enough that the heater didn't shut off, trying to keep the water hot enough. Plus it turned out there was a problem with the flue pipe that vented the heater. The opening was blocked outside and there was a very small gap between two sections of the ductwork."

Mr. P. glanced at the rest of us. "It would have been

the same as if a car engine had been left running in a closed garage for several hours."

"Why did the police suspect you?" Rose asked. "Was it just because you were Leila's husband?"

Mac pushed the cup away and shifted in his seat to face Rose, who had taken the chair to his right. "That was part of it. The spouse being the bad guy became a cliché for a reason after all. But that's not the only reason. Leila was—is a beneficiary of a trust set up by her great-aunt. The other beneficiary is her cousin, Stevie. For now, they each receive a monthly payout from the interest earned, but on Leila's thirty-fifth birthday, which is just a few months from now, she'll receive half of the trust just as Stevie will a bit more than a year from now when she turns thirty-five. If Leila dies before her birthday, all the money in the trust will go to Stevie."

"What happens to the money if Leila dies after her thirty-fifth birthday?" Mr. P. asked, adding a bit of milk to his tea. "I'm assuming it goes to her next of kin, which is you."

"It does," Mac said. "And yes, I know how bad that looks."

"If you were going to kill your wife for her money I think you would have been smart enough to wait until she actually had it," Liz commented, raising an eyebrow at him. She was elegantly dressed in a cream-colored shirt and a pink-and-yellow-flowered skirt. Her blond hair looked like she'd just left a stylist's chair—which she probably had—and as usual she was wearing ridiculously high stiletto heels, which would have left me with a broken ankle if I'd had them on for very long.

Mr. P. shook his head. "I don't think so, Elizabeth. If

Mac waited until his wife inherited from the trust, at best he'd end up with half of the money if their marriage ended and that would only be if the courts decided it was joint property—which I doubt they would have. On the other hand, if she were incapacitated, he'd have control of the current payout and if she were to die after her thirty-fifth birthday he'd get all of her share." He looked over at Mac. "Not that I think for a moment you'd do anything like that."

"Could Leila's cousin have been behind what happened to her?" Rose asked as she got up to get the teapot. "If Leila had died, all the money would have been his."

"Hers," Mac said. "Stevie is short for Stephanie, and I don't believe that she would have hurt Leila. They were close."

Rose refilled my cup and patted my arm as she moved past me.

"Why are you here in North Harbor and not with your wife?" Liz said. She looked at Mac across the table and I saw no recrimination in her gaze, just curiosity.

Rose shot her a withering look but Liz ignored it, deliberately or possibly because she hadn't seen it. I wasn't sure, but I suspected the former.

Mac explained about his in-laws and the lawsuit.

"Why are you and Leila still married?" Liz asked.

"You don't have to answer that," Rose said sharply.

"I'm sorry. But it's a valid question," Charlotte said. It was the first time she'd spoken.

Tall, with the posture and focused gaze of the high school principal she used to be, Charlotte was often the voice of reason in the group. Like Nick, she was one of the first people to step up when there was a problem, but unlike her son she was a lot more easygoing.

Mac looked at Rose. "It's okay. Charlotte's right." He put both hands flat on the table and shifted his attention back to Liz. "I promised for better or for worse when I married Leila. And even though I agreed to her parents being in charge of her care *for now*"—he put extra emphasis on the last two words—"I didn't give up the right to change my mind. As long as I'm her husband, I have the option to change things if I feel that's what she needs. And I didn't stop loving her, just because the person I knew is . . . gone."

Liz nodded. Taking care of the people you cared about was important to Liz, to all of them. I knew they'd understand Mac's reasoning.

"Mac, may I ask what Leila did for a living?" Mr. P. said as he added a little sugar to his tea.

"She has an MBA from Northwestern and an undergraduate degree in chemistry before that. She actually did two years of art history before she changed her major." I saw the beginning of a smile on his face. "She ran her own organic beauty products company, du Mer. She bought seaweed and sea salt produced here in Maine. In fact, the first time I saw North Harbor was on a trip to Maine with Leila to source sea salt for a body scrub she wanted to add to her line."

"Who's running the company now?" Rose asked as she sat down again.

"Leila has a half sister, Natalie Welland, who's ten years younger. She's the result of an affair that their father had. Natalie worked summers with Leila while she was in college and she's been running the company since . . .

since Leila's accident. Leila's share of the profits goes into the trust that helps fund her care." Mac shifted in his seat again. I knew him well enough to know the conversation was making him restless. "I know what you're thinking," he said to Rose, sending her a sideways glance. "Leila and Natalie didn't grow up together but they were very close and I just don't believe Natalie had anything to do with what happened."

He studied his hands for a moment. "I can't think of anyone who would have wanted to hurt Leila. Even though she hadn't made art her career she never lost her love for it. She was warm and creative. Everyone loved her. She was that kind of person." He looked up, looked around the table and then focused his attention on Mr. P. "Alfred, go ahead and dig into my life and Leila's. I don't think you're going to find anything. I still think what happened to her was a horrible accident. I've told you everything. There are no secrets to uncover, so go ahead and look."

Even though it was a warm evening I felt goose bumps rise on my arms at Mac's words, that feeling my father called "A goose just walked over my grave." I didn't believe in omens or signs, good or bad, but if I had, this wouldn't have been a good one.

Chapter 5

The next morning I dropped Rose, Elvis and Mr. P. off at the shop and went to pick up Charlotte. We were going out to Clayton McNamara's house to begin an inventory in the house itself on the things we were going to sell for him. His daughter, Beth, had come for a visit earlier in the summer and convinced her father that it was time to declutter his small story-and-a-half house and the other buildings on the property. It hadn't taken much persuading after Elvis had cornered and dispatched a very large and furry squatter in a second-floor closet.

"I'm not gettin' any younger," Clayton had said to me on my last visit. "I might just sell up, move into that seniors' place in town and let all the widows fight over who's gonna make me dinner every night." He'd given me a mischievous grin. "I'm a catch, you know. I've got my own car, my own teeth and all of my parts are still in good working order." With that he'd headed back to his woodpile.

Beside me, Glenn, his nephew, had started to laugh. "I could have gone pretty much the rest of my life without having that information," he'd said as we turned toward the house.

"We've cleared out several places that belonged to older people," I'd said with a sly grin. "I could tell you stories about some of the things we've found."

Glenn had made a face.

I'd bumped him with my hip. "C'mon, when you're Clayton's age don't you want to have your own teeth and all your parts in working order?"

"I absolutely do," he'd said, holding the back door of the little house open for me. "Including my mouth, which I hope I'll have the good sense to keep shut."

"What are you smiling at?" Charlotte asked now from the passenger seat of the SUV.

"I was thinking about the last time I was out at Clayton's with Glenn. Clayton told me that maybe he'd sell the house and move into Legacy Place and let the ladies chase him." I shot her a sideways look. She was smiling now.

"They would, you know," she said. "Clayton McNamara is a charmer and as your grandmother would say, he cleans up well."

"Is that your way of reminding me that he could have been my grandfather?"

"Roads not taken, Sarah," Charlotte teased. "Roads not taken."

She and Liz had been teasing me about my grandmother and Clayton's very short-lived romance since Clayton had told me about it.

"You were quiet last night," I said, as much to change the subject as because I was curious about her reaction to Mac's revelations.

"So were you."

"I knew most of the story already."

"You didn't know Mac had a wife, though, did you?"

I shook my head, slowing down as the car in front of me turned. "Not before he told me, no." I had suspected that Mac had been married at one time, but it had never entered my mind that he still was. I looked in her direction again. She was watching me, her brown eyes thoughtful. "But you knew," I said.

I heard her exhale softly. "Not for sure," she admitted. "I suspected there was someone in his past—Mac has always kept pretty much to himself—but I had no idea the truth was this complicated."

Neither had I. Mac was a very private person and I hadn't asked any questions. Truth be told, maybe I hadn't wanted to hear the answers.

"I'm hoping to kill two birds with one stone this morning," Charlotte said.

"What do you mean?" I asked.

"I think it might help if we knew a little more about the company Mac's wife owns, the one her sister is running now."

"And for some reason you think that Clayton gets his body wash and moisturizer from them?"

Charlotte laughed. "Well, as I said, according to Isabel, he cleans up well."

I tried to get a mental image of big, burly Clayton dabbing moisturizer on his face but my mind seemed to reject the idea.

"Several years ago—quite a few years ago, actually—Clayton worked for a seaweed harvester in Steuben," Charlotte continued. "Mac said his wife's company bought both sea salt and seaweed here in Maine. I thought it wouldn't hurt to understand a little more about the process before we went out asking questions."

"Good idea," I said, putting on my blinker and turning into Clayton McNamara's driveway. We both got out of the SUV. I could smell the ocean on the breeze and the sun was warm on the back of my neck. Somehow I couldn't see him leaving this place for a seniors' apartment in town anytime soon.

"Charlotte, why is it that Gram is the only one who had a romance with Clayton back in the day?" I asked with a teasing smile. "What about you?"

Charlotte shook her head. "It was pretty much a love-at-first-sight thing with them. The first time he laid eyes on her he was hit over the head." She clapped her hands together. "Like that."

I frowned at her. "Are you trying to say that it was love at first sight for a couple of first graders?"

"No," she said. "I'm saying the first time Clayton saw Isabel he tried to look up her dress on the swings and she hit him over the head with her book bag." She cocked her own head to one side. "Now that I think about it didn't she meet John when she hit him over the head with something?"

"Gram knocked a library book off a shelf and it hit him in the head, so technically, yes."

"I'm starting to see a pattern," Charlotte said with a grin.

I laughed as we started up the driveway. "Me, too. I'm so glad Gram is finally coming home. I have a lot of questions to ask her."

We found Clayton in the backyard, working on his

never-ending woodpile. He was a big man like his nephew Glenn, with a barrel chest and beefy arms in his blue plaid shirt. Now that Clayton had shaved his beard the two men looked even more alike.

"Charlotte Elliot, it's damn good to see you," he said, taking both of her hands in his. "You're as pretty as ever."

"And you're as full of it as ever," she replied, but she was smiling.

Clayton must have been a charmer when he was a younger man. Heck, he was a charmer now. He turned his smile on me. "Sarah, how are you? It's good to see you, too."

"I'm fine," I said. "Charlotte and I are planning to start an inventory of the upstairs this morning. No second thoughts?"

"Not a one. I won't live long enough to use half the stuff that's in that house and I'll be damned if I'll leave it all to be dealt with by Beth and Glenn."

"That's what we're here for." I smiled at him. I couldn't imagine Clayton getting steamrollered into giving up his stuff by anyone but I'd wanted to ask, just to be sure.

"Clayton, could I pick your brain for a minute before we get started?" Charlotte asked.

"I figure the pickin's are pretty slim," he said, "but go ahead."

"Years ago you worked down in Steuben, didn't you?"

"Yes, I did. Raking seaweed for the Lawrence brothers." He shook his head. "Good money but hard work." Two frown lines formed between his bushy eyebrows. "Now, Charlotte, don't tell me that you've been taken in by that damn fool commercial that runs during *Elmyra's House of Horrors Midnight Movie*?"

"What commercial?" I said. Somehow we'd gone from seaweed harvesting to late-night TV and I wasn't sure how we'd gotten there.

"Dr. Ho's Miracle Moisturizer with Botwilla," Charlotte said, as though that should clear up my confusion.

"They claim their secret wrinkle-reducing ingredient is seaweed," Clayton said in a voice heavily laden with skepticism. He looked at Charlotte. "You're a damn fine-looking woman and you don't need any so-called wrinkle-reducing cream for twenty-eight ninety-five plus shipping and handling."

Charlotte smiled at him. "Thank you and don't worry. I wasn't planning on ordering any of Dr. Ho's products but I will admit to a little curiosity about them. Do you think there's actually any seaweed in that skin cream?"

"I think there's a pretty good chance that there's a little. Back in the day the Lawrence brothers were selling most of what we harvested to some spa in New York that used the seaweed for some sorta body wrap. They claimed it restored mineral levels in the body."

"Okay, that has to be some sort of scam," I said.

"Not so fast," Clayton said. He held up one finger. "How much do you know about seaweed?"

"I've had dulse," I said, pushing my bangs back off my face. I'd been eating the dried red seaweed since I was a kid.

"So pretty much nothing," he said with a laugh.

I nodded. "Pretty much."

"Seaweed's story really starts on land. Minerals leach into surface water and get washed down to the sea. They end up as part of the seaweed and people believe that eating it has all kinds of health benefits. Look at the

Japanese. They live a lot longer than most of the rest of us do, and their diet has a lot more seaweed in it. Course they eat a lot less fast-food crap, too."

"Okay," I said. "I can see how eating seaweed could be a good thing, but a wrinkle cream? Really?" I made a face.

"Hold your horses," Clayton said. He smoothed a hand over his bald head, brown as a nut from all the time he spent working outside without his hat. "The idea's not as far off the bubble as you might think. I told you there are minerals in seaweed—iodine, iron and copper among others. Well, it's the copper that gets people excited."

Beside me Charlotte nodded. "Copper peptides help with tissue regeneration. Wounds heal faster and cleaner."

"So why couldn't it do the same for wrinkles?" Clayton said.

"So does it?" I asked.

He laughed, a warm, booming sound that seemed to echo around the yard. "Damned if I know, but my guess is no."

"Why no?" Charlotte said.

Clayton held out his gnarled, wrinkled hands. "These mitts of mine handled a heck of a lot of seaweed back in the day and they don't exactly have that youthful glow, now, do they?"

"They look like they've done plenty of hard work and there's nothing wrong with that," Charlotte said.

That sly grin stretched across the old man's face again. "Flattery," he said, a teasing edge to his voice. "For the record, it works on me." He winked and Charlotte's cheeks flushed.

I made a gesture toward the house. "Well, these hands should probably go in and get started."

"I'll give you a yell in a while when I put the coffee on," Clayton said. He turned back to his woodpile and Charlotte and I headed inside.

"Have you been taking lessons from Liz?" I asked as we started up the narrow staircase to the second floor of the house.

"Lessons? What kind of lessons?" A frown furrowed Charlotte's forehead.

"Flirting lessons. Usually it's Liz who's using her feminine wiles to get information."

Charlotte glared at me. "I did *not* take any lessons from Liz on how to use my feminine wiles," she said, squaring her shoulders and jutting out her chin.

I held up both hands. "I'm sorry. I stand corrected," I said.

Charlotte opened the bedroom door to our left. Then she looked back over her shoulder, slid her glasses down her nose and raised an eyebrow. "I already know how to use all the tools in my toolbox," she said.

Charlotte and I headed back to the shop at noon. We had gone through everything on the second floor. Items for the yard sale we were planning had all been marked. The furniture that I was taking on consignment and the pieces I was buying outright were tagged as coming to the shop.

There were some items of clothing—several men's fedoras, two woolen peacoats and some men's suits—which I planned to send to Jess to sell on consignment for Clayton. The rest—with his agreement—was going to two different charity clothing stores.

"I'm going to bring this armoire back here," I said to Mac, showing him the photo I'd taken of the large, mirrored piece of furniture. "And one of the bedroom sets. I think we'll get more from them in the shop than we will at the estate sale. Glenn offered his cube truck and I think I'll take him up on that."

Mac looked around the shop. "Where are you going to put everything?"

"I think we can rearrange things and find room for the armoire." I gestured at a tall, narrow dresser. "That's going to be picked up tomorrow morning. And as for the bedroom set, I'm thinking about getting Avery to do some kind of window display based around it. Do you think the bed will fit?"

Mac pulled out his metal tape and took a couple of measurements. "If we turn it on an angle it'll work."

I smiled at him. "Perfect. I'll get Avery to start thinking about what she wants to do when she gets here."

"That should be interesting," he teased.

"Remember how popular her kiss window was for Valentine's?"

Avery's idea for a Valentine's window display had turned out to be vintage mannequins dressed as the members of the band Kiss, complete with wigs and full makeup. She'd stenciled A KISS IS STILL A KISS in red letters on the window.

Mac folded his arms over his chest, tipped his head to one side and regarded me thoughtfully. "What I remember was you coming in here early before it was completely daylight, forgetting what was in the window and almost taking out the entire display with the lance that came with that suit of armor you bought from Cleveland, all because you thought someone had broken in."

I laughed. "Good thing you were here to save me and the band."

"You nearly skewered me like a shish kebab."

I tried to make a straight face but failed miserably. "The fact that you took one (almost) for the team is duly noted."

His phone buzzed then. He took it out and checked the screen. "It's Josh," he said.

I moved a few steps away to give him some privacy. Rose was arranging three teddy bears in a doll carriage that I'd just painted a few days ago. "This turned out really well," she said, pointing to the carriage that I'd painted a soft woodsy green on the underside and a creamy pale yellow on top.

"I like the bears," I said. Each one of them wore a seersucker baby bonnet. One pink, one blue, one yellow.

"The hats were in the bottom of that bag of linens you got at the flea market," Rose said. "When you were little you had a carriage like this. You used to take that stuffed monkey you had for a ride."

"Cheeky Monkey," I said, smiling at the memory.

"You put one of Isabel's tea cozies on his head for a hat."

I laughed. "That was so he didn't get sunstroke."

"You were a very imaginative child," Rose said, reaching over to tuck a strand of hair behind my ear.

"You think I was imaginative? Liam used my doll carriage as a transport vehicle to get his G.I. Joes across the brook. He got the bottom all wet and muddy. I was so mad."

"Why do I have the feeling that wasn't the end of the story?"

I hung my head. "I might have done some bodywork to G.I. Joe's jeep," I said, looking at her from under my eyelashes. "So Barbie could use it."

Rose's lips were pressed together and she was trying not to laugh.

"Sarah Grayson, what did you do?" she asked.

"I swiped a bottle of Gram's nail polish and tried to paint the jeep pink."

Rose shook her head, her lips still twitching. "Oh dear, what did your mother say?"

I made a face. "Let's just say she wasn't happy," I said. "In my defense if she hadn't interrupted me I could have gotten the whole thing finished and it would have looked a whole lot better."

Rose gave up then trying to keep a straight face and laughed as she reached down to adjust the blanket in the carriage. "What on earth did you give your mother for an explanation?"

"I told her Liam had asked me to paint the jeep."

"And what happened when she asked him?"

I could tell by the knowing smile on Rose's face that she already knew the answer. "He told her he had. Then later he held Barbie upside down in the toilet and gave her a swirly, because, you know, I'd tried to paint G.I. Joe's jeep pink." I smiled at the memory.

My mom and Liam's dad had gotten married when Liam and I were in elementary school. By rights we should have been bickering stepsiblings. We were both slightly spoiled only children who had lost a parent and weren't used to sharing the one we had left. But to everyone's surprise, from the beginning we were, as Gram put it, "thick as thieves." Liam could drive me crazy at times and I was sure he'd say the same thing about me, but I knew he always had my back and I always had his.

Out of the corner of my eye I saw Mac put his phone away. I turned around. "Is everything all right?" I asked.

"That was Josh," Mac said. "The police have a few more questions."

"Michelle," I said.

Mac nodded. "Probably. Josh didn't say. We're meeting at his office at four thirty." His expression was unreadable.

"I'll drive you over."

"Alfred and I can close up and Elvis can come with us," Rose said as though everything was settled, and I knew that if Mac didn't agree he'd have an argument on his hands.

"You don't have to do that," he said.

Rose gave him her I'm-humoring-you smile, not to be confused with her I'm-pretending-to-be-a-sweet-befuddled-little-old-lady smile, which also usually got her whatever she wanted. "At my age, Mac, I rarely do things I don't have to do," she said.

I opened my mouth to confirm the truth of that comment when Rose—who seemed to have read my mind—fixed her gray eyes on me.

"Did you have something you wanted to add to this conversation, Sarah?" she asked.

I cleared my throat. "No, ma'am," I said. I patted my chest. "Just a little frog in my throat."

"I hope you're not coming down with something," Rose said, brushing lint only she could see from the front of her apron. "Like I told you, we need to get you a neti pot, but for now, I have some Fisherman's Friend in my purse. I'll go get you one. They can knock a germ dead in its tracks." She headed for the stairs.

I screwed up my face. "Those cough drops of Rose's can take down a buffalo."

"The fact that you're going to take one for the team is duly noted," Mac said with a smile, echoing my earlier words.

Midafternoon, Rose knocked on my office door and poked her head into the room. "Do you have a minute?" she asked.

"I do," I said. I had just finished updating the store's Web site with absolutely no help from Elvis, who had managed to add two zeros to the price of a vintage quilt when he put a paw on the keyboard as he leaned around the laptop to look at the screen. "What do you need?"

"Could you come down to the sunporch? Alfred may have found something."

"Just let me shut down the computer," I said. Elvis jumped down from my desk and went over to Rose. It seemed that he thought he'd been invited to come, too.

I followed the two of them downstairs. Charlotte was showing a wooden rocking chair to a man in his twenties with a thick mass of brown hair and a couple of days of stubble. I noticed him eyeing one of the guitars on the wall, his right hand tapping against his leg, and wondered if he'd look at it.

Mr. P. was at his desk in the Angels' sunporch office. Mac was with him, leaning back against the wooden table.

"What did you find?" I asked. I could see the tension in Mac's arms and shoulders. Rose patted his arm as she moved past him.

"There's a five-million-dollar life insurance policy on Leila with her sister Natalie as the beneficiary." Mr. P. nudged his glasses up his nose.

"I told Alfred that's because of the business partnership," Mac said.

Rose shook her head.

"No," Mr. P. said. "I'm sorry, but I think you may be wrong. The policy pays out to Natalie personally, not the business, and I can't find any record of a similar life insurance policy on Natalie that would have paid out to Leila in the same way."

Mac looked away for a moment then looked at Alfred again. "I see your point but you didn't know Leila. That's exactly the kind of thing she would do. Her father kept Natalie a secret until she was almost seventeen years old. Leila thought Natalie had been cheated out of all the things she'd gotten herself—vacations, clothes, social connections." His mouth twisted into a semblance of a smile. "It wasn't her job to fix any of that, but it didn't mean she wasn't going to try. So if that's it—" He stood up.

"It's not," Mr. P. said. He glanced at me and then his eyes shifted to Rose.

"Go ahead and tell us whatever you've found," Mac said. "Like I told you, I don't have any secrets from Sarah—or any of you. Not anymore."

"Du Mer is being sued over the quality of some of their products."

Mac frowned in confusion. "That doesn't make any sense. Leila always used quality products. I told you that she purchased sea salt and seaweed here in Maine. Natalie was running things the same way. Nothing changed."

Mr. P. cleared his throat. "At the time of Leila's accident the Federal Trade Commission had just opened an investigation into the company for deceptive advertising practices. You didn't know?"

I didn't need to hear him say no. It was clear from the expression on his face.

"Could Leila have known?" Rose asked.

Mac shook his head. "There's no way Leila knew because she would have told me. We talked about the business pretty much every day. She wouldn't have kept that kind of thing to herself."

"I'll see if I can find out a little more information," Mr. P. said. He and Rose exchanged a look and I made a mental note to ask them later what they hadn't said.

I put a hand on Mac's shoulder. "Do you have a minute to look at that table I'm working on?" I asked. "I could use a second opinion on the casters I'd like to use."

"Umm, yeah, sure," he said.

"Let me know if you find anything else," I said to Mr. P. He nodded.

Mac and I went out the back door and started across the parking lot to the garage workshop. He squinted at me in the sunshine. "Do you really want a second opinion or were you just trying to get me out of the Angels' office before Rose told me I didn't know my wife as well as I thought I did."

I stopped walking. "Rose would never say that, Mac."

Silence hung between us like a curtain, then Mac exhaled softly. "You're right. I guess I'm the one who's wondering if Leila was keeping secrets from me."

"She didn't say anything to you about the insurance policy?"

He shook his head.

"Maybe she forgot to tell you." I tipped my head to keep the sun out of my eyes. "Maybe she'd just gotten the policy and didn't get a chance to tell you. Don't jump to conclusions. Let them find you."

"What is that supposed to mean?"

I shrugged. "I don't know. It's something Rose said to me once. I think it means just wait and see how things work out. It was the only thing that I could think of that was vaguely appropriate."

He gave me a genuine smile then. "I appreciate the thought." His expression grew serious once more. "I'm sorry you got tied up in all of this."

I bumped him with my shoulder and we started walking again. "How many times have you gotten tied up in one of the Angels' cases because *I* got tied up in it? Think of this as me returning the favor."

Mac smiled again. "I'll try." He pointed at the garage. "So do you really want my opinion on the casters?"

"I really do," I said, stopping to unlock the door to the former garage. "Because I don't have a clue which ones to use or how I'm going to attach them."

"In other words you were hoping that I'd say I'll do it for you."

I gave him a sheepish grin. "I was and I guess I wasn't nearly as subtle as I thought."

"It's just because I know you," Mac said. "Let me see the bottom of those table legs."

He laid the small metal table on its side and crouched down to study the legs.

Mac did know me well, but I couldn't help wondering if he'd known his wife nearly as well as he thought.

Chapter 6

We got to Josh's office about five minutes before the scheduled appointment time. Josh was waiting. His suit jacket was off and he was wearing purple suspenders with his gray trousers. "Hi, Sarah," he said. He turned to Mac. "Come on in. Michelle should be here any minute."

Mac hesitated. "Is it all right if Sarah joins us?"

"I don't need to," I said.

"I'd like you to." Mac looked at Josh. "Is there any reason she shouldn't?"

"It's fine," Josh said. "Everything you say will be on the record so there's no problem with Sarah being there if you want her."

"I do," Mac said. He looked at me again. "Please. I want you to know everything that's going on."

I nodded. "All right."

We followed Josh into his office. The entire space was painted a soft white and the room was flooded with afternoon sunshine, which made it seem less intimidating. The office had high ceilings and the wall behind

Josh's desk was a bank of tall, wide windows with the original detailed trim from when the building had been built over a hundred years ago. To the left of his dark wooden desk were floor-to-ceiling bookshelves with a rolling library ladder to reach the highest volumes. To the right was a wall of exposed brick. In front of the desk an oriental rug in shades of navy, red and gold covered part of the pickled oak floor and there were two chocolate brown leather chairs for guests.

"Michelle asked for this meeting because she says she has some new information about Ms. Fellowes's death," Josh said. "She's always been straight with me so I don't have any reason to disbelieve her, but that doesn't mean she isn't looking for more information."

The phone on his desk buzzed then. Michelle had arrived. Josh's assistant showed her in. She was wearing a black skirt with a short-sleeve lavender blouse, and her hair was pulled back from her face. "Hi, Josh," she said with a smile. "Thanks for fitting this in today."

"I'm happy to accommodate the police department whenever I can," he replied.

I knew that Michelle had wanted the meeting at the police station and Josh had insisted it be at his office. Her comment and his response made it sound as though she'd asked for a small favor instead. If Liz had been with us she would have called it "territory marking." Actually she would have made a comment more appropriate to dogs and fire hydrants.

"You said you had some new information," Josh said.

Michelle nodded. "I do. I wanted you to hear it from me and I wanted to give Mac the chance to amend his statement."

"We appreciate that," Josh said. He gestured to the leather chairs set around a round glass-and-metal table in front of the brick wall. "Let's sit down."

We all took a seat, Josh on one side of Mac and me on the other.

Michelle directed her attention to Mac. "We have a witness—a very credible one—who saw you arguing with Erin Fellowes the night she was killed."

"It's not possible," Mac said. "I told you I couldn't find her."

"Wait a minute, that's it?" Josh said, interrupting him. "That's nothing new. You told us last night that someone thinks they *might* have seen Mac talking to your victim."

I noticed how he put extra emphasis on the word "might."

So did Michelle. "Did see him," she corrected. Her eyes flicked to me for a moment. "The witness heard Erin Fellowes call Mac by name."

"They're wrong," Mac said. "I left Erin some voice mail messages and I went to the Rosemont Inn. She wasn't there. I checked the restaurants in the area and I walked around the nearby streets looking but I didn't find her. Your witness is lying or mistaken."

"Maybe Erin was mugged," I said.

Michelle shook her head. "She had her wallet and her cell phone and she was wearing a pretty expensive pair of diamond earrings."

"Is there anything else?" Josh asked. He'd made a note on the yellow pad in front of him and now he set his pen down.

Michelle shook her head. "Not unless there's any-thing else you want to tell me." She spoke to Josh but I saw her glance at Mac and I realized her words were more for him.

"Have you released cause of death yet?" Josh said.

Michelle's mouth moved for a moment before she spoke. "Ms. Fellowes was smothered," she said.

Mac's hand tightened on the armrest of his chair but he didn't speak.

Josh stood up. "Thank you for keeping us updated. I appreciate that." He held out his hand.

Michelle got to her feet as well. Her gaze flicked over to me for a moment. Then she shook Josh's hand. "Thanks for your time," she said. "I'm sure I'll be talking to you again soon."

Josh walked around the table and showed her out. After his office door had closed behind her, he turned to face us.

Mac rubbed the back of his neck and shook his head. "Smothered. That's horrible." His voice was rough with emotion.

"That kind of violence suggests a lot of anger," Josh said. "Can you think of anyone who might have felt that way about Erin?"

Mac shook his head. "I haven't seen Erin in a long time, but when I knew her there was no one that would have wanted her dead. No one who would have done something like that."

"Just the same, put together a list of friends and colleagues for me, please."

"I said too much again, didn't I?" Mac asked.

Josh nodded. "Yes, but there's no real harm done. You said the same thing you said last night, so it's already on the record."

"You don't seem that worried about this witness," I said.

"Given the weather and the time of night, I'm not. Eyewitness IDs are known for being unreliable, and overheard conversations even more so." He rolled his eyes. "How many times have you heard that some *reliable eyewitness* spotted Bigfoot somewhere in the state?"

"It wouldn't hurt to find out who this person is, though."

"No, it wouldn't," Josh agreed. "I take it the Angels are on the case."

"They are."

"I'll call Alfred, then." He turned to Mac. "Could someone be setting you up? Does anyone have a grudge against you?"

"Other than my in-laws," he said. "No. And Leila and Erin have been friends since they were kids. They would never do anything to hurt Erin." He shook his head. "I can't think of anyone."

"Think harder," Josh said.

Mac shook his head. "No. It's impossible."

There was nothing more to say. Josh said he'd keep in touch and we left.

Mac didn't say a word until we were headed in the direction of the shop. "Why do you believe in me?" he asked. "Why do you just accept what I've said without question especially since Michelle clearly thinks I'm lying?"

My eyes flicked away from the road for a moment. He was looking at me with a genuine questioning expression on his face. I turned my attention back to the road in front of me. "I'm a pretty good judge of character and you haven't given me any reason not to believe you. My dad says you trust someone until they give you a reason not to and then you stop. You haven't given me a reason not to."

I remembered the argument I'd had with Nick and his accusation that I had different standards when it came to his actions and behavior than I had for anyone else's. In the end I trusted Mac because some feeling, some instinct, told me I could. I had an uncomfortable thought that maybe . . . *maybe* what Nick had said might be true.

"What was Erin like?" I asked.

Mac smiled. "Smart. Funny. She worked for a commercial bank. She spoke three languages—English, Spanish and Mandarin—four if you count Klingon."

I shot a look his way. "Okay. You're not serious," I said.

The smile grew wider. "Yes I am. She was a serious *Star Trek* geek—all the incarnations. One year for a Halloween party she dressed up as Lieutenant Uhura; the original one with the go-go boots and the little thing in her ear."

"What about you? Who did you dress up as?"

Mac gave me a sheepish grin. "Leila and I were Buffy and Spike from *Buffy the Vampire Slayer*. She liked that show."

I glanced over at him again. "So you had the white-blond hair?" I couldn't quite picture that.

He nodded. "Temporarily. At least it was supposed to be temporary." The grin faded. "It seems like a long time ago," he said, quietly.

When we got back to the shop Rose, Mr. P. and Elvis

were still there. Rose was at the workbench sorting through a box of teacups with a little—very little—help from Elvis. "Why are you all still here?" I said. "I thought Liz was picking you up."

"She was already here," Rose said, "but the people who bought that dresser called and they're coming after all in about"—she looked at the watch on her arm—"fifteen minutes. I knew you wanted to get it out of the shop so you can bring the furniture from Clayton's place so I told them we'd wait for them." She looked at Mac. "How did the meeting go?"

He made a face. "The police have a witness who saw me with Erin."

"That doesn't mean anything," Rose said, waving away the words like she was shooing a fly. "Eyewitness testimony is appallingly inaccurate. Read Elizabeth Loftus's work on memory recall."

"I'll do that," I said. I looked at Mr. P. "Josh said he'll call you. He wants to know who the witness is."

"I have a couple of ideas, my dear."

I didn't ask what they were because I really didn't want to know.

Mac reached out to stroke Elvis's fur. "I didn't kill Erin and I didn't hurt Leila," he said. The cat's expression didn't change.

"You didn't need to do that," I said, putting my hands on my hips and shaking my head at him.

"It's important that you all know I didn't do this."

Rose reached up and patted his cheek with one hand. "We don't need Elvis's lie-detecting skills to know that," she said.

It was more like half an hour before the man and

woman who had bought the dresser showed up to get it, and then it took time to get it loaded securely in their borrowed half-ton truck. Elvis, Rose and I were an hour late leaving the shop.

"Did Mr. P. find out anything more about the FTC investigation?" I asked.

"Not yet," she said. "But he's going to do a little more digging around tonight."

Mr. P. had the computer skills of a first-class hacker. I knew what "digging around" could really mean.

"Rose, do you think that life insurance policy is important?" I asked.

"I'm not sure," she said. "It could be that Mac is right and Leila bought it to protect her sister. It certainly seems as though she cared a great deal about Natalie."

"But," I said. "I know there's a 'but.' I saw the look you gave Alfred when Mac said that he and Leila talked about everything."

Rose sighed softly. "It's just that we want to believe the best of family but it doesn't always mean that's what we get."

When we got home Elvis followed Rose down the hallway. "Do you two have plans?" I asked, standing in front of my own front door.

"We're making egg rolls," Rose said as if it was perfectly logical that my cat would be helping her.

"Umm, okay, then. Have fun."

"You, too, dear," Rose said as she stuck her key in the lock of her front door. "And try not to dump any food on Nicolas because salsa is so hard to get out of a light-colored shirt." She smiled sweetly at me and she and Elvis disappeared inside the apartment.

Since I was running late I had a quick shower and pulled on shorts and a blue-and-white-striped tee with loose sleeves that I'd bought in the spring when I'd injured my hand and had to wear a brace, and then hadn't worn it since. I left my hair down and was looking for my favorite sandals when there was a knock at the door. Rose, I guessed, probably bringing something I could have for breakfast, but when I opened the door Nick was standing there.

"I need to talk to you," he said.

"I'm meeting Jess in a few minutes," I said. "How long is this fight going to take?" Jess and I—and quite often Nick—had a weekly date at The Black Bear for Thursday Night Jam.

He braced one hand on the doorframe. "No fighting, I swear. I already had an argument with my mother over the Angels working on Mac's case and I don't want to fight with everyone in my life."

"I thought you said you were going to stop squabbling with your mother and Rose about their cases."

"I was," he said. "I am. I—" He let out a breath then he stepped inside the apartment, closed the door and leaned back against it.

"You're assuming the worst about Mac," I said. "You know him. You know he's a good guy."

"Sarah, he's lying. No matter what Mac says, he did meet Erin Fellowes right before she was killed. Michelle has a witness."

"The witness is mistaken," I said flatly.

"No. The witness isn't wrong."

"You're going to take the word of a stranger over Mac?" My voice was getting louder. I stared up at the ceiling for a moment and took a couple of deep breaths. I didn't want Rose coming down the hall to separate us again.

"The witness knows Mac."

My frustration got the better of me. "I don't care who it was," I said. I repeated the words, enunciating each one carefully. "I. Don't. Care. Whoever it is, they're wrong."

"No, I'm not," Nick said.

I'm not.

I stood there, body rigid, just staring at him. His cell rang then. "Let it ring," I said. I couldn't pull my eyes away from his face.

"I can't," he said, pushing away from the door. "I'm on call." He answered the phone, spoke briefly and then ended the call. "I have to go."

"And we have to talk." I felt desperate to hear more, to understand why Nick was so sure he'd seen Mac.

"I know." He made a helpless gesture. "There's a body. I have to go."

"Go, then," I said.

"You can't tell anyone, *anyone*, what I told you."

"I won't." I knew if I said anything it would cause problems with Michelle for both of us. Nick gave me a long, searching look and then he left.

I stood there in the middle of my living room, unsure of what to do now. I knew Nick wouldn't lie and given his keen observation skills I didn't see how he could be mistaken.

But.

But I knew in my gut that Mac wasn't lying. I rubbed the middle of my forehead with the heel of my hand and thought that I was starting to think like Rose.

I realized that I needed to leave if I wanted to make it to the jam on time. It seemed like a better alternative to sitting at home eating a carton of mocha fudge and trying to figure out why Nick was so sure he'd seen Mac. I gave up on my pretty sandals, stepped into my red Keds and left.

Jess had gotten us a table close to the front. I slid onto the empty chair. She took one look at me, raised a finger and somehow even with the crowd, a waiter appeared at our table. "What would you like?" she asked.

I hesitated, my mind a blank.

"Fish tacos and vinegar coleslaw for both of us," she said, giving the waiter a smile that had him tripping over his own feet as he headed for the kitchen. Jess had that effect on men. She was curvy in all the right places, with thick, dark hair and a smile that could make a guy forget his own name.

"What's up?" she said to me, reaching for the glass of wine in front of her.

I gave her a brief rundown on what was going on, how Mac had a wife in a coma and how her friend had come to town to see him and now she was dead.

"And let me guess," Jess said. "Rose and her cronies are on the case and Nick's got his man panties in a wad."

I couldn't help it, that last part made me laugh. "In a nutshell, yes."

"Nick being the nut."

I slumped against the back of my chair. "I feel like my loyalty is being pulled in two opposite directions." I made a face. "I wish I were an amoeba."

Jess frowned. "How exactly would being a micro-scopic, single-celled organism help? Aside from the fact that if no one was able to see you they wouldn't be able to pull you in any direction."

"I could undergo binary fission and then there would be two of me so I wouldn't have to pick a side."

Jess shook her head. "Yeah, but you couldn't eat fish tacos if you were an amoeba and the ones I see coming look pretty darn good."

Our waiter was back with our food and Jess was right, the fish tacos looked delicious and smelled even better.

"Wanna know what I think?" she asked around a mouthful of crispy battered fish, corn taco and salsa.

"Yes," I said, reaching for my fork so I could try the coleslaw. "Because otherwise I've just been whining to hear the sound of my own voice."

"Don't take a side and yes, I do know how hard that is. Just for now, follow the facts and see where they go."

I laughed. "I thought you were going to say something like 'follow your heart.'"

She shrugged and gave me a smile. "That's not a bad idea, either."

Chapter 7

The next morning, just after Elvis and I arrived at the shop, Liz showed up with Avery. The teen hugged Charlotte and me tightly. She'd had more layers cut into her dark hair and the shaggy style suited her.

"I missed you so, so much!" she said. She bent down, picked up Elvis and kissed the top of his head. "And I missed you."

He nuzzled her chin, cat for "I missed you, too."

"We all missed you," Mac said. "It was way too quiet around here."

"Nonna told me about your wife and her friend," Avery said. "I'm really sorry. And anyone who thinks you would hurt anybody is a moron." She glanced at her grandmother. "I'm sorry, I know you don't like the word, but it's true."

Mac gave her a smile. "I appreciate that. Thank you."

Avery looked around and spotted the collection of empty teacups waiting on the workbench. Turned into tiny planters, they were always popular with tourists.

"Sarah, do you want me to start working on those?" she asked.

"Please," I said. "The haworthia is out in the garage."

Avery threw her arms around Liz. "I have work to do," she said to her grandmother. "I'll see you tonight."

Liz kissed the top of her head. "Have a good day," she said.

Avery headed outside and Liz walked into the store with Mac and me. "You're right," she said. "It was quiet while she was gone. It was worth having one of those hideous smoothies for breakfast just to have her back."

"So what's on your agenda for today?" I asked, putting an arm around Liz's shoulders.

"I have a meeting at the bank and I'm having dinner with Channing Caulfield tonight," she said.

"Business or pleasure?" I asked, raising an eyebrow. I saw Mac try to stifle a smile as he moved across the room to unlock the front door.

"You're a saucy miss," she said tartly.

I put a hand on my chest and tried to look aggrieved. "I was just curious."

"Curiosity killed the cat," she said, pointing a warning finger at me.

"And satisfaction brought it back," I countered.

"I knew I was going to regret teaching you the rest of that."

I laughed. "So is this a date with Mr. Caulfield?"

"It most decidedly is not," Liz said firmly. "I'm looking for more information on du Mer. Small New England companies are one of Channing's areas of expertise. I thought he might know something."

"I appreciate this," Mac said.

She reached out and laid a hand on his shoulder as he came level with her. "You're family," she said. "This is what we do." She looked at the watch on her left arm. "I need to get going."

"I'm not going to have to start calling Mr. Caulfield 'Uncle Channing,' am I?" I called after Liz.

She kept on walking but over her shoulder she said, "Watch it, missy. You can be replaced with one of those self-driving cars and a robot that vacuums."

Mac had been watching us, arms folded over his chest. Now he smiled at me. "What would I do without all of you?" he asked.

I smiled at him. "Given the tenacity that the Angels have shown on other cases I don't think you're ever going to find out."

Charlotte and I spent the first part of the day back out at Clayton McNamara's house, continuing the inventory on the main floor of the house. There was so much furniture stuffed into the little rooms.

"This house is like one of those little cars at the circus that has about twelve clowns inside," I said to Charlotte.

"Ah, but I bet none of those cars ever had a Big Mouth Billy Bass," she said, holding up the musical prop which looked, from a distance, like a mounted trophy fish. In reality it was an animatronic novelty that had been very popular in the early 2000s.

"Does it still work?" I asked.

Charlotte pushed the button under the rubber fish and it lifted its head and began to sing "Don't Worry, Be Happy."

I buried my face in the crook of my elbow so Clayton wouldn't hear me laughing. I knew the musical fish would sell quickly, but I was thinking maybe I'd hang it in my office where I could make it sing to me the next time I got caught up in one of the Angels' cases.

Midmorning, Clayton brought us coffee and I got a kick out of how he flirted with Charlotte—and how she was flirting back.

A bus tour stopped in at the shop late afternoon, which kept us all busy. We sold every one of the teacup planters Avery had made, along with several quilts and other small kitchen items. The man with the great hair who had been in the shop the previous day came back and I sold him a guitar, a 2006 Takamine cutaway. The acoustic-electric came with the original hard-shell case, and the buyer didn't quibble over the price I was asking, but I felt confident we were both getting a great deal. Sam Newman had helped me set the price and he knew more about guitars than anyone I knew. I'd known Sam my whole life and he'd been playing a lot longer than that.

After the tourists had gone Mr. P. came downstairs with a cup of coffee for me. "Thanks," I said. "I needed this."

He smiled. "It's my pleasure."

"Have you come up with anything?" I asked after I had taken a long drink from the mug he'd handed me.

"As a matter of fact, I have." He had a bit of a *cat that swallowed the canary* look about him. I'd seen that expression before. It meant that he was particularly pleased with whatever he'd unearthed. "I found Leila's cousin, Stephanie. She's living in Carrabassett Valley."

"That's easily doable," I said, taking another sip of my coffee. "It's just a couple of hours' drive. When do you want to go?" I knew Liz would be happy to make the trip but truth be told I wanted to meet Stevie and I had the illusion—even though I knew it was probably misplaced—that if I went along Rose and Mr. P. would get into at least a little less trouble.

The latter smiled at me now. "I was hoping you'd say that, my dear. Will tomorrow morning work for you?"

Mac had been getting the vacuum out from under the stairs. I knew he'd heard the conversation. I looked over at him.

"I'll open," he said. "Avery and Charlotte will be here. We can take care of everything."

Avery and Charlotte were just coming in from the workroom.

Charlotte nodded. "Of course we can," she said. Then she looked at me and frowned. "What are we taking care of?"

"Here, Saturday," Avery said. "So Sarah and Rose and Mr. P. can go talk to Mac's wife's cousin."

We all looked at her.

"Yeah, I was eavesdropping." She shrugged. "You all know I do that so if you don't want me to know stuff you should talk quieter."

"Saturday's covered," Mac said with a smile.

Mr. P. turned to look at him. "Thank you, Mac," he said.

Mac brushed off the front of his jeans and came over to us. "I don't need any thanks," he said, "but I owe them to you."

"We're happy to be able to help," Mr. P. said.

Mac shook his head. "I know I sound like a broken record but I can't believe that Stevie would hurt Leila. They spent a lot of time together as kids and Stevie was very supportive of Leila when she started the company. And why would she kill Erin?"

"We aren't going to see Stephanie to prove she killed Erin," Mr. P. said, hiking up the waistband of his pants. He had an unfortunate tendency to wear them up in his armpits. Given that I'd once rocked overalls with one strap hanging down and combat boots—in the summertime—I wasn't going to criticize. "We're going to see Stephanie to learn more about Leila from someone she grew up with. We're fact-finding. You've seen us do that before with other cases. *Scientia potentia est*."

"Thomas Hobbes," Charlotte said approvingly. "Knowledge is power." Charlotte had coached the high school debate team and I knew the quote was one of her favorites.

Avery had her head under the table where she'd been changing the linens before going out to the workroom to help Charlotte find a box of snow globes Jess and I had bought at an auction. "Actually the quote was used hundreds of years before Hobbes by a seventh-century imam who wrote 'Knowledge is power and it can command obedience.'" Avery straightened up and looked at us. "That's the English translation. He wrote in Arabic." She smiled at us and headed back out to the workroom to get something. "I love knowing things," she called over her shoulder. "It freaks out adults."

After we closed I took Elvis home. I had a plate of sundried tomato and chicken pasta salad that Charlotte had made. Elvis had a little chicken and then headed for the bedroom to get settled for *Jeopardy!* I put my dishes in the dishwasher, brushed my teeth and put on a little lip gloss. The TV in the bedroom was on a timer, set to come on for *Jeopardy!* and shut off when the game show was over. I had no idea why Elvis liked to watch the show. Maybe it was something he'd done with his previous owner. I kept thinking he'd get tired of the routine but after more than a year of living with me he was still a faithful viewer.

"I'm leaving," I called from the living room. I was going to pick up Jess. We were taking part in a trivia/Pictionary–style contest at McNamara's. It was a charity challenge and Jess and I were playing for the hot lunch program at the elementary school.

"You ready for this?" Jess asked as she climbed into my SUV.

"Well, I can draw a pretty wicked stick man," I said as I pulled onto the street. "You, on the other hand, were born for this." Jess had a head for odd bits of trivia. The odder, the better.

She grinned and nodded in agreement. "Yes, I was." I could see her eyeing me out of the corner of my eye. "How many planets are there?" she suddenly asked.

"Nice try," I said. "But I know this. Eight. There used to be nine and then Pluto got demoted."

"Pluto was reclassified."

"Isn't that the same thing?"

"No," Jess said, vigorously shaking her head. "Pluto didn't meet all the criteria to be a planet."

"In other words the cool planets didn't want Pluto hanging out with them anymore."

"The International Astronomical Union altered the definition of what constitutes a planet."

"Like I said. The cool planets didn't want Pluto hanging out with them so they changed the rules."

Jess nodded. "Pretty much." She shifted in her seat. "How many dwarf planets are there?" she asked.

"Are you going to quiz me all the way there?" I flipped on my blinker to turn right.

"That was my plan," she said. "How many dwarf planets?"

"Seven," I said.

"No!" Jess said. "Seven dwarves is *Snow White*. There are five dwarf planets. You're not taking this seriously."

I nodded in agreement. "You're right. I'm not. I don't need to know any of this because you do and you're on my team. All I have to do is draw great stick men and be gracious when we win."

And that was all I had to do. Although I did ace the question "How many planets are there?" We moved on to round two in two weeks.

"You two are a great team," Glenn said.

"We pretty much clicked from the moment we met back in college," Jess said. "Sarah stuck an ad up looking for a roommate."

"Which Jess immediately took down because she didn't want anyone to answer it before she could," I finished.

Jess tilted her head in my direction. "If Sarah were a guy I would have broken her heart at least once by now."

"Or maybe you would have had a great romantic love story," Glenn said.

Jess and I looked at each other. "Nah," we both said at the same time.

Glenn had half a dozen blueberry muffins for the two of us for winning our first round.

"Thank you," I said. "You didn't have to do that."

Glenn's blueberry muffins were delicious, full of juicy berries with a hint of lemon and a crumbly streusel topping.

"I figured you deserved some sort of prize," he said with a shrug. "You could stack them up and make a little trophy with them."

"A trophy I can eat. I like that," Jess said. Something across the room caught her eye. "There's a customer I need to talk to," she said, making a vague gesture in my direction. "Just give me two minutes and I'm ready to go."

"Take your time," I said. I turned back to Glenn.

"Rumor has it that there's a connection between Mac and the woman whose body was found down on the boat dock," he said. "Is everything all right?"

I rubbed the back of my neck with one hand. "Yeah, for now."

"So the Angels are on the case?"

"You couldn't pry them away from it with a crowbar," I said.

Glenn brushed crumbs from the front of his apron. "I don't know if this is important or not, but the woman who was killed was in here just a few hours before she died. She was looking for directions to your shop."

"Did you see anyone with her?" I asked. I knew it was a long shot even as I said the words.

Glenn shook his head. "No."

He hesitated, just for a moment before he answered.

I squinted up at him. "There's something you're not saying. What is it?"

"It's probably nothing."

I gave him a half smile. "I'm pretty sure Rose has

some words of wisdom about this but I can't think of them. Please, just tell me what 'probably nothing' is."

"Okay," he said. "I gave the woman directions. I was standing right there." He pointed toward the front window. "I saw her head up the street. There was a car parked on the other side, just down a bit. A gray Toyota. The driver turned and went the same way."

"Did you notice whether the driver was a man or a woman?"

"Man, I think," Glenn said. "The body type was right and he was wearing a baseball cap. It's probably just a coincidence the guy happened to turn and head in the same direction."

"Probably," I said, because most likely it was a coincidence. They did happen sometimes. On the other hand maybe there were security cameras somewhere on the street that Mr. P. could get a look at.

Jess came back then, we said good night to Glenn and left.

I'd told Alfred and Rose that I wanted to hit the road at quarter to eight Saturday morning. I stepped into the hallway five minutes before that to find Rose coming out of her apartment with Mr. P. I decided I didn't want to know if he'd walked over early for breakfast or spent the night. Liam liked to tease that Rose had more of a love life than I did. I was pretty sure she did, but I didn't need confirmation. It seemed like everyone had more of a love life than I did. Liam's solution to the problem was, as he'd put it while he sprawled on my sofa, to "lay a wet one on Nick."

Nick. I hadn't heard from him since his confession that he was Michelle's witness. Maybe he was just tied up with the case that had called him away. Maybe he was avoiding me.

Stevie Carleton's home was off the grid outside the Carrabassett Valley ski area in the western part of the state. The weather was gorgeous, not too hot or too humid and we made good time. It was about quarter after ten when Mr. P. directed me to turn left. We drove down a tree-lined road and pulled into a cleared parking area.

Off to the right I caught sight of the house. "Oh wow," I said.

Stevie Carleton's home was two stories, built of stone with a saltbox roof and wide, high windows. Beyond it I could see cultivated fields and beyond them trees. It was a beautiful spot.

We got out of the SUV, grateful to stretch and shake the kinks out of our legs. A curvy woman in her early thirties wearing a tie-dyed T-shirt and gray cotton shorts was coming down a path from the house to meet us, wiping her hands on her shorts. Her dark, curly hair, streaked with blond highlights, was pulled back into a messy knot at her neck. She had the same dark eyes and light brown skin as Leila did in the photo Mac had shown me. This had to be Stevie Carleton.

"Alfred, you found us," she said.

Mr. P. smiled. "Your directions were excellent." He indicated Rose and me. "Stephanie, this is Rose Jackson and Sarah Grayson."

"It's a pleasure to meet you," she said.

"Your house is beautiful," I said. "I've never seen anything like it."

Stevie smiled with pleasure. "Thank you. My partner, Davis, and I collected all the rocks that make up the outside walls." She laughed. "We picked the rockiest section of land to buy and build on so there were plenty." She gestured in the direction of the building. "You've had a long drive. How about a glass of iced tea?"

"That would be wonderful," Rose said. "Thank you." Mr. P. and I both nodded.

We followed Stevie back along the path. The house almost seemed to be rising from the land. There was a low platform, like a deck with no railings, in front of the house.

"These boards are from an old barn that was on the property," Stevie said.

Mr. P. leaned forward for a better look. "Douglas fir?" he asked.

She nodded. "We salvaged everything we could. I have a table inside that's made from the same wood." She indicated several chairs grouped around an octagonal wooden table. "Have a seat, or would you like to see the house?"

Rose smiled. "I'd love to see the house if you don't mind."

"So would I," I said.

"I think we all would," Mr. P. added.

"Okay, then, let's take the tour," Stevie said.

The main floor of the stone building was one open space. There was a kitchen at one end and a living/family room at the other with a central woodstove. The wall that faced south was almost completely windows and Stevie showed us the insulated shades that she and her partner had set up on a pulley system so they could be lowered at night or on bright days when the sun made the inside of the house too warm. She explained that the nearby solar panels provided all the energy they needed to power everything in the house. Stairs led to the second floor, where there were two bedrooms. The house was filled with light even with the shades partly drawn and I was captivated by how many things had been repurposed in the well-organized space.

Stevie got a glass pitcher from the refrigerator. There was a tray on the counter with glasses, cloth napkins, and a plate of cookies.

"I can bring this," I said, indicating the tray.

"Thanks," she said.

Stevie led the way back outside. Once we were all settled in our chairs with our tea she looked at Mr. P. "First of all, I need to say that I didn't try to kill Leila."

"That's not why we're here," he said.

"Although we appreciate your frankness," Rose added.

"Hey, it would make sense for you to suspect I had something to do with what happened," Stevie said. "I know how it looks. I'm the one who benefits if Leila is dead." She stopped speaking and cleared her throat, blinking several times. It was clear that she was emotional about Leila. "What I want is for Leila to wake up and come back to us. No amount of money is better than that."

"When was the last time you saw Leila?" Rose asked, leaning forward in her seat.

"You mean before she ended up in the hospital?" I noticed that, unlike Mac, Stevie didn't use the word "accident." Did she think Mac had had something to do with what had happened?

Rose nodded.

"I saw her the day before she went into the coma. I was in Boston for a conference. We made plans to get together again in a few weeks. There was an exhibit coming to the Museum of Fine Arts that she wanted to drag me to: Japanese woodblock prints and those little carved figures—netsuke. Leila had a thing for Asian art." Stevie shifted in her chair, pulling both legs up so she was sitting cross-legged. "I was at a lecture on hydroponic greenhouses at the time the heating system in the house would have been tampered with. *And* for the record I have the skills to mess with the heating system. I've learned how to do a lot of things since Davis and I started building this homestead. You can't exactly just call a repair person when something goes wrong out here."

So she didn't believe what happened to her cousin was an accident.

"When I get my share of the trust on my thirty-fifth birthday I plan to start a charitable environmental foundation to promote the kind of lifestyle I'm living and help people learn about sustainable building and farming. It'll be more than enough to do what I want. I have no designs on Leila's share. I don't need it." Her voice was emphatic.

"Do you mind telling us what Leila was like?" Mr. P. asked.

I reached for a cookie as much to have something to do with my hands as because they looked delicious. I'd been wondering what Leila was like since Erin had first said her name.

A smile spread across Stevie's face. "She was funny. She was a tiny person but she had this huge laugh and when she started laughing pretty soon you were laughing, too, just because she was. She didn't take any crap from anyone, but on the other hand she was so kind-hearted she wouldn't even kill a spider in the bathtub."

Leila sounded like someone I would like, I realized.

"She was only a year older than I am but she always acted like a big sister," Stevie continued. "I talked to her about guys, about life, everything." She pressed her lips together for a moment. "I miss that."

"What was Leila's relationship like with her sister, Natalie?" Rose asked.

Stevie reached for the pitcher of iced tea and refilled Mr. P.'s glass.

"Thank you," he said softly. The tea was very good, lemony with a hint of sweetness.

"It's a good indication of the type of person Leila was," Stevie said. She paused for a moment. "The type of person she is. She welcomed Natalie and insisted from the beginning that everyone else in the family do the same or stay away. She was angry with her father for keeping Natalie a secret for so long, but Leila never took it out on her."

She was still holding the pitcher and she turned to me and raised an eyebrow. "Please," I said, holding out my glass.

She filled it and set the pitcher back on the low table.

"Leila always had a strong sense of what's right and wrong. When she invited Natalie to work at her business Leila bought a life insurance policy with Natalie as the beneficiary, so if anything ever happened to her, Natalie would have the money to buy Mac out."

The policy Mr. P. had discovered. Rose and I exchanged a look. It seemed Leila had had some secrets from Mac.

"What were things like between Leila and Mac?" I asked.

Stevie grinned. "They were crazy about one another from the moment they first saw each other. I was there. It was a party and they literally saw each other across a crowded room and it was magic." Her expression changed, the smile fading from her eyes. "Does Mac know you're here?" she asked.

"Yes," Rose said. "And for the record he told us there was no way you could have hurt Leila."

Stevie hung her head for a moment. "He's kinder to me than I was to him. I bet he didn't tell you that we had words when Leila ended up in the hospital."

"It must have been a very emotional time," Mr. P. said, his voice warm and kind the way it always was. "Things are said that no one means at times like that. I doubt Mac holds it against you."

"Maybe he should," she said. "I'm ashamed to say that I asked him if he had anything to do with what happened." She gave her head a shake. "I was wrong. Mac loved Leila more than anything in the world. He wouldn't have hurt her. Of everyone who knew her you can be sure Mac isn't the guilty one."

I suddenly felt that the questions we'd been asking were way too personal. Mr. P. was looking at me, I realized.

"Thank you for telling us about Leila," he said. "I'm wondering if you mind sharing something a little lighter? I'm curious about how you and your partner ended up in the wilds, so to speak, of Maine. I confess the idea of being so independent intrigues me."

I tried to get a mental image of Mr. P. living off the grid, growing his own vegetables, making bread and getting his electricity from the sun. He'd probably be good at it. The more I got to know the man, the more he surprised me with what he knew and what he could do.

Stevie smiled. "I don't mind at all. Being self-sufficient is one of my favorite things to talk about."

She explained that they grew their own organic vegetables as well as apples and pears. "We don't eat much meat but what we do eat comes from a small farm a few miles west where the animals are free-range."

We spent another twenty minutes or so with Stevie, sitting in the sunshine and learning more about her desire to get her pear and apple butters business going. Finally Rose looked at me and said, "I think we need to be getting back on the road." We all stood up. Rose took one of Stevie's hands in both of hers. "Thank you for talking to us and thank you for letting us see this beautiful place."

"You're welcome," Stevie said. She handed Mr. P. a piece of paper. "That's the contact information for the registrar and several people who can tell you where I was the night Leila was hurt. I'd feel better if you confirm I've told you the truth."

She shifted from one foot to the other. "I'm afraid I don't have an alibi for the night Erin Fellowes was killed, unless you'd take the word of a couple of raccoons. I was here by myself. Davis has been away in Nova Scotia at a course on organic farming methods for the last couple of weeks." She stopped and frowned. "I did have a flat tire earlier in the day. I'm not sure if that matters."

"Thank you, my dear," Mr. P. said.

"Had you spoken to Erin recently?" I asked. We still didn't know how Erin had located Mac.

Stevie shook her head. "No. I barely knew her. She was Leila's friend." She brushed something from the front of her shorts. "Would you . . . tell Mac I'm thinking about him?"

I smiled. "We will."

"You're welcome to visit, you know," Rose said.

Stevie smiled. "Maybe I will."

As we started for home I glanced in the rearview mirror at Mr. P. in the backseat. "Do you think Stevie is telling the truth?"

"I want her to be," he said.

Beside me Rose nodded. "I like her."

"Neither of you answered my question," I said.

Rose exhaled softly. "She had answers to all of our questions and all the right emotional responses."

"But . . ."

I glanced at Rose. Her hands were folded in her lap and her expression was serious. "Well, sweet girl," she said, "I've been around the block enough times to know that money makes people do things you just wouldn't believe they'd do."

"I'm afraid Rose is right," Mr. P. said from the back.

"So we keep on digging," I said.

Next to me Rose was nodding. "We keep on digging," she echoed.

Chapter 8

We got back to the shop about one thirty. I was glad to get out of the SUV and stretch my legs. We'd stopped at a farm stand for tomatoes, green beans and new potatoes.

"You made good time," Charlotte said as I handed her a bag of vegetables.

"That's because Sarah needs glasses," Rose said.

I turned to look at her. "I do?"

"Well, it would explain why you didn't seem to be able to see any of the posted speed limits."

I put my hands on my hips. "Are you implying I was speeding?" I said.

Mr. P. noisily cleared his throat.

Rose shook her head as she headed for the stairs. "I guess I'm getting old. I didn't think I was being overly subtle."

"I wasn't speeding," I said. "I may have accelerated several times to pass other cars that were going too slow, but I wasn't speeding." I might have been just a little self-righteous in my denial.

Rose kept going. Charlotte's lips were twitching.

"Liz drives faster than I do," I said.

Rose stopped on the bottom step and looked over her shoulder at me. "And if Liz drove off a cliff would you do that, too?" she asked. She started up the steps.

I'd been hearing some version of that line from her and Liz and Charlotte *and* my grandmother since I was five. "Well, if I did it wouldn't be because I was speeding!" I called after her.

Rose started up the steps but I could tell from the way her shoulders were shaking that she was laughing.

Liz came in later in the afternoon to report on her dinner with Channing. He'd used his contacts in the business world to find out more about the lawsuit and the fraud investigation into du Mer. The quality of the products was the problem. Customers were claiming the products were not organic and natural and didn't contain the ingredients listed on the label.

"That's impossible," Mac said. "Leila graduated with a bachelor of science in chemistry before she got her MBA. She understood the manufacturing process and she'd put quality control checks in place." He shook his head and grimaced. "I know I keep saying this, but nothing, *nothing* makes sense."

Liz patted her blond hair. "Let us figure things out. We're pretty darn good at it if I say so myself."

"You are pretty darn good at it," he said. "I'm glad you're on my side." He looked at me. "I'm going out to the shed to take another look at that old bed frame."

I nodded. Once Mac was gone I put my arm around Liz and kissed her cheeks. She smelled like spring flowers. "Thank you for having dinner with Channing," I said. "I know it was a sacrifice." I tried not to grin but it got away from me.

Liz turned her head and gave me the stink eye. "You're not too old to spend five minutes in the corner," she warned.

I laughed. "Did you know that Gram still has the naughty chair in storage?"

"And clearly we still have the girl who used to sit in it."

"Liam spent as much time in that chair as I did," I protested.

Liz squeezed my cheeks between her thumb and middle finger. "What I remember is how many times you were both in it at the same time."

I grinned at her, remembering the big upholstered chair in Gram's living room where she would put Liam, or me, or most often Liam and me for a time-out. We were supposed to think about whatever it was we'd just done. Mostly we'd poke each other with our elbows and smack the sides of our sneakers together, and the time in the chair would end up getting extended by several minutes.

"So when are we going to see Liam again?" Liz asked.

Charlotte came past us with a box from under the stairs and smiled. "Is Liam coming?" she asked. My tall, blond brother with his little boy good looks was popular with women of all ages, and Charlotte and the others loved to spoil him.

When my mom married Liam's dad not only did he get me, and a stepmom who loved him like crazy, he also got a grandmother and *three* fairy godmothers. When I reminded him of that he'd pretend to get thoughtful for a moment and then say it was worth putting up with me to get all of them.

"I think he's coming around Labor Day," I said. "He's still consulting on the harbor front development."

The downtown project, which was going to add a hotel and several new shops to the waterfront, had already had several stops and starts. Now the start date had been delayed from the end of the month to the beginning of October because the town still got a lot of visitors during September. The developers were trying to cause as little disruption to businesses in the area as possible.

Charlotte set the box she was carrying on the counter next to the cash register and smiled. "It'll be good to see Liam and Isabel will be here in—"

"—ten days!" I finished, grinning at her. "I can't believe Gram and John have been gone so long."

"It'll be good to have them home," Liz said. "And it would be nice if we could have this business with Mac settled by then." She held out her hand and studied her nails for a moment. "I think I need to go do a little more fact-finding and maybe get French tips." She waved at us and left.

I walked over to join Charlotte and she put her arms around my shoulders and gave me a knowing smile. "I think Chuckie Caulfield is beginning to win Liz over."

I looked around, somehow expecting that Liz had heard and would come through the door to tackle Charlotte. "Do not say that in front of Liz!" I hissed. "I'm not saying it might not be true but don't say it out loud."

"Don't worry," Charlotte said, still smiling as she released me from the hug. "I didn't just fall off the turnip truck." Then her expression turned serious. "I know this is none of my business," she began, "but that's never seemed to stop any of us before. Did you and Nicolas argue over this case?"

I sighed softly. "What did he tell you?"

She smoothed the front of her apron. "Nothing, but it was pretty clear from his mood when I saw him that something was wrong. You can call it mother's intuition if you want."

I shook my head.

"You have to know that he loves Rose and Liz just as much as you do. They're just as much his family. I know that he can be overprotective in the extreme. But it comes out of love."

"I probably shouldn't be talking about Nick with his mother," I said. I didn't have the heart to tell her that we hadn't argued about the Angels being on the case. And I couldn't tell her about Nick's insistence that he'd seen Mac with Erin Fellowes right before she was killed. He'd asked me not to tell anyone.

Charlotte gave me a look I couldn't read. It was almost a mix of love and . . . sadness? "I'd love it if you could talk to me as my daughter-in-law," she said.

A lump formed in my throat. Before I could say anything Charlotte spoke again. "But knowing you were with someone who makes you happy would be just as good."

I leaned my head against hers. "I love you," I said, my voice raspy with emotion.

"I love you, too, sweetie," she said. "Always."

I straightened up just as a couple of customers came through the front door.

"I'll take care of them," Charlotte said.

I escaped to my office, closed the door and leaned against the desk. I loved Charlotte and Liz and Rose. I knew they all wanted Nick and me together. It would be the perfect happy ending as far as they were concerned, but I wasn't so sure it would be for the two of us.

I went to the staff room and got a cup of coffee, then I sat down at my desk and called my dad.

"What's wrong?" he asked.

"What makes you think something is wrong?" I said.

"My Dad Spidey Sense and, by the way, you don't have to be bitten by a radioactive spider to get it."

Talking to Dad always made me feel better. Technically, Peter Kennelly was my stepfather, but to me he was just Dad. And I was his child just as much as Liam was. Like Liam he had the ability to make me laugh no matter how bad I felt and I knew I could always count on him to chase the monsters out from under the bed no matter how old I got.

"There's no such thing as Dad Spidey Sense," I said, leaning back in my chair and propping my feet on the corner of my desk where I could admire how cute my sandals were.

"Is, too," he insisted. He hummed the *X-Files* theme. "And it has determined that the Angels have a case."

I laughed. "That's not Spidey Sense, that's reading the North Harbor newspaper online."

"Hey! Good reading skills are one of my superpowers."

"Yes, the Angels have a case."

"Who's the client?"

I hesitated but I knew if I didn't tell Dad he'd just call

Rose or Charlotte and find out. "Mac," I said. I filled him in on the background.

"What do you need?" he asked. I knew he'd grabbed a pen and a pad of paper and was making notes. I pictured him writing, his mouth twisted to one side.

"You hold your mouth funny when you think," Mom liked to tease him.

"Anything you can find out about the incident that put Mac's wife in a coma. In the end what happened was ruled accidental, but for a while, as far as the police were concerned, Mac was the main suspect. The only suspect, I think."

"I'll use my contacts and see what I can find out. It might take me a day or two."

"That's okay," I said.

"Sarah, Mac's a good man," Dad said. "This'll work out."

"Love you," I said.

"You, too," he said. "Talk to you soon."

I hung up and slid down in the chair so I was sitting on my tailbone. He was right. Mac was a good man. Was that why he was in this mess?

I leaned my head against the back of my chair and closed my eyes. Now that I'd called Dad I didn't know what to do next. There was a soft knock on my door then.

"Come in," I called, opening my eyes and straightening up.

It was Mr. P. "Am I interrupting?" he asked.

"No," I said. "All I was doing was beating my head against a metaphorical brick wall."

"Sometimes those can be as painful as the real thing."

I nodded. "Have you confirmed Stevie's alibi yet?"

He pushed his glasses up his nose. "It's going to be Monday before I can do that, but there are a couple of things I wanted to talk to you about."

I leaned forward and gestured at the love seat on the other side of my desk. Mr. P. sat down. He cleared his throat. "First of all, I managed to get some security camera footage from Glenn McNamara's neighbor across the street."

"Did you find anything useful?" I asked. On the drive out to see Stevie Carleton I'd told Rose and Mr. P. the story Glenn had told me, that Erin had stopped in at McNamara's looking for directions to Second Chance. Based on his serious expression I thought I knew what his answer was going to be. I was right.

"No," he said. "The camera is old and the quality of the images is poor—dark and grainy. I have a piece of software that cleaned up the image a little, but in the end all I can do is confirm the car is a gray Toyota and it appears to be a man in a baseball cap in the driver's seat. If you'd like to look for yourself I'd be happy to show you what I have."

"If you can't see anything I doubt that I would." I rubbed the bridge of my nose with two fingers. I'd been hoping the car Glenn had seen would turn out to be a clue even though I knew the chance was pretty remote.

Mr. P. was studying me, his expression thoughtful behind his wire-framed glasses.

"You said there were two things you wanted to talk about," I said.

"It's about the witness who supposedly saw Mac talking to Erin Fellowes."

I could suddenly hear my heartbeat thudding in my ears.

"At some point Detective Andrews will have to provide that information to Josh."

I nodded slowly. "I think so."

A furry black paw poked around the office door followed by the rest of Elvis. He padded into the room, jumped up beside Mr. P. and looked expectantly at him. The old man reached over to stroke the cat's fur. "I don't think it makes a lot of sense to put any effort into digging up that name when we'll have it soon, anyway," he said.

He knew Nick was the witness. And somehow, someway, he'd guessed or figured out that I knew as well.

"I think you're right," I said, trying to keep my tone as offhand as his had been.

Alfred got to his feet, giving Elvis one last scratch on the top of his head. "I'll let you get back to work," he said. He started for the door.

"Thank you," I said.

He turned and smiled at me. "Things have a way of working out, my dear," he said. "Have faith."

Elvis launched himself from the love seat to the top of my desk. My chin was propped on one hand and he walked across the top of the desk to nuzzle my cheek. "Mr. P. said to have faith," I told him.

The cat cocked his head to one side and gave me a look of skepticism. Even he knew I wasn't very good at that.

Chapter 9

I'd planned to stay and work on the metal cart but by the time we closed up I'd lost my enthusiasm for that idea.

"Let's go home," I said to Elvis.

"Mrr," he agreed, heading for the back door.

As soon as I opened the apartment door Elvis retreated to his cat tower. I changed my clothes and went for a run. I remembered when Nick had come running with me. He was slow and his form was terrible but I'd laughed the entire time we were out. I wondered when I was going to hear from him. We were all working to prove Mac had had nothing to do with Erin Fellowes's death. My stomach felt unsettled when I thought that maybe Nick was working to do the opposite.

When I got back to the house Liz's car was parked out front. I stepped inside and she poked her head out of Rose's apartment. "Dinner's in fifteen minutes," she said.

I turned to look at her. "It's Saturday night. Maybe I have plans."

Liz rolled her eyes. "You're hilarious," she said. She

looked down at her watch. "Dinner's in fourteen minutes." She closed the door again.

I had a shower, put on a T-shirt dress and flip-flops and went out into the living room to find Elvis waiting by the door. "How do you know we were invited for dinner?" I said. "Were you over here with your kitty ear pressed to the door, listening?"

He put a paw on the door for a moment, then looked at me and meowed loudly. Sometimes I got the feeling the cat was messing with me—and enjoying it.

As always dinner was delicious—chicken with leeks and tomatoes, new baby potatoes and green beans. "How was your manicure?" I asked Liz over a second helping of green beans.

She held out a hand. She had a pretty pink French manicure. "Channing was correct," she said. "Everything he found out about du Mer is true. Six or seven months before Leila's accident there were rumblings that the product quality had gone way down. I talked to Elspeth."

Elspeth was Liz's niece, her brother's daughter. She owned Phantasy, a spa and hair salon and a pretty good source of North Harbor gossip.

"She confirmed that the products haven't been the same since." Liz reached over and swiped a green bean from my plate.

I made a face. "Then either Leila knew what was going on or . . ."

Rose finished the sentence. "Or her sister was defrauding the company. Given that Mac knew nothing about the problems at du Mer it's not too much of a stretch to think maybe Leila didn't, either."

"You think it was Natalie," I said, gesturing with my fork.

Liz held out a hand and admired her nails. "'Blood is thicker than water' doesn't always mean a damn thing," she said.

I was restless and up early the next morning. I made breakfast, checked the store's Web site and cleaned the bathroom all with Elvis's supervision. I still had energy to burn. I decided to head over to the shop and work on my table for a while. I grabbed my keys and bag and turned around to find Elvis waiting by the door. "You don't even know where I'm going," I said.

"Mrr," he said. I got the feeling he didn't care.

The cat was almost always up for going out. He was very social, I'd discovered. He'd quickly made himself at home in the shop, charming customers—even those who weren't cat people.

I'd had Elvis for over a year now. He'd just appeared one day, down along the harbor front, managing to get fed at several different places, including The Black Bear. Sam and his pickup band, The Hairy Bananas, were doing their Elvis medley when Sam swore he saw the cat sitting just inside the front door of the pub. He claimed Elvis stayed put through the entire set and left only when they started on "Satisfaction."

No one seemed to know who owned the small black cat. Sam had named him Elvis because he seemed to like the King's music. On closer inspection he'd discovered a scar that sliced diagonally across the cat's nose, and a couple of others hidden by his black fur.

Sam had managed to convince me to take the cat and it had been hard to say no once Elvis had climbed in my old truck and settled himself behind a guitar case. I grinned at the memory.

I leaned into the truck to grab him, but he slipped off the seat, onto the floor mat. With the guitar there I couldn't reach him.

Behind me, I could hear Sam laughing.

I blew my hair out of my face, backed out of the truck and glared at Sam. "Your cat's in my truck. Do something!"

He folded his arms over his chest. "He's not my cat. I'm pretty sure he's your cat now."

"I don't want a cat."

"Tell him that," Sam said with a shrug.

I stuck my head back through the open driver's door. "I don't want a cat," I said.

Ensconced out of my reach in the little lean-to made by the guitar case Elvis looked up from washing his face—again—and meowed once and went back to it.

I looked down at the cat now. "I think you and Sam were in cahoots," I said.

Elvis seemed to shrug. It was as close to an admission as I was going to get.

As I came level with the shop I caught sight of a man in the parking lot, leaning against a red SUV. "Is that a customer or is that TV crew coming back to try to hijack our parking?" I said to Elvis. He craned his neck to see out the windshield and made a huffy sound through his nose. Okay, his vote was the TV crew.

I took another look at the man. He was a couple of inches shorter than Mac, which put him at maybe five ten or so, with the same dark skin and cropped dark hair, plus a closely trimmed mustache and goatee. He was wearing a lightweight, gray summer suit and was a little heavier than Mac, with broader shoulders.

I parked by the back door. "Stay here," I said to Elvis. His ears twitched but he sat down on the seat again.

I walked over to the mystery man, who had pushed away from the car and straightened up when I'd pulled in. "Hello," I said. "Can I help you?"

"You're Sarah Grayson, aren't you?" he said. He was wearing a white shirt with the gray suit. The top button was undone and he didn't have a tie.

"I'm sorry," I said. "You have me at a disadvantage. Should I know you?"

He extended his hand. "I'm Jackson Montgomery. Mac and I are friends." He had gorgeous blue eyes and a ready smile. The gray suit was expensive. Thanks to Liz I could recognize quality when I saw it. But I noted that he was wearing an inexpensive Timex on his left arm.

"I came to see Mac," he said. "Is he here?"

"I'm sorry, Mac isn't available," I said. Just because the man said he was a friend of Mac's didn't mean he was. "Would you like me to give him a message?"

"It's okay, Sarah." Mac was standing in the garage doorway. He walked over to us.

Jackson Montgomery smiled at Mac. "Man, it's good to see you. I heard about Erin. I was in trial or I would have been here sooner."

So he was a lawyer. That explained the expensive suit and the inexpensive watch. Together they said successful but not elitist.

"Why are you here at all?" Mac said. "I've been in North Harbor for more than a year and you haven't made any effort to contact me. Go back to Boston, Jackson."

"I can help," Jackson said. His eyes didn't move from Mac's face.

"I have a great lawyer and friends I can depend on. I don't need anything from you." Mac's tone was cold, his body tightly controlled. "I have work to do. Excuse me." He headed across the parking lot.

Jackson exhaled loudly and pulled a hand down over the back of his head. He swore softly just under his breath. I stood silently watching him. He glanced at me. "Mac's angry," he said.

I folded my arms across my body. "What he said was true," I said. "Are you really surprised? Mac has been here for over a year but this is the first time I've seen you."

He looked away for a moment then faced me again. "You're right. I should have come sooner—a lot sooner—but I'm not leaving town now that I'm here." He pulled his keys from his pocket. "It was a pleasure to meet you, Sarah."

I watched him drive away, then I collected Elvis from the car and went inside. Mac was at the workbench. "He's gone," I said, setting the cat down.

Mac didn't look up. "He'll be back. Jackson doesn't take no for an answer the first time he hears it—or the second or third time." He set down the screwdriver he'd been holding and finally faced me. "I'm sorry for just walking away. I didn't want to say something I'd be sorry for later."

"It's okay," I said. "You should know that he said he's not going anywhere."

Mac gave me a half smile. "That doesn't surprise me.

Jackson has a bullheaded streak I always half admired. Now I'm seeing the other side of it." He gave his head an abrupt shake as though he were trying to get rid of the feelings the conversation had stirred up. "You're up early," he said.

"You know what they say; the early bird gets the worm."

He made a face. "No worms, but how about coffee?"

"Even better," I said.

"I haven't made any coffee here but I have a pot in my place," he said. "I should warn you, it's strong."

I shot him a look.

He laughed. "Right. I forgot who I was talking to."

Elvis followed us into the shop. We started for the stairs. He went to nose around a collection of baskets Charlotte had arranged by the front door.

"When I was a kid I'd sneak tastes of my grandmother's coffee," I said. "I think I was about twenty years old before I figured out that not everyone made it as strong as she did."

Mac's apartment was on the second floor overlooking the old garage. This past winter the building where he'd rented an apartment had been sold. We'd ended up renovating part of the second-floor space and now he had a small apartment with its own private entrance at the back and I worried a lot less about security for the store. Not to mention that most mornings the coffee was on when I arrived. It seemed to be working out well for both of us.

"Have a seat, I'll get the coffee," Mac said, gesturing at the round, wooden table by the window. We'd found the table in an old barn. It had been painted a bilious shade of olive green. Mac and I had removed all the old finish, Avery had helped with the sanding, and a rich walnut stain had brought out the wood's natural beauty.

I ran my hand over the gleaming wood surface. The table was one of my favorite projects. Mac and I worked well together.

He set a mug in front of me and took the chair on the opposite side of the table. "Did Jackson say anything to you?"

"No," I said. "Just that he needed to talk to you." I picked up my cup and took a sip. As promised it was strong and hot, just the way I liked it. "I take it you and Jackson used to be close."

He nodded. "We were. Jackson was like Jess is to you."

I couldn't imagine not being in contact with Jess for more than a year. Even when I'd been working in other parts of the country we'd always stayed in touch. "What happened?"

He looked past me for a moment then his gaze came back to my face. "Hypothetical question?"

"Okay," I said, folding my hands around my mug.

"What would happen, what would Jess do, if someone suggested that you'd tried to kill someone?"

"You know Jess. She'd be all over the person. You know how loyal she is. I could rob a bank and Jess would say, 'Well, what did they expect, keeping all that money in it?'" As I said the words I knew where the conversation was going.

"I would have said the same thing about Jackson," Mac said, slowly turning his cup in circles. "And I would have been wrong."

"He sided with Leila's parents."

"He did more than that. He helped them when they sued to take over Leila's care. How am I supposed to forget that?" He sighed. "Erin, I get. She and Leila had been friends since they were kids. But Jackson?"

"Maybe he's sorry. Maybe that's why he's here now—to try to make up for that," I said. I held up both hands. "I'm not taking his side. I'm not taking anyone's side other than yours. I'm just playing devil's advocate. You know I haven't always been the best friend to Michelle. I know what it's like to screw up and not be able to fix it."

Michelle Andrews and I had been fast friends until the summer we were fifteen, the same summer her father had been sent to prison for embezzling money from the summer camp run by the Emmerson Foundation, the charitable trust set up by Liz's grandparents. Michelle had suddenly stopped speaking to me and I'd spent years not knowing why. It wasn't until the Angels had gotten involved in the murder of Arthur Fenety that I'd learned that Michelle had overheard me talking to Nick the night of my birthday. She'd been sick with chicken pox but she'd snuck out of bed to bring me my present and she'd heard me tell Nick that it wasn't fair that her dad was still here and my father was gone. "I wish he was the one who was dead!" I'd blurted. A minute later I'd taken it all back, but she hadn't stayed around long enough to hear that. And then a couple of weeks later, her father *was* dead.

"It's not the same thing," Mac said. "You said something stupid because you were a teenager. And you never stopped trying to fix things. Don't compare yourself with him." His dark eyes flashed with a spark of anger. "You're nothing like Jackson." His expression softened a little. "Jackson is nothing like Jackson—he's not the friend I thought I had."

He picked up his mug, took a drink and set it back on the table again. "Tell me what your day looks like," he said. It was a clear signal that the conversation about Jackson Montgomery was over. "It's Sunday. Don't spend all of it working."

"I'm not," I said, getting to my feet. "I'm meeting Jess later. What about you?"

"I'll be out on the water," he said.

"Have fun."

He nodded. For a moment I thought he was going to say something but the moment passed.

I decided to head out to the old garage to work on my table project for a while. I'd been at it for about an hour when Dad called.

"What did I take you from, my girl?"

"I'm trying paint samples on a table."

"Green," he immediately said.

"You don't even know what colors I'm trying."

"Did I ever tell you one of my ancestors was a gypsy fortune-teller?" Dad asked. "I have some psychic ability."

Grinning, I walked out of the garage work space into the sunshine. "I thought one of your ancestors was a French pickpocket."

"What? I can't have more than one ancestor?" I could hear the laughter in his voice.

I laughed as well. "So I take it you've found some information about Mac's wife," I said.

"I did," he said, his tone turning serious. "But there

really wasn't anything to find. There's no scandal around Leila's family other than the birth of her half sister, Natalie—she was the product of a brief affair Leila's father had and she was a secret until she was a teenager. I did learn that it seems for at least a short period of time Leila and her father were estranged, but from the beginning she insisted that people treat Natalie with respect."

I thought once again that Leila sounded like someone I could have been friends with.

I heard Dad shuffle some papers on the other end of the phone.

"A colleague of mine covered the investigation into Leila's accident," he continued. "I talked to him last night. It was eventually ruled an accident but the police did look pretty closely into Mac and his movements. In the end they concluded the timing wasn't right for Mac to have tried to kill Leila. And they couldn't show for sure the heating system had been tampered with."

I rubbed the back of my neck with my free hand. I thought about what Mac had told me about Jackson. "Do you have any idea why so many people were unconvinced?"

Dad sighed softly. "It's pretty clear that Leila's family didn't like Mac. Apparently he and Leila met at a fundraiser for a charity that provides scholarships for low-income inner-city kids." I remembered Stevie saying Mac and Leila had literally seen each other across a crowded room. The story had seemed very romantic.

"Both Mac and Leila's great-aunt were on the charity's board," Dad said. "It seems her family had a bias against Mac from the beginning."

"Why?" I said.

"I don't know." I pictured my dad shaking his head. "I don't think it helped when Leila's great-aunt replaced her father with Mac as her financial adviser. She disapproved of his affair, although she was welcoming to Natalie."

I had a feeling I would have liked Leila's great-aunt as well.

"Sarah, what do you know about Mac's family?"

The sun was warm on my arms and the back of my neck. I moved back to the garage doorway, where there was some shade. "I know he has a younger brother, Jameis, and their parents are dead. His brother's a nurse. He's working in Central America with some organization that provides medical care in remote places that don't regularly see doctors or nurses—Honduras, I think."

"Did you know that Mac was in college when his parents died?"

I glanced over at the shop. "I didn't." There were still so many things about Mac that were a mystery.

"Mac became his brother's guardian. Raised him through the rest of high school. I can't find anything that says he was involved in what happened to his wife. Mac's a good guy."

"Thanks, Dad," I said. "I appreciate this."

"Anytime, sweetie," he replied, and somehow I could feel the warmth of his smile through the phone.

"Love you," I said. "I'll talk to you soon."

I worked on the metal table for the next hour or so, smiling when I realized that Dad was in fact right: Green was the best color choice.

Jess and I spent the afternoon driving around to flea markets. She found some bolts of vintage cotton prints and a couple of jean jackets to refurbish. Jess had a great sense of style. All she needed was her sewing machine, some thread and a pair of scissors and she could make magic out of just about any old item of clothing she found. What she didn't keep to wear herself ended up in the funky little used and vintage clothing shop along the waterfront that she was part owner of.

Jess wasn't the only one who found some treasures. I bought a box of glass fishbowls, some copper baking dishes and an old metal nursery cart. We had supper at a little mom-and-pop restaurant just this side of Rockport and I felt that my batteries had been recharged when I got home.

Monday morning Mr. P. and Rose drove to the shop with Elvis and me.

In the backseat Mr. P. was humming to himself. I glanced in the rearview mirror at him. "You're in a good mood," I said.

"Does that mean that sometimes I'm not?" he countered with a twinkle in his eye.

I smiled. "No. But you do seem a little like the cat that swallowed the canary this morning."

Beside me Elvis meowed and looked around, seemingly puzzled.

Everyone laughed.

I glanced down at him beside me on the seat. "I wasn't talking about you," I said.

He stared at me unblinkingly for a moment and then went back to watching the road. Elvis took his backseat driver status very seriously. Rose reached over and stroked his fur.

"It's possible that I may be onto something." Mr. P. put his hand on the back of my seat and leaned forward. "But I don't want to jinx myself."

Rose turned partway around to look at him. "Is it what we were talking about?"

"It is," he said.

She clasped her hands together like a little girl. "Splendid!" she said.

"Bring me in the loop when there's something to share," I said. As usual I didn't have a clue what was going on, which experience told me might turn out to be a blessing—or might turn out to be a curse.

The shop was very busy for a Monday morning, probably because the sky was dull and cloudy and rain was threatening. I sold a mandolin and a small shopping cart I'd repurposed into a plant stand and house numbers display. The woman who bought the refurbished cart offered twenty dollars for the three pots of geraniums I'd used for display in the cart. I immediately said yes, tucking the two tens she gave me into my pocket to give to Charlotte, who had grown the plants and who I knew would argue that they hadn't cost anywhere near that much to grow. Since my thumb was more black than green it was an argument she was going to lose.

Avery sold a small rectangular table to a tourist Sam had sent over. I had stripped and whitewashed the top, but painted the legs a creamy off-white. The woman decided she wanted to buy the dishes that Avery had used to set the table as well. I eavesdropped as Avery made several suggestions for tablecloth and napkin combinations. After the woman left, the table padded with old blankets and secured in the bed of the enormous half-ton crew cab she was driving, I put my arms around Avery's shoulders and hugged her. "Good job," I said.

She grinned with pleasure. "You don't think I was being pushy when I told her having everything matchy-matchy is kind of 1980s, do you?"

I shook my head. "No. She asked what you thought. By the way, I like your idea of using one main color to pull it all together."

"Yeah, that stuff always seems kind of obvious to me but I get that it's not like that for everyone." She slid the stack of bracelets she was wearing up her arm. "You know, I might be a designer after college."

Avery was wearing a funky jungle print sundress from Jess's shop with a lime green dyed denim vest over the top and the ubiquitous stack of bracelets on one arm. "I could see you doing that," I said.

She nodded. "Yeah, that or nuclear physicist. I haven't decided yet."

It was the first time she'd mentioned either occupation. "I, um . . . I'm sure you'd be good at both."

She smiled and gestured at the empty place on the floor. "Which table should come in to fill the space?"

Tables were very popular with our customers so as quickly as we sold one I tried to get another in its place.

"You and Mac can decide," I said. "Go see what he says."

Avery headed for the old garage, where Mac was

working, passing Rose and Mr. P. coming in from the back. "I sold that table," she said to Rose.

"Wonderful!" Rose said. They exchanged high fives as the teen went by.

Mr. P. smiled as they joined me. He still had a bit of a self-satisfied gleam in his eye.

"You're ready to share?" I asked, raising an eyebrow.

He nodded. "Yes, I am, my dear."

"You've found something."

"Security footage," he said.

"Of?"

"Of Mac at four different restaurants, looking for Erin Fellowes, just as he told the police he was, just when he said he was. Depending on the timeline the police have established, it might help show that Mac couldn't have had anything to do with her death."

I felt like doing a little victory dance but I settled for grinning at both of them.

"I've already left a message at Josh's office," Rose said.

Now Mr. P.'s expression grew serious.

"Is there something else?" I asked.

He nodded. "I did a little more digging and it's possible that Stephanie Carleton wasn't at the hydroponic workshop that's her alibi for the time the heating system at Mac's house could potentially have been tampered with."

I sighed softly. I'd liked Leila's cousin and I hated the idea that Stevie may have had something to do with Leila's death. "So you think she wasn't at the workshop at all, or that she just wasn't there the night of Leila's accident?"

"The latter, I'm afraid," Mr. P. said, nudging his

glasses up the bridge of his nose. "I talked to several people who confirmed that she was there, but very quickly I realized how fuzzy they were on time and how big the seminar was."

"And how much most of them had to drink at the hotel bar afterward," Rose added with a roll of her eyes.

"They used swipe cards at the conference center," Mr. P. continued.

"And?"

"The system keeps track of who has each card and every time it's swiped."

"I take it they store that information somewhere," I said.

Rose smiled. "Isn't it wonderful how much computers can keep these days? Just think how many trees have been saved."

The conversation was about to veer off into the ditch. I eyed Mr. P. "I take it you've seen that information."

"Only with respect to Stephanie's movements," he said, adjusting his glasses again.

"Freddie would never violate someone's privacy," Rose added.

"Freddie?" I asked. Despite my best efforts it seemed the conversation had gone off course.

"Don't tell me you don't remember Freddie Calhoun?" Rose looked at me as though the name should have made sense to me.

Freddie Calhoun.

"Josh's friend?" I said. I remembered a skinny, gangly kid, his blond hair buzzed close to his scalp, helping Josh Evans launch a rocket in the Evanses' backyard.

Josh's mother, Jane, had had to draw eyebrows on Josh for the rest of the summer.

Rose beamed at me. I'd clearly given the correct answer. "He has his own cybersecurity firm now. Such a helpful young man." Freddie had been one of Rose's students. Pretty much everyone within ten years in either direction of my age had been one of Rose's students. "Oh, and he goes by Ric now—no 'k'—not Freddie," she added helpfully.

"We know that Stephanie left early, in plenty of time to have tampered with that water heater," Mr. P. said.

"You still think what happened wasn't an accident?" I'd shared what my dad had confirmed—that the police couldn't prove that the leaking water heater had been tampered with.

Mr. P. and Rose exchanged a look. He cleared his throat. "I managed to get a look at those reports as well. The police couldn't prove the heater had been tampered with but they couldn't say it hadn't been, either."

I nodded. "Okay." I didn't ask how he'd managed to see those reports. I looked at some of Alfred's fact-finding the way I did Rose's favorite breakfast sausage. I liked the end product but I was happier not knowing exactly what went into it.

I looked at my watch. "We can leave in about ten minutes," I said. "I just need to call Clayton and tell him I won't be there this afternoon."

"We appreciate the offer, dear," Rose said. "But Alf has something else he wants to try first. He's set up a Skype session with Stevie in about fifteen minutes. He told her he wants to know more about Leila and Stevie's great-aunt." She looked at Mr. P., giving him a warm smile.

"You mean the one who set up the trust for them?"

Mr. P. nodded. "Leila and Stephanie are the only girls in the family on that side of the family and from that generation, aside from Leila's half sister, Natalie. I really would like to know more about Marguerite Thompson-Davis. And of course I want to see Stephanie's face when I tell her what I found out." He hiked up his pants, which were already almost up in his armpits. "Not that I told her that, of course. You're welcome to join us, Sarah, if you're free."

Could Stevie really have put her cousin in a coma over money? I knew it was possible; I just didn't want to believe it had actually happened. Mr. P. wasn't the only one who wanted to see Stevie's face when he told her what he'd unearthed. "Thank you," I said. "I think I just might do that."

He glanced at his watch. "I'll be at my desk. I'll see you in a few minutes."

Both Rose and I were in the Angels' office when Mr. P. opened his Skype session with Stevie.

"What would you like to know about Aunt Margie?" she asked.

"She had no children of her own?"

Stevie shook her head. "My mother seemed to think that she'd lost a baby but it wasn't something that was ever talked about." She smiled. "She spoiled us—Leila and me. She paid for music lessons, she took us for long weekends in New York City and she encouraged us to go after our dreams."

"She sounds like a very special person," Rose said, leaning sideways so Stevie could see her.

"Hi, Rose," Stevie said with a smile. She waved at her computer screen. "And yes, you're right. Aunt Margie was special." She turned her attention to Mr. P. again. "You knew she was pretty much a self-made woman."

Mr. P. tipped his head to one side like a curious seagull. "I know that Marguerite and her husband ran their own business."

Stevie nodded. "I'm not trying to imply that she grew up poor, but Aunt Margie's father thought her only purpose was to be a good wife. The only reason he agreed to let her go to university was that he felt she'd meet a better class of potential husbands."

"Goodness," Rose said softly, shaking her head in dismay.

"Her grandmother had what they called at the time 'her own money.' She left several thousand dollars to Aunt Margie and that's what she and her husband used to start their business." Stevie turned her attention back to Rose. "I don't know if Alfred told you, but they took a small business teaching language and customs to businesspeople traveling overseas, and turned it into a multimillion-dollar corporation they later sold. Leila always said we got our business chops from Aunt Margie." She looked away from the screen for a moment and closed her eyes briefly before turning back to the camera and pasting on a smile. "So, anyway, Aunt Margie became very much a philanthropist after the business was sold. She said it was more fun giving money away than it had ever been making it."

Stevie leaned back and put both hands on the desktop next to her computer. "I heard from a couple of friends, Alfred. They said you'd been in touch to check out my alibi." She made air quotes around the word "alibi." "So now you know I had nothing to do with what happened to Leila."

"On the contrary, now I'm a little suspicious because I know you lied about where you were. I know you swiped out of the conference center much earlier than you said you did." His voice was as even and nonconfrontational as it would have been if he were at McNamara's putting in a sandwich order.

Stevie pressed a palm to her forehead. "Big Brother is always watching," she muttered, exhaling loudly. "I didn't do anything to Leila," she said, her expression pained. "I would never hurt her."

"Telling the truth would go a long way toward making that seem credible," Mr. P. said.

Stevie gave an almost imperceptible nod. "Fine," she said. She reached for her smartphone. "I thought this might happen. I'm e-mailing you some photos. They're time-stamped. There's probably some way to show they haven't been faked because they haven't been. I don't know how to do that kind of stuff."

It was only seconds before we heard the ping of an arriving message. Mr. P. opened his e-mail. There were four photos attached. They were all of Stevie in a '50s-style diner. She seemed to be eating some kind of sundae.

"Are those Pop-Tarts in that dish?" Rose asked, leaning closer to the screen to get a better look at the pictures.

Stevie hung her head. "Yes. And three kinds of ice cream plus strawberry sauce and whipped cream."

"Where on earth were you?" Rose said. She and Mr. P. exchanged another look.

Stevie actually smiled. "This little place that serves the most amazing junk food I've ever had."

"Why did you lie?" Mr. P. said. He frowned at the screen. "It appears that you have a perfectly good alibi. So why pretend to be somewhere you weren't?"

"You have to understand that Davis and I are this close to signing a deal to see our organic apple butter and pear butter in a major, high-end department store chain." She held up her right thumb and index finger about half an inch apart. "But part of the deal is our image as an all-organic, healthy-eating couple—not someone who scarfs down Pop-Tarts and whipped cream from a can. I couldn't take the chance." She shrugged. "No, I wasn't at the seminar all evening but I wasn't killing Leila, either. All I was doing was gumming up my arteries and sending my cholesterol levels through the roof."

Mr. P. smiled and took off his glasses, pulling a small gray cloth out of his gold shirt to clean them. "As long as these photos check out, I don't see any reason why we need to share your affection for whipped cream in a can."

Rose leaned into the frame again. "Although I would like to suggest you try making your own whipped cream with the addition of a pinch of sea salt and tiny bit of vanilla bean paste."

I pressed my lips together so she wouldn't see the grin I was working hard to hold back. Rose thought basic cooking skills were as important as being able to read and write, change the oil in a car and curtsy—or bow if you were a man. The latter because you never know when you might meet royalty and one doesn't want to look like an "uncouth hooligan."

Mr. P. thanked Stevie for the photos and said he'd be in touch. He signed out of the Skype session and leaned back in his chair.

"I'm guessing you have some kind of software program that can tell whether those pictures have been altered," I said, pushing away from the table where I'd been leaning during the conversation with Stevie.

He nodded. "I have a couple, but I tend to believe she's telling us the truth. This time."

"Why?" I asked.

"That day we went to visit her I noticed that she wiped her hands on her shorts before we shook hands. She'd been eating Cheetos and a bit of the orange powder was still on her fingers." He smiled. "You might say her story has junk food fingerprints all over it."

Chapter 10

Rose and I spent the afternoon out at Clayton McNamara's house finishing the inventory.

"I should have a recommendation for you and Glenn on what to sell and how in about a week," I told Clayton as we stood in his driveway.

"I appreciate that," Clayton said. "It'll be good to get things cleared out so Beth and Glenn don't have a pile of junk to deal with when I'm gone." Then he grinned. "Not that I'm planning on taking that final drive anytime soon."

"I should hope not," Rose said with a smile.

Clayton pointed a finger at me. "And I don't want to see any friends and family discount when all this gets added up. I can be a cantankerous old coot when I set my mind to it."

I gave his arm a squeeze. "And have you forgotten who my grandmother is? You're not the only one who can dig their heels in."

Clayton laughed. "Lord help us," he said.

I told him I'd be in touch soon and Rose and I headed back to the shop.

The rest of the afternoon was quiet, which didn't surprise me. The weather was beautiful and there weren't that many summer days left.

"Would you like a ride home?" I asked Rose as I went to lock the front door at the end of the day.

"Thank you, dear, but Alfred and I are going with Liz." She handed the floor attachment to Avery, who had just pulled out the vacuum cleaner.

"We're making peach cobbler," Avery added. "I'll try to save you some but you know how Nonna is when it comes to dessert."

"I heard that," Liz said. She was standing in the doorway to the workroom.

"I know," Avery said as she plugged the vacuum into the wall outlet. "That's why I said it." She gave her grandmother an exaggerated smile and started the vacuum.

I headed for the workroom, pausing to give Liz a kiss on the cheek as I passed her. "She's going to run the world one of these days," I said, glancing back in Avery's direction.

"I know," Liz said. "I don't know whether to be proud or terrified."

Liz had just pulled out of the parking lot about fifteen minutes later when Nick pulled in. I'd been set up, I realized. I headed outside to intercept him.

"Hi," he said, taking off his sunglasses and giving me a tentative smile. He'd been to court. He was wearing a white shirt with the sleeves rolled back and no tie. His dark suit jacket was draped over the back of the passenger seat. He smelled faintly of spearmint chewing gum and Hugo, the aftershave he'd been wearing since we were teenagers.

I glanced down the street half expecting to see Liz's car at the curb with Rose watching out the back window, but there was no sign of them. "What pretext did Rose use to get you here?" I said.

"No pretext," he said. "I called her and asked her to make sure you were alone so we could talk." He held up both hands. "I conspired with Rose, Sarah. That should tell you how much I want to fix this thing between us."

Nick looked so earnest standing there that I couldn't help laughing. "Now you owe her," I said.

He gave me a wry smile. "Which shows just how important this is to me. Please, tell me what I can do to fix things."

I wrapped one arm over my head, digging my fingers into my scalp. "I don't know. I just don't want to keep arguing with you over the same things."

"I don't want that, either."

"So what now?"

Nick's mouth worked as though he were trying out what he wanted to say before saying the words out loud. "Just for now, just until the murder of Erin Fellowes is solved, can we set aside our differences?"

"Nick, we're working at cross-purposes. How can we set things aside?"

He was shaking his head before I finished speaking. "No, we're not," he said. "We both want the truth. Give me a chance. Please."

I tried to let go of my aggravation, consciously loosening my shoulders, which seemed to be hunched up by my ears. He was right. I wanted the truth and I knew Nick well enough to know that he was after the same thing. "There's something I want to ask you first."

"Anything," he said.

"You said you saw Mac with Erin. Did you see Mac as in you saw his face, or did you just see someone with the same color skin?" I knew what I was potentially accusing him of, but I had to know.

Nick took a deep breath. He shook his right hand as though he were trying to loosen his fingers. "I saw a man. He was wearing a gray hoodie and his hands were in his pockets so I didn't see what color skin *or hair* he had. But I heard Erin Fellowes call him Mac. For the record I don't think Mac is a murderer but I do think he's keeping secrets and it's very possible those secrets are why Erin Fellowes is dead." His eyes were glued to my face. "She said, 'Mac, leave me alone.' I heard her clearly, Sarah. I'm sorry."

I felt a surge of relief. Nick's ID of Mac was far from certain. "All right," I said slowly.

His eyes searched my face a little uncertainly. "All right what?"

"I will try to put aside our differences *for now*, until Erin Fellowes's killer is found. After that I'm not making any promises."

He smiled. "Okay," he said. He glanced at his watch. "I'm sorry. I have to go." He hesitated and then put his arms around me. It was an awkward hug, which told me things weren't really completely okay with us.

"I'll talk to you soon," he said.

I nodded and watched him get into his SUV and drive away.

I went back inside to get my bag and Elvis. The latter I found sitting on Mr. P.'s desk in the Angels' office, looking idly out the window. He looked up at me and licked his whiskers.

"Ready to go home?" I asked.

"Mrr," he said, then his gaze darted to the window again for a moment.

"I was talking to Nick." I folded my arms over my chest. "Which I'm sure you knew. Did Rose tell you to spy on us to make sure I didn't whack Nick with my purse?" I knew that wasn't nearly as preposterous as it sounded. The cat suddenly became engrossed in washing his right front paw.

Elvis and I headed home. There was no sign of Rose so I couldn't tell her I knew what she'd done. Elvis and I ate supper and then he went into the bedroom to watch *Jeopardy!*

I sat on a stool at the counter and called Liz. "Hi," I said when she answered on the sixth ring, slightly out of breath. "Did I take you from something? I was going to come over for a minute."

"Where are you?" Liz asked.

"I'm home. I know what you and Rose and probably Avery as well were up to and I will give you all an A for effort—and sneakiness."

Liz gave a snort of derision. "If the two of them had listened to me you wouldn't be home right now. At least not by yourself."

"You do know that whole chloroform-on-ahandkerchief thing only works in the movies, right?" I said, grinning in spite of myself. I really wanted to be mad at their attempts at matchmaking between Nick and me, but I couldn't seem to manage it.

"Speak for yourself," she retorted.

"I'm leaving now," I said, getting up to grab my bag from the arm of the sofa. "So if Channing is dancing in your living room in his boxers and a feather boa you might want to get him out of there." I hung up laughing before Liz could answer.

"I'm going to Liz's. I won't be long," I called to Elvis.

"Merow," he answered after a moment.

Liz let me in and I made a show of peeking into the living room with one hand up to shield my eyes.

She glared at me. "Don't start, missy," she warned.

I gave her my best wide-eyed look of innocence, which was pretty darn good.

"Channing wasn't here and if he had been it certainly wouldn't have been in a feather boa." She looked down her nose at me as only Elizabeth Emmerson Kiley French could do and then led the way into the kitchen. "You know feathers make me sneeze," she added over her shoulder.

Liz didn't ask if I wanted a cup of tea. She just got out two cups and poured one for each of us. There was a plate with two lemon tarts in the middle of the table. I reached for one. Liz set my tea in front of me and I set the tart on the edge of the saucer.

She turned to the cupboard and handed me a plate. "Were you born in a barn?" she asked.

I broke a bite off the tart and popped it in my mouth, putting the rest on my plate. "No. I was born in a hospital, although rumor has it I was *almost* born in the backseat of a Toyota Tercel."

Liz grinned as she sat down opposite me. "Front seat, the way I heard it," she said.

I made a face, wrinkling my nose at her. "You've been looking into Mac's background," I said.

She didn't deny it. She simply nodded and reached for her teacup. Liz had connections in the business world from her work with the Emmerson Foundation.

I waited. She took a sip of her tea and set the cup down again. "It probably won't surprise you to learn that Mac was an excellent financial adviser, by all accounts."

"It doesn't."

She reached for the other tart. "I would have hired him," she said.

High praise.

"Did you find out anything about Leila's family?" I asked, licking my finger to pick up the crumbs of short-bread crust on my plate.

"Old money and many of the clichés that go with it," Liz said with an edge of disdain in her voice. "Mac's clients, his coworkers, no one other than Leila's family, believed he had anything to do with what happened to his wife."

"You think there were hard feelings when Mac took over as Marguerite Thompson-Davis's financial adviser."

"There was a"—Liz cleared her throat—"a conversation that got a little heated between Mac and his future father-in-law right after the account was moved, heated at least on Leila's father's part."

"How heated?" I asked, reaching for the other half of my lemon tart.

"There were pigeons in the parking lot that heard him. Or so I was told." Liz tapped a nail on the top of the table. "I know that Alfred has eliminated Leila's cousin, Stevie, as a suspect, but I did find out an interesting piece of information about her."

I raised a curious eyebrow since my mouth was full of lemon tart.

"That property you visited, that house, all mortgaged to the hilt. They've been trying to get this organic food business of theirs off the ground for the past two years. They don't have a pot to—"

I shot her a look across the table.

Liz narrowed her eyes at me. "Bake beans in," she finished.

"Money," I said with a sigh. "None of these people knew what it was like to go without and yet it seemed to mean so much to them."

Liz reached for her tea again. "You know what the good book says. Love of money is the root of all evil."

I nodded as I picked up my own cup. I wasn't sure if anything Liz had found out was going to help Mac, but as Mr. P. liked to say, information is power.

There was a white bankers box on the chair between us. It seemed like a good time to change the conversation. I dipped my head in the direction of the carton. "Have you found anything?" I asked.

Liz had agreed to help Michelle in her quest to prove that Michelle's late father, Rob Andrews, had been framed for embezzlement. When I'd found out what they were doing I'd asked Liz if I could help as well. It was, I hoped, my chance to really restore our friendship.

Liz played with the china cup in front of her, tracing the rim with a finger. "I've been going over notes from the board meetings from that time."

"And?"

"And I haven't found any indication that anything was wrong or anything was even suspected of being wrong. We all liked Rob. He'd had great references and he was doing a good job." She leaned over, lifted the lid of the box and handed me a manila folder. "Would you take a look at these?"

"Sure," I said. "What am I looking at?"

"Financial documents from the time period when Robert Andrews assumed directorship of the Sunshine Camp."

"What am I looking *for*?"

"Just take a look," she said.

I spent about ten minutes going over several pages, line item by line item. Finally I leaned back in my chair. "I don't really know what I'm looking for," I said. "The numbers look fine to me. The only thing I did see were a couple of projects I don't ever remember you talking about."

"Which ones?" Liz asked.

I took the second page from the folder and turned it to face her. "That one," I said, tapping the paper with one finger. "And that one."

Liz nodded. "That's because I have no memory of either one of them and there's not a damn thing wrong with my memory."

Liz had a memory like the proverbial elephant. She could remember every embarrassing story from my childhood.

"And I can't find any paperwork associated with either project." She glanced at the single page in front of me and then looked at me again. "That first one, at the top of the page, turns up in some paperwork from before Robert was hired."

I raised an eyebrow at her. "That means . . ."

She nodded. "Michelle could be right about her father."

There was something more. Her expression was troubled, with tight lines around her mouth and eyes.

"There's something else," I said. I tapped a finger on the sheet of paper. "Spit it out."

"That project, the first time I can find any reference to it in the budget is right after we added new board members."

She didn't have to say anything else. I knew why she looked troubled.

"John," I said. John Scott, my grandmother's new husband. Back then he'd been Bill Kiley's grad student. History professor William Kiley had been Liz's first husband.

She nodded. "Yes. We have to talk to him as soon as he and Isabel get home."

My tea was cold. I got up for another cup. "So we have to tell Gram that her husband just might be involved—even if it's indirectly—in sending an innocent man to jail? There's a great welcome home." I leaned against the counter.

"I know. I don't really want to think about it," Liz

said. She looked at me thoughtfully. "So let's talk about you and Nicolas."

"There's nothing to talk about," I said, hating how defensive I sounded.

Liz swiped her finger through a dab of lemon crème on her plate and licked it clean. "One question," she said. "When Nicolas walks into a room after you haven't seen him for a while do your toes curl?"

"Do my toes what?" I asked.

"Do your toes curl?" she repeated with just a touch of annoyance in her voice.

I reached for the teapot and poured a fresh cup for myself. "That's not how things are with the two of us."

Liz got up, walked over to me and took the pot from my hand. "I'm going to say one thing and it's the last thing I'm going to say about this."

I shot her a skeptical look.

"Tonight," she added.

"Go ahead." I folded my arms over my chest. "Not that I can stop you."

"No, you can't," she agreed. Then her smile faded. "Sarah, a lot of people say passion is overrated but I disagree. That kind of heat between two people can keep you warm when life gets cold. And it's going to get cold." With that she turned back to the table to refill her own cup.

I thought about the way Stevie Carleton had described Mac and Leila's first encounter, how she claimed they had locked eyes across a crowded room. If it was true it gave me some perspective on just how much Mac had lost.

Chapter 11

It was raining when I woke up in the morning. I lay in bed watching the rain make tiny rivers down the window. I'd set the clock earlier than usual so I could get a run in before work. Ever since Nick had shown up at the shop I'd been filled with a restless energy that I needed to burn off but I didn't want to burn it off running through puddles and getting splashed by cars.

A loud meow came from the chair by the window.

"I know I said I was going running but it's raining." I pulled the pillow over my head. Half a minute later Elvis landed on my chest. I lifted the pillow so I could see him. Was I imagining the reproach that seemed to be in his green eyes?

"It's raining," I said again. "Wet feet. Wet everything. I'm not a duck."

"Mrr," he said.

That could have been a reminder that I'd said I was going for a run, *no excuses*. It also could have been his way of pointing out that I did have all the rain gear I needed to go for a run no matter what the weather was like.

Elvis leaned forward and butted my chin with his furry head.

Or it could have been his way of saying, "Get up; it's time for breakfast." Either way I wasn't going to be able to go back to sleep.

"Fine. You win. I'm getting up."

I swear the cat smiled at me. I picked him up with one hand and sat up. "I'll get your breakfast," I said, giving the top of his head a scratch.

He nuzzled my hand, then wriggled free, jumped down to the floor and headed for the kitchen.

I was tempted to stretch out again but I knew I had a maximum of five minutes before Elvis would be back to roust me again.

I stretched, went to the bathroom, and padded out to the living room in my new fuzzy ladybug slippers. Elvis was sitting on a stool at the counter. My favorite running shoes had been nudged almost into the middle of the floor.

"What are you? The exercise police?" I asked.

He gave what seemed to me to be an indifferent shrug. "You're as single-minded as Nick sometimes," I said as I went to get his breakfast.

Nick. Thinking about our truce of sorts made me antsy all over again.

I got Elvis his breakfast and headed back to the bedroom to put on my running clothes. He was still eating as I sat on the living room floor and reached for my shoes.

"This doesn't mean you won," I said.

He didn't so much as lift his head from his bowl but he did make a rumbly noise low in his throat, which I knew meant in fact he knew he had.

Because it was so wet and because as I had pointed out to Elvis I was not a duck I decided to run the second-floor track at the hockey rink. There were a few die-hard walkers who smiled hello at me but by the time I was approaching my last few circuits I had the place to myself.

I was on my second-to-last lap when Michelle came in carrying two take-out cups. She smiled at me and I held up two fingers to let her know I had only two more laps left.

When I finished I walked over to Michelle, who held out one of the cups. "From McNamara's."

"Bless you," I said. This counted as rehydrating, didn't it? I took a long sip of the coffee and gave a small sigh of happiness. "How did you know I was here?"

"I called your cell and when it went to voice mail I figured you'd gone for a run. I took a chance that you'd be here instead of outside."

"I'm glad you did," I said, taking another drink. "What's up?"

We headed toward the coat hooks where I'd left my nylon Windbreaker.

"Liz called me last night," Michelle said. "She told me what she'd learned about Stevie Carleton's finances."

I nodded. Liz had told me she would.

"I know there's no point in me giving you the speech about how they all shouldn't be involved in this case."

I held up both hands. "I can't stop them, not even if I had the Patriots' entire defensive line behind me."

"I know," she said. "But please, do what you can to rein them in. This case is personal and I don't want Rose or any of them to do something stupid and end up getting hurt."

"I'll do what I can," I said.

"Liz also said you found a couple of questionable projects in some old budget projections from the Sunshine Camp."

I used the edge of my T-shirt to blot the sweat from my neck. "We did, but I'm not sure if it means anything. Liz said that sometimes ideas were floated that didn't go anywhere, but at least it's somewhere to start." Liz was adamant that there was no point in telling Michelle about John's possible connection to those budget inconsistencies until we'd had a chance to talk to him. I had (very) reluctantly agreed.

Michelle nodded. "Thank you for helping. I can't tell you how much it means to me."

I smiled at her. "You don't have to tell me and I'm glad you're willing to let me help. Liz and I are going to start sounding out the people who were involved with the Emmerson Foundation during the time your dad was camp director."

"What are you going to tell them?"

I set my take-out cup on the bench and pulled on the thin nylon rain jacket. "We aren't going to tell them what we're looking for. If someone set your father up it would be bad to tip that person off. So we're going to say that Liz wants to put together a history of the foundation." I picked up my cup and we headed for the stairs to the main floor of the building.

"You think people will believe that?"

I noticed that Michelle hadn't taken a single sip of

her own coffee. She was holding on to the cup almost as though she'd forgotten she was supposed to drink what was inside. "Liz can sell anything," I said. "And I actually think she's considering the idea for real."

"And when we find the person who set up my dad that can be part of the story."

I nodded. I wondered if Liz and Michelle were right. Was Rob Andrews wrongly convicted or did he do what he was accused of? Either way I knew Michelle wouldn't get what she was really looking for because her dad would still be gone. But I wasn't going to lose this chance to be a better friend to her.

We walked down to the entrance and as if she could read what I was thinking Michelle bumped me with her hip. "I mean it," she said. "Thank you for getting involved in this whole thing. Thank you for being there for me. I owe you."

"Hey, how many times have you been there for me, especially since the Angels began their business?"

A cloud seemed to pass over Michelle's face. "Nick told me that he admitted to you that he's the witness that saw Mac with Erin Fellowes."

"He saw someone with the same build as Mac, wearing a similar sweatshirt, that Erin may, *may* have called Mac—not exactly a neon arrow with a sign saying 'killer' pointed at Mac's head."

"I know," Michelle said.

My surprise had to show on my face. "You do?"

Michelle nodded. "A decent attorney, like Josh, for instance, could get that ID tossed very easily. Nick didn't see the man's face and he was far enough away that it would be easy to argue that he didn't hear what he says he heard." She held up one hand. "We're still investigating so it doesn't mean Mac is in the clear."

"What about that security camera footage Mr. P. found?"

"There's still a big enough window, timewise, that Mac could have gotten downtown and killed Erin."

"He didn't kill anyone," I said.

Michelle finally took a sip of her coffee and then made a face. The coffee had to be cold now. "I really want to believe you're right," she said.

We said good-bye and I headed home to change and collect Elvis. He refused to move beyond the apartment door and I had to shield him inside my raincoat to get him to the truck.

Rose didn't come in until late morning. She was dwarfed by the oversize yellow slicker and big green gum rubber boots she was wearing. I took her jacket and hung it on one of the hooks by the back door where it could drip and not leave a trail of puddles through the building.

"I think even the ducks would find this a little too much," Rose said, smiling at me.

"You set me up," I said, skipping all pleasantries.

Rose didn't even try to play innocent. "Yes, I did. Nicolas, of all people, asked for my help. Nicolas! Do you really think I was going to say no to his request when it's something I want as well? You know me better than that."

I folded my arms over my chest. I was angry, I reminded myself. At least I had been. All of a sudden I couldn't seem to muster up any of the righteous indignation I'd felt before. Rose was smiling at me, and all I could think about was how much they all wanted Nick and me together and yet it never seemed to happen. "What if it's not what I want?" I said, as much to myself as to her.

Rose picked up her canvas tote, which she'd set inside a clear plastic shopping bag. "Oh, that's fine," she said, "but you can't take forever to decide." She patted my cheek as she moved past me. "You know what Liz likes to say, sweet girl—'Pee or get off the pot.'"

Liz called about fifteen minutes later to say she was bringing lunch so we could all talk about our progress such as it was. It was getting to be something we did whenever the Angels had a case.

The rain had let up a little by the time Liz arrived, but she was dry under a gigantic blue-and-white-striped golf umbrella. Her concession to the rain was a pair of bright yellow pumps instead of open-toe sandals. No green gum rubber boots for her.

She handed me a paper shopping bag and I made a mental note to add it to our stash of bags behind the front counter. It was just the right size to hold one of Avery's teacup planters. I peeked inside the bag although my nose had already told me what was inside—pasta pesto salad from Sam's and breadsticks.

As usual Avery would watch the shop while the rest of us ate and hashed over the case so far. As she got her food she looked around. "Can I ask a question?" she said.

Liz shot her a look.

Avery rolled her eyes. "Oh, excuse me," she said. "*May* I ask a question?"

"Of course," Mr. P. said, wisely choosing to ignore the sarcasm that had laced her voice.

She looked at Mac. "That woman who got killed—I heard Sarah say that her message to you was that she believed you, right?"

Avery never missed anything.

"Yes," Mac said.

I found myself nodding.

"That means she believed you didn't try to kill your wife anymore, but she did before, because what else could it be?"

Again Mac agreed.

Avery picked up her plate, grabbed a piece of corkscrew pasta and popped it in her mouth. "So what happened so that she changed her mind? Maybe if you could figure that out you could figure out why someone wanted to kill her."

She headed for the front.

"Out of the mouths of babes," Mr. P. said softly.

"Follow the money," Liz commented, pouring a cup of tea from the pot Rose had made and brought downstairs. Would anything get done if we ran out of tea? I wondered.

"What money?" Rose asked.

Charlotte had just dished out a plate of pasta. She handed it to me. "You mean the money in the trust."

Liz nodded. "Yes. It's too much of a coincidence that Leila's part of the trust is going to be released soon and Stevie needs money."

"Stevie wouldn't have done anything to hurt Leila," Mac said. He seemed to have that sentence on permanent repeat.

"And I thought she had an alibi," Charlotte said.

I looked at Mr. P. "She does. The photos she sent me were not doctored in any way I could determine. In one Stephanie is visible and there's a clock in the background showing the time. She pretty much has an ironclad alibi."

Liz waved a breadstick at us. "So? What about her partner or husband or whatever he is?"

"Davis Abbott," Mr. P. said.

"Yes, whatever his name is," Liz said dismissively. "It seems to me that he would also benefit if Leila were dead and Stevie got all the trust instead of half of it." She looked at Mr. P. "Alfred, what exactly do we know about this Abbott person?"

A flush of color warmed Mr. P.'s cheeks. "Elizabeth, I am embarrassed to say, very little, but I will rectify that right after we eat."

Rose beamed at him. Liz reached for her tea, catching my eye with a self-satisfied smile. Charlotte leaned over to ask Mac something.

Both Napoléon and Frederick the Great are credited with saying an army marches on its stomach. I was pretty sure the Angels detected on theirs.

It turned out to be a busy afternoon. Because it was wet, people were happy to be inside browsing around shops like Second Chance. It was still raining when Elvis and I headed home. Since it was cool enough to have the oven on I was going to try to put together a chicken and rice dish Rose had taught me to make a couple of weekends ago. Every time I made something I was amazed that it was even close to edible. Not to mention that no fire extinguishers had been used.

The cheesy chicken and rice was delicious and I ate a huge bowl, sharing a bit of chicken with Elvis. Then he watched *Jeopardy!* while I ran the dishwasher and cleaned up the kitchen. We had a date with must-see TV—the summer finale of *Restless Days*.

I used the remote to turn off the TV and slumped against the back of the sofa. Elvis and I had just spent the last five minutes literally on the edge of our seats. I looked at the cat, sprawled now beside me. "Well, I didn't see that coming, did you?"

"Merow," he said. It seemed that Elvis had been blindsided by the two-hour, cliff-hanger summer finale just as much as I had. He had seemed to enjoy watching the dramatic nighttime sudser for the last couple of months, settling himself beside me on the sofa whenever he heard the theme music for the show. It wasn't that surprising, considering he was a faithful viewer of *Jeopardy!* every weeknight, missing an episode only for special circumstances like dinner with Rose and Mr. P. at Rose's apartment.

All at once Elvis sat up, craning his head to look at the front door. I'd given up trying to figure out how he knew when someone was going to knock at the door. Maybe it was the fact that cats have hearing vastly superior to ours. Or maybe he had X-ray vision or cat ESP. He just seemed to know. Of course being a cat, he let me in on it only when it suited him.

I got to my feet just as we heard a knock. "It's probably Rose," I said. "She had some kind of meeting about the library book sale. Maybe she's bringing us the leftover cookies."

But it wasn't Rose. It was Michelle. She was dressed in flip-flops, cropped jeans and a green and gold T-shirt with an open Windbreaker, which told me she'd come from home and not from work.

"Hi," I said.

"Is this a bad time?" she asked.

I shook my head. "No. C'mon in."

She glanced over her shoulder and then stepped inside. "I'm sorry to show up like this so late," she said. "I saw your light and just took a chance you'd be by yourself." Her expression was serious, her green eyes troubled.

I took her jacket and we both sat down on the sofa. Elvis jumped up between us. "Something's going on," I said. "What is it?"

"I've been taken off Mac's case."

I took a moment before I said anything. Just that morning she'd told me not to worry about Nick seeing Mac with Erin Fellowes and now she wasn't involved in the case herself. "Do you know why?"

She gave me a grim smile. "Because I'm too close to it—too close to all of you."

I sighed. "I can see that. I don't like it but I can't argue with the reasoning."

"That's not all," she said. She hesitated for a moment. "Tomorrow they're going to charge Mac with Erin Fellowes's murder."

"How . . . how can they do that?" I stammered. "They don't have any real evidence."

Elvis put his front paws on Michelle's leg and she began to absently stroke his fur. "We have a witness who saw Mac and Erin together right before she was killed. Remember?"

"That wasn't Mac," I said, biting off the words. I almost added, *Even you're not sure of that,* but caught myself.

"It's not just that," she said.

"It's Leila."

She nodded. "The police in Boston may have decided that what happened to her was an accident but that doesn't mean it's been settled in everyone's mind. There's been some . . . pressure."

I felt a sour taste in the back of my throat. The pressure had to be coming from Mac's in-laws. They had money and influence and they'd put up roadblocks to keep him away from their daughter. It made sense that they would use any connections they had to try to have Mac arrested.

"It's not as bad as it sounds," Michelle continued. "Do you know Cal Barnes?"

I got a mental picture of the burly police officer: stocky and solid, built like the hockey goalie he'd been since high school. I nodded.

"He's taking over the case. Cal's a straight arrow and he's fair and he's honest. He won't stop looking for more evidence."

I'd twisted the drawstring of my cutoff sweatpants so tightly around my finger the tip had turned a deep purple-red color. "Mac didn't do this," I said. "I swear to you he didn't."

"I believe you," she said. "The ADA owes me a favor so she agreed to let Mac surrender himself at the station tomorrow morning. He'll be arraigned right after lunch. They're going to want bail. I'm assuming Liz will take care of that."

I nodded. Liz had taken care of bail when Maddie Hamilton had been wrongly accused of murder. I didn't have to ask to know she'd do the same thing for Mac.

"Mac shouldn't be held for more than a few hours. He won't have to spend the night in jail or anything like that. I know it sounds intimidating but it'll be all right. I promise." She tried to smile but didn't quite get there.

"Thank you," I said. The words didn't seem anywhere near enough.

Michelle picked up Elvis and set him on the sofa. Then she stood up. "I have to go," she said. "For obvious reasons I won't be there tomorrow, but I promise Cal won't be the only one still looking for evidence."

I'd gotten to my feet as well and now I hugged her, hard. "I mean it," I said, my voice almost overcome with emotion. "Thank you for everything you've done."

She pulled back and looked at me. "We're friends," she said. "Remember?"

I felt the prickle of tears and had to swallow hard before I could speak. "Yeah, I remember," I said.

My cell phone was on the counter. It rang then. I glanced over my shoulder.

"That's probably Josh," Michelle said. "Go ahead and get it. I'll talk to you soon." She actually managed a small smile. "Go. It'll work out all right."

She headed for the door and I turned to pick up my phone.

Michelle was right. Everything went just the way she'd told me it would. Mac—with Josh—turned himself in at the police station first thing in the morning. He was scheduled to go before a judge right after lunch.

I'd shown up at his door with Elvis and a couple breakfast sandwiches at seven a.m. Looking past him I saw two mugs on the table. "You expecting someone?" I asked.

"Just you," he said with a hint of a smile. "And Josh in a little while. I already made the coffee."

We settled at the table with our coffee and breakfast. Elvis jumped up onto the wide windowsill and looked down to the parking lot.

Mac seemed so calm, so accepting of what was about to happen. It seemed to me that I was angrier than he was and I said as much.

"I expected this to happen," he said. "I'm the most likely suspect in Erin's murder. Hell, I'm probably the only suspect." He played with his mug. "Erin was Leila's best friend. That was where her loyalty lay. I never held that against her. I never would have hurt her."

"We're going to figure this out," I said. I put my hand over his. "We are."

Mac nodded. "I know," he said.

The moment stretched between us and then Elvis meowed loudly. He looked from the window to us.

"I think Josh might be here," Mac said.

Reluctantly, I pulled my hand back and he got to his feet. Whatever might have been about to happen had passed.

Right before we opened I gathered everyone in the store and explained what was going on.

"How could Michelle do something like this?" Rose exclaimed.

Mr. P. put a hand on her arm. "Wait a minute, Rosie," he said. "We may not have the whole story."

I raked a hand back through my hair. "Michelle had nothing to do with this," I said. "She's been taken off the case."

Rose's eyes widened. "Why?"

Liz made an offhanded gesture. "Why do you think? She's too close to everything, to Sarah, to all of us."

I nodded. "Liz is right."

"So who will be taking over the case?" Mr. P. asked, giving Rose a reassuring smile as he dropped his hand.

"Cal Barnes," I said.

"I taught him American history," Charlotte said. "Bright enough but not very imaginative."

"Would he remember you?" I asked.

"I think so," she said. "I did some extra work with him. He was on the hockey team and the coach at that time was a stickler for the boys keeping up their marks." She frowned at me. "Is that important?"

I shrugged. "I don't know. It might be."

"If this new detective had Charlotte for a teacher does that mean we could get him kicked off Mac's case?" Avery asked.

I smiled at her. She cared about Mac as much as any of the rest of us. "I'm sorry, no."

She folded her arms over her chest. "Mac isn't going to have to stay in jail, is he?"

"He most decidedly is not," Liz said. She put an arm around her granddaughter's shoulders and Avery leaned against her.

"Can we be there this afternoon?" Rose asked.

I tucked a strand of hair behind my ear. I couldn't seem to keep my hands still. "Yes, we can. I'm leaving at about quarter to one."

"Rosie and I will ride with you, if that's all right," Mr. P. said. I could see the concern in his eyes.

"I'd like that," I said.

I saw Charlotte glance at Liz, who nodded. "I'll go with Liz," Charlotte said.

Avery broke away from her grandmother and came to stand in front of me. "Sarah, I wanna go, too," she said, her fingers playing with the stack of bracelets on her left arm. "But I'll stay here and watch the store if you want. You can trust me."

Avery had a challenging relationship with her father, Liz's son, so Mac had become very much a father figure to her. "I know I can trust you, but you can come. I'm closing the store for a few hours."

Mr. P. took a couple of steps toward us. "I could stay here and help Avery, if you'd like me to," he offered.

I smiled at both of them. "I appreciate both of you making the offer but the only place we need to be this afternoon is in that courtroom for Mac."

Mr. P. smiled back at me. "Then that's where we'll be, my dear."

At twelve thirty I put a sign on the door that informed customers we were closed for the afternoon. Liz had just shown up, looking the picture of understated wealth in a pale gray suit with darker gray slingbacks and a soft peach shell. Rose and I had gone home just after eleven to change. I was wearing a navy and white sheath with waist-length navy blazer. Rose had put on a yellow, green and blue tunic dress with a three-quarter-sleeve white sweater. We'd dropped off Mr. P. and when we picked him up again he was sporting a brown tweedy sport coat and tan trousers with a crisp white shirt and striped tie. As Rose had explained, it was important the judge know we had respect for the process so we should wear our best things. I wasn't sure that it really mattered whether I showed up in my old sweatpants or my best dress and heels but there wasn't anything else I could do at the moment so I was doing this.

Liz came up behind me and put an arm around my shoulders. She smiled at me and then turned to look behind us. "We clean up well," she said.

I nodded.

Liz held up her gray leather clutch. "Don't worry, child," she said. "In a couple of hours Mac will be back here."

I blew a kiss at her because I didn't want to disturb her perfectly applied makeup. "What would I do without you?" I said.

She leaned in and kissed my cheek. "Lucky for all of us, you're never going to find out."

Avery came down the stairs then with Charlotte. Charlotte was wearing a fitted white top with her pearl choker and a slim black skirt. She looked competent, in charge, and slightly intimidating. Avery was dressed in a flowered black and white skirt with a white cotton sweater. Someone—probably Charlotte—had combed her hair back from her face and tucked it behind her ears. She was wearing her black Doc Martens because she was a teenager, after all, but they had been cleaned and shined.

I looked around at all of us and thought that Liz was right: We cleaned up well.

Chapter 12

At quarter to one we left for the courthouse, Liz following my SUV. Rose talked about the history of the building as we drove, probably as a way to distract me, I realized.

Josh Evans was waiting for us inside the courthouse. In his expensive dark suit and equally pricey haircut, it was hard to find a glimpse of the kid who'd loved to argue. Then he pushed his sleeve back to check the time and I caught a glimpse of his Darkwing Duck watch and somehow I felt a little better. He smiled and walked over when he caught sight of us. "Hi, Sarah. Everything is running on schedule," he said. "I've seen Mac. He's fine." The knot between my shoulder blades seemed to unkink just a little.

Josh said hello to the others. Then he went over what was going to happen in the courtroom. "After the charges are read the judge will ask Mac how he pleads. He'll say not guilty. The ADA and I have already talked about bail." His gaze flicked momentarily to Liz. "I'm going to agree with her suggestion and I don't have any reason to believe the judge will have a problem with it." He gave us an encouraging smile. "Things should go pretty quickly."

"Is it all right if we go in and find seats now?" I asked. I felt a little antsy standing in the hallway and I was guessing Josh probably had things to do.

Josh nodded. "Go ahead. I'll be there in a minute."

I'd been inside the courtroom once before, when Maddie had been arraigned, but I'd forgotten how intimidating the room was. The walls were painted a dark taupe while all the trim, moldings and columns were a glossy white. Vintage brass chandeliers hung from the fourteen-foot ceiling, and what I was guessing were reproduction sconces added more light from the walls. The high, multipaned windows had been restored and refinished in a dark wood stain. The rest of the wood, the railing, the spectators' seating—which reminded me of old wooden movie theater seats—and the judge's bench were a warmer oak finish. The space was formal and serious and I reminded myself that Mac hadn't done anything wrong so there was nothing to be afraid of.

We took the first row of seats behind the low railings so we were as close as we could get to where Mac and Josh would be sitting. We'd been inside the courtroom only a couple of minutes when Rose leaned across Charlotte, who was sitting next to me. "Sarah," she said, gesturing over her shoulder. I turned to see what she was looking at. Jess and Sam had just walked in. Sam was wearing a sport coat and tie with his jeans. Jess had on a wildly patterned red dress.

I stood up and Jess came down the aisle and hugged me. "What are you doing here?" I whispered.

"Where else would I be?" she said with a smile. She gave me one more squeeze and moved into the row behind us.

Sam caught both my hands in his. "No one in their right mind would believe Mac could hurt anyone," he told me.

"Thank you for being here," I said.

"Any time, kiddo." He leaned over and kissed my forehead and then took a seat next to Jess.

I was about to sit back down when the courtroom door opened again and Glenn McNamara walked in, followed by his uncle Clayton. They both smiled and Glenn raised a hand in hello as they took a seat on the aisle four rows back.

I took my seat again but a couple of minutes later I noticed Rose look over her shoulder once more. I turned to see that Channing Caulfield had come in, along with two men I knew that Mac had crewed for several times. Suddenly my chest got tight, like someone had just sat on me, and I had to take several deep breaths to make the sensation go away. By the time we were ready to begin, almost every seat behind me was filled by someone who knew Mac: Vince Kennedy, who played in The Hairy Bananas with Sam, Stella Hall, whose brother's house we'd cleared out back in the spring. I started biting the inside of my cheek so I wouldn't cry. Just before court was in session, Jackson Montgomery slipped in and took a seat in the back. True to his word he was still in town. I nodded in recognition and he raised a hand in return.

Mac came into the courtroom looking serious but collected. I saw him swallow a couple of times when he looked behind us and realized the courtroom was more than half-full of people, all of them there for him.

Josh was right about the process and bail and very quickly we were all in the hallway outside the courtroom.

Rose hugged Mac and then stepped back to look him over. "Are you all right?" she asked, her eyes searching his face. "Did they treat you well?"

He smiled. "I'm fine, Rose."

Avery threw her arms around him then. "Was prison horrible?" she asked.

"It wasn't prison and it wasn't horrible," Mac said. He shook hands with Mr. P., hugged both Charlotte and Jess and as he turned to speak to Sam and Glenn his eyes locked with mine and he smiled.

I looked around but there was no sign of Jackson. His not staying around was probably for the best.

Liz came down the hall with Josh.

"Everything all right?" I asked.

"Mac's free to go," Josh said. He moved to speak to his client while I turned to Liz.

"Thank you," I said.

"No point in having money if you can't throw it around once in a while," she said with a smile.

"I love you," I said, already knowing how she was going to answer.

She waved a hand at me. "Yeah, yeah, everybody does," she said.

There were a couple of things that Josh explained needed to be taken care of, so we all headed back to the shop. Mac arrived about half an hour later. By then I'd made tea and cut the Bundt cake that Rose had taken out of her freezer when we'd gone home to change. Josh was with him, and Rose immediately invited him to stay for cake. I headed upstairs to get a cup of coffee for him and one for Mac.

When I came back down Mac was standing at the bottom of the stairs. I handed him one of the mugs I was carrying.

"Thank you," he said.

I smiled. He'd been gone only a few hours and I couldn't believe how relieved I was to see him. "You're welcome."

"I don't mean for this," he said, holding up the mug. "Well, I do, but I mean for everything working out so well today."

"I didn't do anything," I said. "The people who deserve credit for today are Josh and Liz."

Mac smiled. "And I've thanked both of them, but I also know that I wouldn't be standing here right now if you weren't friends with Michelle. I wouldn't have been allowed to turn myself in this morning the way I did, Josh wouldn't have been able to get a reasonable bail set. Michelle made that happen. She did it for you." He shrugged. "So thank you for being the kind of friend that she'd put herself out for, that lots of people would put themselves out for." He leaned over and gave me a hug.

Before I could point out that all the people who showed up in court today came because of him, not me, we were interrupted by Avery. We stepped apart, a little self-consciously, at least on my part.

"Hey, Sarah, is there any hot water in the kettle?" she asked. She was carrying the teapot in its knitted cozy.

"Uh, yes," I said. "But you'll need to put it on to boil again."

"Okay." She bounded up the stairs. "Rose is looking for you," she said over her shoulder.

"For me or for Mac?" I asked.

"Both of you," she said. "She wants to plan strategy."

"Strategy?" Mac said.

Avery stopped two steps from the top and turned to look at us. "Well, yeah," she said. "We have to figure out who killed that woman. Rose said we can't wait for the police to do it. Right now she thinks they're all a bunch of . . ." She hesitated. "I won't say the word but it rhymes with 'glass bowls.'" She took the last stairs in one long step and disappeared down the hall.

I turned to look at Mac.

"All bets are off now, aren't they, as far as Rose is concerned?"

"Oh yeah," I said.

"Is there any way I can ask her to—" He hesitated. "I'm trying to think of the right cliché."

"Not go off half-cocked? Or get her knickers in a knot?" I shook my head. "Not unless you want to be a 'glass bowl.'" I smiled at him and headed for the workroom.

Just before closing Avery knocked on my office door. "Come in," I called.

The teen poked her head around the door. She looked troubled.

"What's up?" I asked.

"There's a man in a suit downstairs asking for Mac," she said. "I don't know who it is and I wasn't sure what to do."

I knew that Mac was out in the garage working on a bed frame I'd found during the spring trash pick. "What does he look like?" I asked.

"He's tall, very short dark hair with one of those little beards just on his chin. The suit is expensive and Nonna would say he had good posture because you know how she is about that kind of thing." She shifted impatiently from one foot to the other. "He was at court earlier."

It was likely Jackson, I realized. "I'll talk to him," I said. "Thanks for letting me know."

"Mac's not going back to jail, is he?" Avery said. "I thought maybe that man was some kind of police officer."

I shook my head. "He's not a police officer and Mac isn't going back to jail."

"How do you know that?" It was impossible to miss the challenge in her eyes—and the concern.

I got to my feet. "Because he didn't do anything wrong."

She gave a snort of derision and shook her head, looking so much like Liz I had to bite my tongue not to laugh. "Innocent people get put in jail all the time. Don't you watch TV?"

"Nothing's going to happen to Mac," I said. "Josh is a very good lawyer. You know that. And besides, he has a secret weapon."

"What secret weapon?"

"Us."

Her expression cleared and she nodded emphatically. "Yeah. You're right. He does."

I went downstairs and discovered I was right. Jackson Montgomery was standing in the middle of the store. He turned as I approached.

"You're persistent," I said.

He smiled. "I messed up. It's up to me to fix things."

"Thank you for coming to court."

"I didn't stay because I figured it would be awkward."

I nodded. "Good call." Avery was over at the cash desk, not even making an effort to pretend she wasn't trying to eavesdrop.

Jackson looked around. "Is Mac here?"

"He still doesn't want to talk to you," I said.

Jackson's mouth twisted to one side. "I screwed up by staying away so long, I get that. I don't know what else to do except keep trying to talk to him." He stopped and blew out a breath. "Please just tell Mac I was here."

I nodded. "I will."

Once Jackson was gone I went out to the old garage. Mac had the headboard and footboard I'd trash-picked lying on a large tarp spread on the floor along with a set of side rails and slats that had been in the garage when I bought the property.

"I think I can make all these pieces work," he said.

"Hey, it feels like a victory just to find a use for the old rails," I said.

"Tell that to Rose and you can probably get a cake to celebrate."

"You don't have to pretend that everything is fine," I said.

He swiped a hand back over his head. "If it's all the same to you, I'd rather pretend a little than sit around worrying about what's going to happen next."

"In that case, sponge cake with berries and whipped cream."

Mac frowned. "Excuse me?"

"You said I could probably get Rose to make me a cake. I want sponge cake." I glanced over at the shop. "Except she'd probably turn it into a cooking lesson." Rose was the only person who'd had any success at teaching me to cook. Everyone else from two middle school teachers to my mom to my brother Liam had given up after multiple kitchen "incidents." In my defense I don't think any of the fires were really my fault.

"I don't mind eating your cooking," Mac said.

I laughed. "That makes you a member of a very elite—and small—group."

"Fine with me."

I glanced out the door again.

"What is it?" he asked.

"Jackson was here again."

Mac looked down at the floor, then bent down and picked up something. "He's stubborn. I saw him in the courtroom." He flipped a small metal washer over the back of his fingers.

"This is totally none of my business but I've been hanging out with Rose and the rest of them"—I gestured in the general direction of the shop—"and they've been a bad example, so now I'm boundary challenged. Why are you being so rigid when it comes to Jackson? It's not like you."

He met my gaze and shrugged. "Jackson and I have been friends since the sixth grade. He always had my back and I like to think that I always had his. But he seemed to find it so easy to believe all the things that Leila's family accused me of. I can't—I don't—trust him." He shook his head as though he were shaking away some old memories. "Do you think I'm wrong?" he asked. "If you were in my place would you just let it go?"

I laughed. "Mac, how many times have you seen Nick and me argue? Or maybe I should say have the same argument over and over again? You should know by now I'm not exactly good at letting things go."

"Nick's still in your life. It looks to me like you're pretty good at forgiving," he said.

I scraped at a bit of paint on the floor with the toe of my shoe. "It's not the same thing. Talk about stubborn? That's Nick." I held up both hands like I was holding a basketball. "I could take his head sometimes and—" I shook my hands in the air. "But I do trust him. He's never given me any reason not to. You said you don't trust Jackson. That's enough for me. Do what feels right for you and I'll run interference."

"Thanks," Mac said.

I tipped my head toward the shop. "I better go see what's going on."

I stepped inside the back door and automatically glanced into the Angels' sunporch office. Mr. P. looked up and beckoned me inside. His sport coat was hanging on the back of his chair and the sleeves of his white shirt were rolled up. "I just wanted to show you this," he said, handing me a photo he'd printed out. "I left the change on your desk."

I nodded. Mr. P. was scrupulous about paying for the Angels' use of my printer along with "rent" for the sunporch space. I gave the money to the Friends of the North Harbor Library and the Midcoast Animal Shelter because it made me uncomfortable to make money off them. Trying to argue my way out of the payments had left me with a giant headache and a new wrinkle in the middle of my forehead.

"Hey, that's Kale," I said.

Mr. P. frowned. "Excuse me?"

"The guy that was blocking the driveway when the TV people were filming. The one in the *Kale Yeah!* T-shirt. Why do you have a photo of him?"

His expression changed as if something had just fallen into place for him. He gave me a small smile. "Sarah, your 'Kale' is Stephanie Carleton's partner, Davis Abbott."

Chapter 13

I stared at Mr. P., eyes wide with shock. I hadn't seen this coming.

"Interesting turn, don't you think?" he said.

Rose came in then. "What's going on?" she asked.

I handed her the photo without comment. She studied it for a moment and then looked at me, a frown creasing her forehead. "What are you doing with a photo of that young man with the deplorable manners?" she asked.

"That young man is Davis Abbott," Mr. P. said.

"Stevie's partner," Rose said.

I nodded. "Yes."

"I wouldn't be surprised to learn he's involved." She handed the picture back to Mr. P. "I found him crude and rude. He definitely isn't a person of good character." Manners were very important to Rose.

"Exactly what did Davis say to you that morning?" I asked.

Rose raised an eyebrow. "Let's just say he made a suggestion that is anatomically impossible."

"The miscreant!" Mr. P. exclaimed, getting to his feet.

For a moment I thought he was going to head out to look for Davis Abbott to defend Rose's honor. Not that she needed anyone to defend it.

She caught his arm. "Don't worry, Alf. I heard a lot worse when I was teaching. And I put that young man in his place." She turned her attention to me. "Did you notice that Davis's truck had one taillight not working and his rearview mirror appeared to have fallen off? Just think how dangerous those things could be."

I'd seen that guileless look in her gray eyes before. I couldn't hold back a smile. I knew where the conversation was going. "Did you call the police on Davis Abbott?" I asked.

"Heavens, no," Rose said, and her surprise at my question seemed genuine. So maybe I didn't know where the conversation was going. "That would have been petty." She fluffed her soft, white hair. "However in an interesting coincidence I did happen to see that nice Charles Sullivan later that morning at McNamara's and when he asked how we were making out with filming on our street I did mention how you and I had arrived to find this very rude driver blocking the lot."

"That nice Charles Sullivan" was Officer Charles Sullivan from the North Harbor Police Department and one of Rose's former students.

She glanced at Mr. P. "He was appalled when I confided how Mr. Abbott spoke to me. So when he asked if I could describe the truck I told him about the broken taillight and the missing mirror and the license plate number, which coincidentally I'd happened to write down, because it would be wrong to keep things from an officer of the law."

I leaned over and kissed Rose on the cheek. "I love the way your mind works," I said.

"What a lovely thing to say," she said. She brushed a bit of dust from the front of her apron. "What we need to do now is concentrate on what Stevie's partner was doing in North Harbor the very day Erin Fellowes was killed."

"As I recall, Stephanie told us that Davis had been in Nova Scotia for some sort of workshop on organic farming techniques. Did she lie to us or did he lie to her?" Mr. P. asked.

"I know you'll figure it out," I said.

He smiled, his previous outrage gone. "I'll see what I can find out about that workshop."

"Keep me in the loop," I said. Rose and I walked through the workroom toward the shop.

"Stevie and her partner are tied up in this somehow, aren't they?" I said.

"I'd like to say I think you're wrong but at this point I'm just not sure." Rose gave her head a little shake. "Both of them certainly seem to be lacking as far as good judgment is concerned."

I nudged her with my hip. "I have faith that you and Mr. P. will figure out what's going on."

"That reminds me," she said, raising one finger in the air, "Liz and I are going to the salt works in Marshfield tomorrow. I switched shifts with Charlotte."

"Is there anything I can do?" I asked. It was the most diplomatic way I could think of suggesting I should go with them. Rose and Liz together on a road trip could get very . . . interesting.

"Thank you, sweetie," Rose said with a smile. "Liz

and I can handle this. Clayton explained the process and he told me what questions to ask."

I frowned at her. "I remember when Charlotte and I talked to Clayton about harvesting seaweed but I don't remember any conversations at all about sea salt, with or without you."

Rose was patting her pockets, looking for something, her phone or her keys probably. She looked up at me. "Oh, I called Clayton. I had some questions."

"What are you trying to find out?"

She seemed to find whatever she'd been looking for in the right-hand pocket of her skirt and gave a small nod of satisfaction. "It occurred to me that if du Mer was being investigated for fraud it might have to do with ingredients. The sea salt seemed the logical place to start."

"That's a good idea." I held the door so Rose could move into the store ahead of me. "You think Erin Fellowes's murder is somehow connected to Mac's wife's accident, don't you?" I asked.

"Yes," she said. "Both Alfred and I do."

"Because?" I nudged.

She reached over and brushed a bit of lint off my shoulder. "Well, dear, it's really the only logical conclusion." She held up one finger. "First of all, we know she wasn't mugged because she had her money, her credit cards and her cell phone."

I nodded. "True."

Rose held up a second finger. "And secondly, there hasn't been an assault on the harbor front in two years and that was just a couple of young men who'd indulged way too much."

"Also true," I said. "Is there a number three?"

Rose smiled and patted her hair. "Of course there is. Alfred and I never rush to judgment."

I decided to just let that go unchallenged.

"The only person Erin Fellowes knew in North Harbor was Mac," she continued.

"As far as we know, yes."

"Their connection was Mac's wife, who's now in a coma, which Erin blamed on Mac."

I wasn't having any trouble following her logic. Everything she said made sense.

Rose cocked her head to one side, looking like a tiny, white-tufted bird. "Don't you think it's too much of a coincidence that just a few hours after she got here—after she told you to tell him she believed him—that she ended up dead?"

"I do," I said, because I did. "There's no faulting your logic."

She smiled again. "I'm not just another pretty face, you know," she said, raising an eyebrow.

I grinned and gave her a hug. "You absolutely aren't," I said.

Rose and Liz left just before eight the next morning. Liz dropped off Avery when she came to pick up Rose. Once Avery was out of earshot, on my sofa talking to Elvis, I propped my chin on Liz's shoulder. "Don't stop for strangers, don't speed and remember to wear your seat belt," I said with a teasing smile.

"I've been driving longer than you've been alive, missy," she said, reaching up with one hand to give me a light smack on the forehead.

"Did you have one of Avery's green smoothies for breakfast?" I asked, lifting my head.

Liz rolled her eyes. "Luckily the child adores Mac, so no, I did not have a glass of green sludge for breakfast. I had a scrambled egg, English muffin and a bowl of berries." She gave me a warning look. "And before you ask, no I don't need to visit the washroom."

"You know what Gram would say," I teased. "Never turn down a chocolate chip cookie or a chance to pee."

Liz made a face at me. "It think that was more likely Rose and not Isabel," she said.

"And do you know the way to where you're going in Marshfield?" I asked sweetly, reaching over to straighten her collar. She had to know what I was up to. When I'd driven up to Carrabassett Valley to see Stevie Carleton Liz had reminded me to check my tire pressure, carry a bottle of water and wear my seat belt.

Liz batted my hand away. "I'd be happy to tell you where to go."

I laughed.

"I heard all about your lead foot from Rose and Alfred," she continued. "So don't get the idea you have some kind of superior driving skills. I've driven on the autobahn. I think I can find Marshfield just fine."

I'd driven with Liz and I knew compared to her I was the proverbial, poky little old lady behind the wheel. I wrinkled my nose at her. "People who live in glass houses," I said.

"Shouldn't walk around the house naked," she finished.

Rose came out of her apartment then, which effectively ended the conversation—not that I was going to win against Liz, anyway.

"I just have to grab my bag and my keys and I'm ready," I told Avery after Liz had pulled away from the curb. "Do you want to stop at McNamara's for a muffin and lemonade?" I asked.

She was holding Elvis and he immediately murped his agreement. "Please," she said. "Only, could I have hot chocolate instead?"

"I don't see why not," I said.

"I have money," Avery said. "Nonna told me not to be a freeloader."

"I appreciate that," I said as I locked the apartment door. "But this is my treat."

We stopped at Glenn's and chose the blueberry muffins that were still a little warm. I got a cinnamon raisin muffin for Charlotte and orange spice for Mac. Glenn made Avery's hot chocolate and it smelled so good I decided to have the same thing, telling myself the day wasn't that warm yet.

"I should have the proposal for Clayton's house soon," I told Glenn as he dropped three marshmallows on the top of my drink.

"Thanks," he said, smiling as he handed me the cup. "Clayton seems to be getting enthusiastic about the idea. He's even talking about moving in to town."

"Don't hold your breath on that one," I said. "I think he talked to Rose about Legacy Place."

"Oh, he did," Glenn said. "Pretty much the only thing he cared about were how many good cooks there were in the building." He laughed. "You can probably tell from looking at him that Clayton likes to eat. He's the personification of 'the way to a man's heart is through his stomach.'"

It was another gorgeous day and the shop was quiet. I sent Avery back to the workroom to cover more lamp-shades with the stash of old maps I'd bought at a yard sale. The shades had turned out to be popular. Charlotte and I started dusting and making small changes in the front window display. Avery was still working on a couple of ideas for changing the display entirely.

While we worked we talked about my idea for offer-ing classes similar to the one I'd taught at Legacy Place, the one where I'd met Mr. P.—as Charlotte put it—"just the way the good Lord had made him" for the first time.

"My plan was to teach in the old garage space but now that it's been finished I realize I don't have enough space out there now that the area has been turned into work space," I said.

"Have you thought about contacting Legacy Place to see about renting space from them?" Charlotte asked. "They have classes there for more than just seniors."

Elvis, who was sitting up on the cash desk, meowed his agreement.

"See?" Charlotte said. "I'm not the only one who thinks it's a good idea."

"Well, then, how can I disagree?" I said.

We worked in silence for a few minutes. Charlotte's mind seemed to be somewhere else. I had to ask her twice to pass me a cloth. "I'm sorry," she said, shaking her head and handing me the duster.

"Where were you?" I asked, lifting down a lamp that I had decided I was going to move to a small bookcase on the end wall.

Charlotte brushed a strand of hair off her cheek. "Thinking about this case, about Mac. I keep wondering why Erin Fellowes came all the way from Boston to North Harbor. If what she wanted to talk to Mac about was so important, why didn't she call?"

I shrugged and set the lamp on the floor by my feet. "I just assumed Mac had changed his cell number and Erin didn't have it."

Charlotte frowned at a teapot and moved it about an inch, nodding with satisfaction. Then she looked at me again. "But she showed up *here*, she knew he worked *here*. Why didn't she just call him here?"

I shook my head. "I have no idea." We hadn't figured out how Erin had learned where Mac was.

"You know, we're all assuming Erin found out something that made her change her mind about Mac's guilt. She told you to tell him that she believed him."

I nodded, remembering the intensity in Erin's face.

"And we're assuming the person who tried to kill Leila followed Erin and killed her as well."

I nodded again. "It's the best theory we have right now."

"Maybe Erin didn't find out something that cleared Mac," Charlotte said. She picked up a small china cream pitcher and turned it over in her hands. "Maybe she found something else."

I wasn't sure what she was getting at. "What do you mean?" I asked.

"Maybe Erin found something." Charlotte gestured with the pitcher. "Some*thing*, that somehow implicated the real would-be murderer. Something she brought here to show to Mac. Maybe because she hoped he would recognize it."

Her reasoning made sense. "So what was the thing?"

"I think it had to be something small. Something she could have picked up and carried around without drawing attention to herself. Did she have a purse or a bag with her?"

I closed my eyes for a moment and pictured Erin Fellowes getting out of her small sports car and walking over to me. "Yes," I said. I opened my eyes again and looked at Charlotte. "A small multicolored cross-body bag. And her dress had a full skirt with pockets."

Charlotte was nodding.

"You think she had whatever this evidence was in her bag or in her pocket."

"Yes."

"We need to find it, whatever it is."

"We do," she said.

I just had no idea how to do that.

Chapter 14

"There's no way that Michelle would tell me what was with Erin's body," I said. "Even if she was still on the case."

"It would be pointless to ask Nicolas," Charlotte said, setting the cream pitcher on the seat of a folding wooden beach chair. She glanced toward the door to the workshop—and the Angels' sunporch office.

I knew what she was thinking and I had no doubt Mr. P. could get the information but I also knew I didn't feel comfortable with the methods he'd likely have to use.

"I'm going to call Josh," I said, pulling my phone out of my pocket. "He may have some way to find out."

Luckily Josh was in his office and available. I explained Charlotte's reasoning and what we were looking for.

"Let me see what I can do," he said. "I'll be in touch as soon as I have anything."

"All we can do now is wait," I said to Charlotte as I tucked my phone back in my pocket.

"I'll cross my fingers," she said.

I shrugged. "It can't hurt."

Mr. P. showed up at lunchtime. Charlotte and I were

sitting by the back door with our sandwiches. Avery was watching the shop and working on a display of perfume bottles. Mr. P. was wearing a straw fedora with a red and navy hatband and a red golf shirt. And he was smiling.

"You've had a good morning," I said.

He nodded. "I have some information about Davis Abbott." One eyebrow went up. "He wasn't at that workshop."

"Not at all?" Charlotte asked.

"Not at all," Mr. P. said. "It turns out Davis and the workshop organizer are old friends." A huge smile spread across the old man's face. "It turns out that William—the man who puts on these workshops—is a poker player."

Mr. P., with his excellent memory, ability to read people and perfect poker face, was an excellent cardplayer. I'd never actually played with him. I knew better than that.

"We got to talking and eventually I got him to admit he was covering for Davis," he continued, "so Stephanie wouldn't know where he was. William seemed to think Davis was 'stepping out' on her, as he put it. He said she could be pretty intense sometimes."

"What do *you* think?" I asked.

He gave the slightest of shrugs. "I see two possibilities. Either William is right or Davis Abbott may have been plotting to kill Erin Fellowes." He smiled then. "How was your morning?" he asked.

"Charlotte came up with an idea and I think she may be onto something," I said. I explained Charlotte's theory that Erin had brought something to show Mac and how I'd called Josh to see if he could get a list of what had been with Erin's body.

Mr. P. nodded slowly. "I think you could be right," he said to Charlotte. "Good work." Then he looked at me. "I assume you'd like to wait to see if Josh can find out anything before I see what I can do?"

I nodded, suddenly feeling a little uncomfortable.

"I think that's very wise, my dear," he said. "This is Mac. We need to be like Caesar's wife."

"Above reproach," Charlotte said quietly.

He nodded approvingly. "Exactly."

Mac stuck his head out the back door then. "Sarah, by any chance do you have more quilts up in your office?" he asked.

"I do," I said. "There are three that Jess repaired. I was going to get Avery to put them out this afternoon." I set my coffee cup by my feet. "What do you need more quilts for?" I knew there were two on display in the shop.

"Adam and James are looking for four quilts for the inn," he said.

Adam and James were big-city transplants who had restored a gorgeous old house in Camden and were running it as an inn. They'd found Second Chance by accident on their way to a funeral in Portland a few weeks previous and had become good customers since then. "They bought the last two quilts that Jess fixed just a couple of weeks ago," I said.

Mac held up both hands. "I don't know what happened," he said. "All I can tell you is Adam said there was a goat involved."

Charlotte and Mr. P. exchanged a look. "Hedley," they said together.

I turned to Charlotte. "Who?"

"Hedley Forbes," she said. "He keeps goats."

"Why?" I asked.

"He makes cheese."

"From goat's milk?"

"People with sensitivities to cow's milk prefer it," Mr. P. said helpfully.

"I know Hedley has had a problem with them getting out." Charlotte got to her feet, brushing crumbs off her skirt. "At least that's what he told Rose."

"The goats, not the people with milk sensitivities," Mr. P. added.

"Rose likes goat cheese?" I said. Out of the corner of my eye I could see Mac struggling to keep a grin in check. I didn't dare meet his gaze directly or I'd lose it.

Charlotte shook her head. "No. She said it's an acquired taste but when Hedley offered her a bite she didn't think it was polite to refuse, especially since she was looking for information."

I was lost. Was this how Alice felt when she fell down the rabbit hole? "Information on goats or on cheese?" Mac asked.

"Salt," Charlotte said, bending down to pick up my empty cup and her own.

"Hedley Forbes uses all-natural sea salt in his cheese," Alfred continued. "Rosie went to see him to find out where he was buying his salt."

Finally the pieces were sliding into place. "That's how she found the place in Marshfield where she and Liz went this morning." I'd wondered how Rose had found out the name of one of Leila's suppliers. I'd just assumed it was Mr. P. and his keyboard.

He nodded.

"And you think these are the same goats that somehow damaged Adam and James's quilts?" I got to my feet.

Charlotte took my plate. "Well, there aren't a lot of people keeping goats in Camden."

"Good point," I said, hoping that was the end of the conversation.

Mr. P. turned to Mac. "How much do you know about Davis Abbott?" he asked.

Mac swiped a hand over his chin. "Not a lot. I think I've only spent time with him on maybe three or four occasions and it was always some kind of family thing. About all I can tell you is that he's well educated. Leila used to call him a perpetual student because he has multiple degrees. She didn't think he was good for Stevie." His dark eyes flashed. "I can tell you that Davis and Stevie had an on-again, off-again relationship. They dated for a while in college, broke up, got back together again, broke up and then this last time it seemed to stick."

"Goodness!" Mr. P. exclaimed. "The young man seems to have trouble making up his mind."

"Or maybe he thinks the grass is greener on the other side of the fence," Charlotte quipped.

"Do you really think he could have been behind Leila's accident?" Mac asked.

"We don't know yet," Mr. P. said.

"But why would he want to hurt Leila? She and Stevie were close. It doesn't make any sense."

Both Charlotte and Mr. P. looked at me.

"I can think of a million reasons why," I said gently.

Mac shook his head. "That damn money." He made a face. "I tried to convince Marguerite not to set up the trust in the first place. You can imagine how that went over with Leila's family."

Charlotte studied him, shielding her eyes from the sun with one hand. "It's none of my business—of our business," she said, "but I'm wondering why you felt that way."

"Both Leila and Stevie came from affluent families," Mac said. "They had piano lessons and dance classes and learned to ride. They both got a great education without going into debt. I wanted Marguerite to use the money in some way to make a difference in the world—scholarships, a kids' club, fund a music program in the schools, but she was insistent that the trust be set up and left to 'her girls.'" His gaze took in all three of us. "For the record, Leila and I were in agreement on that. She always said she would give the money away when she got it all, but her parents were pressuring her to hang on to her share as a legacy for her own kids someday." His mouth twisted to one side. "Marguerite's heart was in the right place but as far as I'm concerned that money has just brought trouble."

He reached for my chair and then Charlotte's, folding them both.

"I'm going to give Avery a break," Charlotte said.

I nodded. She laid a hand on Mac's arm for a moment as she passed him.

"I'll be at my desk," Mr. P. said, following Charlotte.

Mac brushed a bit of dirt off the leg of one of the chairs. "That was preachy, wasn't it?" he asked.

"Maybe just a bit," I said, holding up my thumb and index finger about half an inch apart.

He smiled. "You were supposed to say that I wasn't

preachy at all, that I'm perfectly justified in hating that damn trust."

I smiled back at him. "I'm sorry. You weren't preachy and you're perfectly justified in hating that damn trust." I said the words in a flat monotone as though I were reading them from a script.

That made him laugh. Then his expression grew serious again. "I hate this cloud of suspicion hanging over my head," he said. "This is how it was after Leila's accident. People looked at me differently."

"Hey, we're going to find the truth," I said. "And get rid of that cloud of suspicion, not that I'm convinced it's even there."

He gave his head a shake. "How? The police in Boston said what happened to Leila was an accident but it didn't convince some people." His expression was troubled.

"We have a secret weapon," I said. "We have Rose. She's a pit bull with sensible shoes and a tote bag full of cookies." I was trying to lighten the mood, but part of me was serious. The Angels and their unorthodox methods of solving crime had worked in the past and I realized that deep inside I wanted to believe they could solve this case, too.

Mac couldn't stop a small smile from spreading across his face.

"Don't give up," I said.

Avery poked her head out the door then. "Is there anything special you wanted me to do now?" she asked.

I cleared my throat and turned to give her my attention. "Umm, yeah. If you can get those canvas beach chairs cleaned I think they'd sell pretty quickly."

"I can do that," she said.

The three of us walked over to the old garage. Mac had already removed the canvas slings from the hardwood frames of the four chairs. The heavy fabric—green, blue and red stripes—was dirty but there were no obvious stains and it was in good shape. They just needed a good cleaning with a scrub brush and some elbow grease.

I showed Avery what I wanted her to do and she listened intently the way she always did when one of us gave her a task. I may have hired her because of Liz, but I'd kept her because she worked hard without complaining and she had a quirky way of looking at things, which was often good for the store.

Liz and Rose got back about an hour later. I'd just sold a '60s vintage record cabinet to a young woman looking for a unique birthday gift for her mother, and Charlotte and I were debating what to bring in from the workroom when they walked in. I could tell by the expressions on both their faces that they had some information. Rose was beaming and Liz had a smug gleam in her eyes.

Before I could ask what happened Liz held up a hand. "I need a cup of tea before anything else. I'm as dry as a covered bridge."

"I'll put the kettle on," Charlotte said.

"Thank you," Liz said. She turned to look at Rose. "I know what you're thinking. They can wait five more minutes to hear about our morning."

"Actually what I was thinking is that I'm glad you mentioned having tea," Rose countered. "I'm a little dry myself."

Liz gave her a sweet and slightly fake smile. "You're welcome, then," she said.

Mac came in trailed by Avery, who stopped to hug

both Liz and Rose before moving to straighten up a selection of old books without being asked.

I went out to the workroom to set out some chairs. Mr. P. came out of his office to help. He took one end of a vintage chrome kitchen table and helped me move it closer to the workbench. "Thank you," I said.

"You're welcome, my dear," he replied with a smile. He tipped his head to one side and with his few tufts of gray hair sticking up from his head he reminded me of an inquisitive bird. "You know, it's occurred to me that we need a more permanent place for team meetings."

"I've been thinking the same thing," I said, surveying our collection of chairs for ones I knew wouldn't collapse the second someone sat down.

"We could fit a table in the sunporch, you know."

"It's too cold in there in the winter." I reached for two wooden chairs I knew were in good shape.

"That is a problem," Mr. P. agreed. He put a hand on the back of one of the chrome chairs that went with the table and raised an eyebrow in inquiry. I nodded and he picked up the chair and the matching one beside it and carried them to the table.

"That's why I've been thinking about renovating the space," I said. I grabbed a couple of folding wooden chairs that were leaning against the back wall. That made enough seating for all of us.

A frown creased Mr. P.'s forehead. "What were you thinking about doing?"

"Nothing fancy," I said. "Some new windows and some insulation in the walls."

He nodded as he took one of the chairs from me and

unfolded it. "That would certainly make that space usable all the time."

It suddenly occurred to me that he probably thought the Angels were going to lose their office. "I mean more usable for you," I said. "And Rose and the Angels in general."

The frown faded. "Are you certain you want to spend money on a space you're not using?" he asked.

I nodded, pressing on the seat of the folding chair to make sure it was open all the way. "Before you set up your office, that was just wasted space. We didn't even us it for storage. And Liam will do the work so that will keep the costs down."

"We'll have to talk about an increase in our rent."

A few months earlier when Rose and the rest of her crew had decided that they were going to pay me rent for the sunporch, I'd explained it was otherwise unused space and I didn't need rent. Rose had countered that the subject wasn't up for discussion. If I wouldn't take their money they'd just have to look for office space somewhere else. I knew that was a very bad idea. So I'd given in.

I'd known that Mr. P. would bring up the rent issue as soon as he found out that I wanted to do some work in the sunporch so this time I was ready.

"I was hoping you might be amenable to bartering your services instead," I said, adjusting the chairs so they were spaced more or less evenly around the table.

Mr. P. nudged his glasses up his nose. "What are you proposing?"

"Instead of raising the rent you do some background checks for me."

"Background checks? Are you thinking about hiring more staff?"

I shook my head. "We're starting to gain a bit of a reputation—a good one—for quality vintage guitars."

He nodded. "Both you and Sam know your musical instruments."

I smiled. I'd learned a lot about guitars from Sam Newman. He joked that he's forgotten more than he knows, but experience had taught me that wasn't true at all. "I've been approached a couple of times by people who have instruments to sell. In one case the guy just gave off a squirrelly vibe and I turned him down flat. But in the other instance, I kind of wish I'd taken the deal. But as Rose would say, I didn't know the seller from Adam."

A smile spread across Mr. P.'s face as the old man began to nod. "You're looking for someone to vet the instruments and the people selling them."

"Exactly." And I was. This wasn't a make-work project, not really. It was a deal that would benefit both of us.

"We'd have to agree on either an hourly or a per-instrument rate and how many hours you'd want to allow for our work."

"Put together some ideas for me and we can talk about all that," I said. Charlotte was coming in carrying a tray with the teapot and cups. Mac was behind her with the milk and the sugar bowl. Mr. P. nodded his agreement and I went to take the tray from Charlotte.

Once everyone but Mac had a seat and a cup of tea—or in the case of Mac and me (bless Charlotte) a cup of coffee, I looked at Liz, turning one hand palm up to the ceiling in a "voilà" motion.

She in turn looked at Rose. "Go ahead," she said,

taking another sip of her tea and nodding approvingly at Charlotte.

"There really isn't any nice way to say this," Rose began. Her gray eyes found Mac, leaning back against the workbench with his coffee, the way he invariably did when we had one of these gatherings. "We found evidence that Leila's sister has been, well, running a scam is the best way to describe it."

"What do you mean 'running a scam'?" Mac asked. To everyone else I'm sure it seemed that he hadn't been affected by Rose's words. He continued to lean against the waist-high bench with one elbow propped on the wooden surface, coffee cup in the other hand. But I knew him well enough to see the tension just under the surface.

"She was substituting cheap ingredients for the pure, organic and more expensive ones Leila chose."

Mac gave his head a shake.

"I'm sorry," Rose said. "But we're sure about this. I saw the invoices."

"How?" I asked. I tried not to sound suspicious but I realized I probably did. The two of them had been known to stretch the rules from time to time.

Liz shot me a look that told me she knew what I was thinking. "How do you think?" she said, flipping a hand in the air. "Just because we're not your age anymore doesn't mean we still don't have a few tools left in our toolboxes. And men have always been susceptible to a little charm." She looked from Mr. P. to Mac. "No matter how old or young they are."

At the same time Rose smiled and fluffed her hair. I got a mental image of Rose charming the owner of the salt works. The poor man probably had no idea what had hit him.

"She replaced the seaweed as well," Liz said.

"Did you charm that information out of someone?" I asked.

"I can be charming," she said. "But direct works, too."

Rose gave her friend an indulgent smile. "Liz found out where Natalie has been buying her cut-rate ingredients."

Liz shrugged. "Never underestimate a pissed-off man with a willing ear to listen to him."

Rose still had what I thought of as Elvis-just-ate-a can-of-sardines smile on her face.

Charlotte picked up the teapot and poured Rose more tea. "Thank you," Rose said.

Charlotte smiled at her friend.

"There's something else you haven't told us," I said.

Rose added a little milk and a bit of sugar to her cup before she answered. "Natalie will be in Maine on Saturday to visit one of her cut-rate suppliers."

Mac and I exchanged a look. "That's an incredible coincidence," I said.

Rose's expression was suddenly all innocence. I wasn't fooled. "The supplier has some new product for Natalie to look at—a onetime, short-term deal," she said.

Liz on the other hand looked smug.

"What did you do?" Charlotte said. She was looking at Liz, not Rose.

"The squeaky wheel gets the grease so I might have greased some wheels." Liz reached for the teapot.

"That doesn't make any sense," Charlotte said.

Liz just shrugged.

"We'll be there Saturday to talk to Natalie," Rose said.

"I'm driving," I said firmly.

"Fine with me," Liz said over the rim of her cup.

Rose turned to Mr. P. to ask what she'd missed while she and Liz were gone.

Charlotte shook her head at Liz. "Liz French, I don't know whether to hug you or smack you with a rolled-up newspaper."

"Hug," Mac said. Setting his coffee mug on the top of the workbench he did just that.

Liz reached up and pressed her hand to his cheek for a moment. Charlotte smiled and gave her friend's shoulder a squeeze. Then she turned to Mac. "Could you help me move that sideboard in the window, please?" She looked at me. "Sarah, I think it would work better if it was in the center not off to one side." She glanced at me.

I nodded. "Go ahead."

Rose and Mr. P. were already on their way to their sunporch office. Liz had gotten to her feet. "So what do you have to say, Miss Sarah?" she asked.

"All this information you and Rose got—were any laws broken?"

She gave me a look. "Honestly, I don't think you trust either one of us to be out by ourselves."

"You're avoiding the question," I said.

She wrinkled her nose at me. "Define 'broken,'" she finally said.

I shook my head even as I was leaning over to kiss her cheek. "That's what I thought."

Chapter 15

Josh called about an hour later. "I've already received the initial police reports in Mac's case."

"That's fast," I said. "Detective Barnes is very efficient."

"I'm hoping it means the prosecutor is overestimating his case," Josh said. "I'm e-mailing you a list of the items that were found with Erin Fellowes's body. I don't see anything significant but maybe you will."

I turned on my computer and printed the list while Elvis watched curiously from the top of the desk. Then I sat next to him and looked over the list. The cat craned his neck over my arm as though he were reading the items as well.

"So what do you think?" I asked him.

"Mrr," he said, wrinkling his nose at me.

I reached over to scratch behind his left ear. "Yeah, nothing sticks out for me, either." I scanned the short list of items again. "Erin Fellowes had a very tidy purse."

Elvis turned and looked over his shoulder in the direction of the drawer where I kept my purse. He licked his whiskers. "Yes, I did notice that she wasn't carrying any cat treats."

Since we'd established that important fact, Elvis seemed to decide I didn't need his help anymore. He jumped down from the desk and disappeared into the hallway.

I looked again at the page I'd printed. The little purse Erin had been carrying held the same kinds of things that were in my purse—her wallet, lip gloss, a comb. Her phone and keys seemed to have been in her pocket and there was also the small, carved wooden bird I noticed her turning over in her fingers. Was it a good luck charm? I wondered, or had it come from one of the small shops on the waterfront? Jess had a similar tiny painted bear on her worktable that she claimed was her good luck charm. I knew she'd bought it somewhere along the waterfront. Had Erin been looking for Mac in the shops down there before she'd driven up here?

I didn't have any more insight than Josh did. I headed downstairs to see what Mr. P. had to say.

He looked up and smiled when I reached around the open sunporch door and knocked on the wall.

"Josh sent me this list of the personal effects they found with Erin Fellowes," I said. "Neither he nor I see anything significant, anything that she might have wanted to show to Mac." I pointed to the tiny bird listed underneath Erin's phone. "I'm thinking she might have been looking for Mac or even trying to locate the shop down on the waterfront before she came here."

Mr. P. looked up at me. He tapped the paper with one finger. "Maybe there was something on Erin's phone."

"The police would have gone through the phone by

now. Wouldn't they have followed up on anything suspicious?"

He gave a slight shrug. "Not if they didn't know what they were looking at."

"We should talk to Josh about the phone. Maybe there was a call log in those police reports he already received."

"It's worth asking," Mr. P. said.

I had a quick supper of chef's salad with extra croutons and French dressing I'd made myself. My cooking lessons with Rose had been sporadic lately but I was looking forward to learning more. I liked being able to make something other than an egg sandwich and have it turn out.

The Black Bear was crowded. I stepped inside and looked around for Jess and Nick. I knew I didn't have to worry about finding a table if they hadn't arrived yet. Sam always kept one for us. He was standing by the stage and when he saw me he raised a hand and headed over.

"Hey, kiddo," he said, putting an arm around my shoulders and kissing the side of my head. "I'm glad I caught you. Can you stop in tomorrow sometime? I found some old photos of your dad. I thought you might want them. You're in a couple of them."

Because my father had died when I was very small there weren't very many photographs of us together. "I'd love to have them," I said.

Sam smiled. "I'll be here all day tomorrow." He gave me another squeeze. "I gotta go round up the guys."

He headed for his office and I looked around for Nick and Jess again, spotting them at a table near the stage.

Nick wasn't wearing a bowl of salsa for a hat so I took that as a good sign.

"Am I late?" I asked as I got to the table.

Jess shook her head. "No, I was early. Nick has been keeping me company." She smiled at him. "And keeping me in chips and salsa." She dipped a chip and raised it in a toast to him before she ate it.

Nick got to his feet and pulled out the chair between them for me. "I've been picking Jess's brain about getting that old quilt of Mom's repaired. You know the one that was my grandmother's?"

I nodded as I sat down. "I know the one you mean."

"I told Nick I could take a look at it but I wouldn't want to do anything with the quilt if Charlotte was uncomfortable with the idea," Jess said.

"I get that," Nick said. He looked at me. "Coffee or a beer?"

"Beer," I said. "I'm not driving."

He shot Jess a look. "Are you ready for another one? I'm buying."

"I'd love another," she said, picking up the empty beer glass at her place. "But I'll get this." She gestured from me to her with a finger.

Nick caught the eye of one of the waitstaff, pointed at Jess's empty and held up two fingers. "Next round is yours," he told Jess as he sat back down.

"Okay, cut the crap," I said.

They both looked at me.

"Have the two of you been replaced with pod people? What's with all the artificial make-niceness between you two?"

Jess looked at Nick. "I told you she'd never buy this."

I glared at both of them, wishing I wore glasses so I could stare over the top at them.

"Don't give me that look," Nick said. "I just asked Jess if we could try a little harder to be nice to each other tonight. I know you hate it when we get into it over something."

"I do hate it," I admitted, "but you went a little too far in the other direction."

Jess shifted sideways in her seat and leaned back so she could talk to Nick behind my back. "Didn't I say this was a dumb idea?" she stage-whispered.

He made a face at her. Then he looked at me and smiled. "I guess if I can't get on your good side by being nice to this one"—he jerked a thumb in Jess's direction—"I'll just have to use my natural charm and charisma."

I smiled back. "Okay," I said. "How exactly is that going to work?"

"Well, first I get a little closer." He put his arm across the back of my chair and leaned toward me a little. "This lets you inhale my male pheromones." He waved his free hand in the air in front of his chest. "You're getting the subliminal message that I'm a strong, sexy man."

Behind me Jess made a noise that was part snort, part cat hacking up a fur ball. When I turned to look at her she wisely turned it into a cough.

I focused my attention back on Nick. I was humoring him, but it was also true that he could be charming and charismatic—when we weren't arguing about something. And while I didn't seem to be affected by his male pheromones, he did smell like Hugo, the same aftershave he'd been wearing when I French-kissed him at fifteen.

"Is this where I'm supposed to ask if you've been working out a lot more?" I reached over and squeezed his upper arm. And found more solid muscle than I was expecting. "Hey!" I said. "You have been working out more."

"Softball season," he said.

I ran my hand over his arm. "Very nice," I said. This close the scent of his aftershave was heady and for a moment I felt like I was fifteen again.

The waiter came over then with our beer and I dropped my hand and straightened up in my chair. "Umm, good to know you're staying in shape," I said.

Nick cleared his throat. "Yeah, uh, well, I try."

I reached for my glass and from the corner of my eye saw Jess give me a *You're so lame* look. I had time for one mouthful of beer and two chips before Sam and the boys started making their way to the stage.

Close to an hour later Sam ended the set with a raucous version of Bob Seger's "Old Time Rock & Roll"—one of my favorite songs. I dropped into my seat and grinned at Jess. There was no way we wouldn't have been up and dancing to that one.

Nick's cell buzzed. He pulled it out of his pocket, looked at the screen and shook his head as he got up and moved away from the table. Whoever the conversation was with it was short. "I gotta go," he said. He smiled. "Have a good night, ladies."

"You, too, Nick," I said. "Thank you for the beer."

"You're welcome," he said. Then he was gone.

"What kind of a thank-you was that?" Jess asked. I knew that teasing gleam in her eye.

"What was wrong with it?" I asked.

"Why don't you just grab him and lay a big wet one on him?"

I punched her lightly on the shoulder. "Who are you? Liam? Things aren't like that with us."

"How exactly are things with you two?" she asked, scooping up what seemed like a quarter of the bowl of salsa with another chip. "Are you just friends, pseudo brother and sister? Or something else?"

"I don't know," I said. "It's . . . complicated."

"You always say that," Jess replied. Her expression had changed from teasing to serious. "The two of you need to figure it out because it's giving the rest of us a headache."

Chapter 16

When I got to Second Chance the next morning Mr. P. was sitting in a lawn chair in front of the open garage door, having coffee with Mac. "Good morning," I said, walking over to them.

"Good morning, my dear," the old man said with a smile.

I set Elvis down. He made his way over to Mr. P., sat in a patch of sunlight next to his chair and began to wash his face. Elvis was very particular about his appearance.

"Morning," Mac said, getting to his feet. He gestured at his mug. "Would you like a cup?"

"I would," I said. "But I can get it myself."

He smiled. "I know you can." He started across the parking lot.

I sat down in the folding chair he'd vacated and turned to Mr. P. "I've been thinking about Davis Abbott," I said. "Do you think that he could have hurt Leila and killed Erin?"

"I think it's a possibility," he hedged. "I did a little

more digging around last evening. The young man has an assault charge that was dismissed during his college years. He's an affluent cliché. He tried a number of things but didn't master any, he likes to gamble a bit too much, seems to like hard work a bit too little, and he has parents who got tired of supporting a dilettante son."

I shifted in my chair. Elvis stretched and wandered into the garage. "Why was the assault charge dismissed?" I asked.

Mr. P. shrugged. "It was a barroom argument that escalated and ended up outside on the sidewalk. It went away when the young man who was assaulted refused to testify."

I raised an eyebrow. "A payout?"

"Yet another cliché but I think so." He took a sip of his coffee.

"And you know all this because?" I wasn't sure I should be asking the question.

"Social media can be very informative. Just because one deletes something doesn't mean it's gone. And Davis and Stephanie share a bank account. She's been very forthcoming with respect to her finances."

I'd expected him to smile, to say something light, but he didn't.

"You found something else."

He nodded. "I'm afraid I did." The breeze ruffled what few wisps of hair he had and he patted them down with a wrinkled hand. "It turns out that Stephanie is one of those people who keeps her bank statements going back several years. And she and Davis share a bank account, as I said. He was in Boston the day of Leila's accident. He used his debit card to buy gas."

"Do you think Stevie knows he was there?"

"I don't. I don't think she would have scanned those bank statements for me if she'd known they could implicate Davis. I do believe she cares about him."

"So he could have sabotaged the heating system?"

He looked at me with one raised eyebrow. "He has the expertise."

Had Stevie's partner tampered with the water heater in Mac and Leila's house? Had Erin somehow found out? Could it have been Davis that Nick had seen talking to her down on the waterfront? I had too many questions and not enough answers.

"So now what?" I asked. "I mean aside from our upcoming visit to the salt works."

Elvis came out of the building behind us, gave an offhand murp as he passed my chair, and headed across the parking lot.

"I do have the name of the hotel where young Mr. Abbott is staying," Mr. P. said. "Perhaps we can pay him a visit at the end of the day."

"Perhaps we can," I agreed. I tipped my face up to the sun for a moment. "Do you have any idea why Davis is still here in town?"

He shook his head. "I'm afraid I don't. I'd also like to know why he came here in the first place, and why he has stayed. And it is interesting that he got here the same day as Erin Fellowes did."

Mac came out then with my coffee, stopping to hold the back door for Elvis. Mr. P. filled him in on what he'd learned about Davis Abbott. He was silent for a moment. "I would have said Davis isn't capable of hurting Leila or, heaven forbid, killing Erin, but I'm beginning to see that I didn't know any of these people as well as I thought I did."

Mr. P. and I exchanged a look.

Mac shook his head. "Could we talk about something else, something normal?"

"Sure," I said. I told him about Charlotte's suggestion to look into offering classes at Legacy Place.

"I think that's a good idea," Mac said.

"I do as well," Mr. P. said. "Despite Rosie's opinion of the place it's a beautiful building in an excellent location."

Rose had gone to live at the seniors' apartment building so her daughter, Abby, wouldn't worry about her, but she'd complained that all the other residents did was talk about their ailments.

My phone rang then. I pulled it out of my pocket and glanced at the screen. It was Avery. I frowned. "That's odd," I said. On occasion the teen would text me but I couldn't remember the last time she'd called me.

"Hi, Avery," I said.

"Oh good, you have your phone with you," she said. "There's kind of a situation going on."

"What do you mean, a 'situation'?" I asked. "Where are you?"

"I'm at the end of Bayview Street, you know, at the far end of the harbor."

I knew where she meant. What the heck was she doing out there? There was no boardwalk, no businesses catering to tourists, no slips for boats. There were several office buildings and a pretty great view of the ocean but that was it. "Avery, what are you doing out there?" I said. I had a bad feeling I knew the answer.

"Well, see, Nonna and Rose are stalking that guy."

I sat bolt upright in my chair. Mac was looking at me, frowning. He'd already figured out that something was wrong just from my side of the conversation. "What guy?"

"You know," Avery said, a touch of annoyance in her voice, even though I clearly didn't know. "The one who told Rose to go you-know herself when he was parked in front of our driveway."

Her explanation may not have made sense to anyone else but it did to me. "Davis Abbott?"

"Yeah, that guy."

By now Mr. P. was also watching me intently, concern etched into the lines around his mouth and eyes.

"Tell me exactly what happened. From the beginning."

"Okay. Nonna and I picked up Rose because she had butter tarts for some awards thing at the library and she said if she brought them to the shop you and Nonna would eat them all."

I took a breath and let it out slowly. "The library is not on Bayview Street. It's not even close."

"I know, but the butter tarts are in a cooler so they're okay," Avery said. "No one's going to get food poisoning or anything." She could go off on a tangent even easier than Rose could.

I took one of those deep, calming breaths Jess was always after me to try. "What happened after you picked up Rose?" I asked. The breath didn't seem to help.

"She asked if she could try my smoothie and I said yes and then Rose said Nonna was wrong, that it didn't taste like feet, it was pretty good and then she saw that guy go by in his truck and she whacked Nonna on the arm and said, 'Turn around, turn around and follow that truck,' and Nonna said, 'What in heck are you talking about?' and Rose said, 'You're letting a killer get away,' and so Nonna did a U-ey right there in the street and we ended up here."

She'd managed to spill out the whole story without taking a breath.

"So where exactly are you now? Are you at the very end of the street?"

"Right at the start of the trail that goes along the water. It's kind of hard to miss because those TV people are here."

I got to my feet. "Stay where you are," I said. "I'm on my way."

Avery promised she wouldn't go anywhere and we ended the call. I took a large drink of my coffee. Both Mac and Mr. P. had stood up as well.

"What's going on?" Mac asked.

Mr. P. put a hand on my arm. "Is everything all right?"

"Rose and Liz are following Davis Abbott," I said. "I have to go see what's going on."

"I'm coming with you," Mac immediately said, moving behind me to close and lock the garage door.

"Good," I said, putting my phone back in my pocket. "Because it will probably take both of us to wrestle down Rose." I glanced at Mr. P. "No disrespect to Rose."

He took my mug and set it over by the old garage door. "None taken, my dear," he said. "I know how Rosie can be when she gets set on something."

We climbed into my SUV and headed across town.

Neither Mac nor Mr. P. said a word about how fast I may or may not have been going. When we got close to the trailhead we discovered cars were parked on both sides of the road. There was only one lane clear. I saw a space that looked big enough for the SUV and managed to shoehorn it in.

We all got out. Mac looked around and then grabbed my arm. "Up there," he said, pointing to a place about seven or eight cars ahead. "Isn't that Liz's car?"

"It is," Mr. P. said beside me.

We hurried up the road. Avery was with the car, leaning against the front passenger door, phone in her hand, one earbud hanging down on her shoulder. She smiled when she caught sight of us. "I'm glad you're here," she said. "I told them it was a bad idea to follow that Davis guy but they didn't listen because I'm just a kid."

I knew they wouldn't have listened to me if I'd been there, but I didn't say that. "Which way did they go?"

Avery pointed up the road.

"Please stay here in case they come back," I said. "If they do, I have my cell."

Mr. P. gestured with one hand. "Go ahead. I don't want to hold you up. I'll be right behind you."

Mac and I headed down the road at a slow run. I could see what looked like a small crowd of people just ahead where the road rose slightly.

"I swear to God I'm going to put both of them on a leash when I get my hands on them. Or maybe I'll weld a bell on a chain around their ankles or stick a GPS chip in their arms," I said.

"I'm sorry," Mac said.

"You have nothing to be sorry for," I said, brushing

my hair back off my face. "I know who the real culprit is."

We finally spotted Rose on the edge of a small cluster of people. Liz was standing in front of her.

Mac pointed. "Sarah, that's Davis," he said about a man at the front of the small crowd watching the reality TV crew.

"That's definitely the man who was blocking our parking lot," I said. Davis Abbott didn't seem to be going anywhere. "I can handle Rose and Liz. Can you . . . ?" I gestured in Abbott's direction.

"It's time Davis and I caught up," Mac said. He veered off to the right and I came up behind Rose from her left.

"What took you so long?" she said without turning around. As a former teacher, she claimed to have eyes in the back of her head and there were times I could almost believe it. "We've been watching that young man for at least fifteen minutes."

"Are you out of your mind?" I whispered.

Rose turned to look at me then. "I most certainly am not," she snapped. "When I got hit over the head a few weeks ago the doctor did tests. He said I was very sharp. And not just for an old lady." She pulled herself up to her full barely five feet, a look of righteous indignation on her face.

I closed my eyes for a moment, took a deep breath, counted silently to five and let it out slowly, another technique Jess claimed would help calm and center me.

It didn't.

I looked at Liz, cool and summery in a yellow flowered blouse while my back was wet with perspiration.

I poked her with my elbow and she turned to look at me. "What's your excuse?" I asked.

"I couldn't let Rose follow that hooligan all by herself, could I?" she said.

I swiped a hand over my sweaty neck. "You know, it's deeply disturbing that of the three people in your car this morning Avery was the most mature." From the corner of my eye I could see Mac, his arm around Davis Abbott's shoulders, moving the man away from the front of the crowd, toward us.

"Let's go," I said to Rose and Liz. We made our way around the clump of people and joined Mac.

Davis Abbott was about average height, dark, curly hair cropped close to his head and even features. A pair of sunglasses hung from the neck of his navy blue T-shirt. His mouth had a dissatisfied sulk. It occurred to me that Jess would have called him handsome in a pretty boy way, which would not have been a compliment. His eyes darted from me to Rose. It seemed pretty clear that he recognized us.

"What do you want?" he said.

Mr. P. had joined us by then. "We want to know what you're doing here," he said.

Davis gave an offhand shrug. "I don't see how it's any of your business where the hell I am or what I'm doing."

Rose was beside me, and it seemed as though I could feel the irritation radiating off her body. "Did you kill Erin Fellowes?" she said. "Because *that* is our business."

He seemed shocked at her words. He turned his attention to Mac. "Erin Fellowes? Leila's friend? She's dead?"

Mac's arms were folded across his chest. "Did you kill her, Davis? Did you hurt Leila?" There was a hard edge to his voice.

"No. Of course I didn't. I barely knew Erin, and Leila was the only person in Stevie's family who was nice to me."

"You're supposed to be at a workshop in Nova Scotia."

"Stevie told you," Davis said. "Look, I changed my mind. I didn't want to listen to her ragging on me about the waste of money so I didn't tell her. I called my buddy Willie and asked him to cover for me, just so I could get a break. I wasn't screwing around or anything. I just needed a break."

It didn't take his nose growing like Pinocchio's to tell me he was lying. His eyes kept sliding away from Mr. P.'s face and he was talking way too much.

"Where were you when Leila was hurt?" Mac stood with his feet apart and his hands behind his back. There was something a little menacing about the posture.

"We know you went to see her right before it happened," Mr. P. said. Was that true or was he bluffing? I wasn't sure.

"I didn't."

I hoped he didn't play poker. Not only was he a liar, he was pretty bad at it.

"We know you were in Boston."

"You're wrong. I haven't done anything."

"You threatened me," Rose said.

"You dented the hood of my truck," Davis countered.

Somehow I doubted Rose's palm hitting the hood of his truck had caused any damage.

Rose got her phone out. "I guess we'll just have to let the police decide."

Davis got a sullen look on his face. "Fine. I went to see Leila. But not at the house. Outside her office."

Mac's expression darkened. "Why?" he asked.

"I wanted to talk to her about challenging that damn trust. There had to be a way to get at least some of the money sooner. I got a copy of the agreement. I figured if Leila was on board then Stevie would agree, too."

"There's no way Stevie would have agreed to that," Mac said, shaking his head. "She adored Marguerite."

"I could have convinced her," Davis said, his tone that of a petulant child.

"Leila told you no." The muscles along Mac's jaw tensed.

Davis nodded.

"Did you try to kill her?" Mac said.

"No," Davis said. "After I left her, I went to this bar. I got drunk and went home with a woman I met there." He held up his phone. "She still texts me. I can send you some of her texts and some pictures of the two of us together if you don't believe me."

"You do that, young man," Rose said.

"Why did you come to town the same day Erin Fellowes did?" Mr. P. asked. There were beads of sweat on his forehead. It was warm standing there in the sunshine. "And why are you still here?"

"I didn't see Erin. I didn't even know she was here. I swear." Davis threw a quick glance over his shoulder.

Just like that I got it. "You've been watching the film crew," I said slowly. "You have an idea you want to pitch to them."

Davis nodded. "Yeah. Stevie and I, the whole back-to-nature thing. We could do a reality show. We're trying to market our fruit butter. This would be perfect." He held up his phone. "I even shot some video."

Behind him Liz rolled her eyes and mouthed the words "pipe dream."

"That wasn't the only reason you came here, though, was it?" I said, keeping my tone conversational.

"I don't know what you mean," Davis said, but I noticed the way his eyes slid off my face.

"It's an awfully big coincidence that you decided to pitch an idea to a film crew working in the same small town where Mac lives."

"Coincidences happen." His Adam's apple bobbed as he swallowed.

The information about the planned filming of the reality show pilot here in North Harbor had been all over the Internet for months.

I moved a step closer to Davis. He shifted from one foot to the other as though I were making him uncomfortable. "I guess that means it was also just a *coincidence*"—I put extra emphasis on the word—"that you ended up parking in the lot for the business where Mac works."

"What are you getting at, Sarah?" Mac asked, his voice tight with suspicion.

"I think Davis was hoping to bump into you. Coincidentally, of course. He needed a backup plan in case his reality show idea didn't pan out. I'm guessing his and Stevie's money problems are worse than we suspected."

Davis's expression darkened and his mouth had a sour twist. I knew I was right.

"I'm guessing he was going to point out that breaking the trust now was the best thing for Leila. That it's what Stevie wanted." Another idea had occurred to me. Rose would say I was going out on a limb, but seeing the kind of person Davis Abbott was, I had a feeling I was right.

"We wondered how Erin knew Mac was here. They hadn't kept in touch and Stevie hadn't spoken to her in ages." I folded my arms over my chest. "Except Erin did call, didn't she? Only she spoke to you." It was a guess but the flush that crept up his neck told me it was a good one. "I doubt she told you why she wanted to talk to Mac, but you thought you better get down here and push your own agenda, just in case."

Davis mumbled something I didn't catch and made a crude gesture with his left hand.

Mac pushed past me and grabbed Davis by the neck of his shirt. He was breathing hard, the veins standing out in his neck. "You scummy little weasel!" he growled. I thought for a moment that he was going to take a swing at Davis and I wouldn't have blamed him if he had. "Stay away from my wife," he said in a voice edged with anger. "Stay away from everyone I care about or so help me I will find you and you'll wish you'd never heard my name!" He let go of Davis's shirt and walked away.

Mr. P. got the contact information for the woman from the bar and gave Davis his e-mail address for the photos he'd offered and told him to call Stevie.

"I'll contact the young woman and check that alibi

but I think it's the truth," Mr. P. said as we walked back to the cars. "I think he lacks the initiative to make up that bar story."

"I think he lacks initiative, period," Liz said.

Mac was waiting by the car. "I can't believe what a lowlife he is." He pulled a hand back over his head. "The first time Stevie brought Davis to a family event Jackson said he was a freeloader," he said quietly to me. "I told Jackson that he sounded like a snob." He shook his head. "I'm thinking maybe I should talk to him, at least listen to what he has to say."

"That's probably a good idea," I agreed.

Avery was still leaning against Liz's car. "Did you find the truck dude?" she asked.

"Yes, we did," I said.

"So did he do it?" She seemed genuinely curious. She wanted to find Erin Fellowes's killer and clear Mac's name as much as any of us did.

"No," Rose said. "It doesn't look like he did."

"Well, that sucks," Avery said as she stuck her cell phone in her pocket.

I agreed. It did.

We all headed back to the shop, with Liz making a detour to drop off the butter tarts. I sent Avery inside to open the shop. We were only five minutes past opening time. I turned to Rose. "What you did could have been dangerous," I said sternly.

Rose smiled. "No, it couldn't," she said. "I knew Avery would call and I knew you would come. There was never any danger." She put her arms around me and gave me a hug. "I'm parched. I'm going to put the kettle on."

I watched her go and when the door to the shop closed behind her I shook my finger at Liz.

"Why are you annoyed at me?" Liz asked. "I was watching over Rose. I should get a reward."

I ran a hand through my hair and held up some strands. "Not only is my hair falling out, I found a gray hair last week," I said. I pointed at her. "You and Rose gave it to me."

Liz gave a snort of disdain. "It's genetic. Isabel went gray very early. You should call Elspeth and have some highlights put in. They'd cover that gray."

I let the hairs flutter to the floor. "I'm going to make coffee. Lots of strong coffee," I said.

"I love you," Liz teasingly called after me.

I knew what I was supposed to say. I lifted a hand but didn't turn around. "Yeah, yeah, everybody does," I said.

Later that morning I was on the way out to the garage just as Mac was on the way in. Mr. P. came to the sunporch door. "Do you both have a moment?" he asked.

"Sure," Mac said.

We followed Mr. P. back to his computer. "I spoke to the young lady Davis Abbott had his assignation with," he said. "I can safely say he has an alibi for his time in Boston. She had some rather"—he paused and adjusted his glasses—"revealing photos with time stamps. I don't think there's any need to show them to you."

"I appreciate that," Mac said dryly.

"I also found photos of Davis out drinking with that reality show TV crew on one of the crew member's Twitter feed. He didn't kill Erin Fellowes, either. I'm sorry."

"Don't be," Mac said.

The list of Erin's personal effects was lying on the table. Mac picked it up. "What's this?"

Mr. P. and I exchanged a look. He spoke before I could. "Those were the things Erin Fellowes had with her," he said gently.

"That was Leila's," Mac said, pointing to something on the list. Mr. P. and I both leaned over to see what he was talking about—the tiny carved bird.

"It belonged to Leila, or at least she owned one. She got it six or seven months before the accident and she kept it in her desk at her office. It was a replica of a nineteenth-century Japanese piece. She was studying Asian art from that time period before she switched her major. She said it was to remind her of the person she wanted to be." He shook his head. "It's probably not the same one."

I looked at Mr. P. wondering if we were thinking the same thing. Could that tiny bird have been Leila's? Was Charlotte right? Had Erin brought it to show Mac? And if she had, why?

Chapter 17

Just before lunch I drove down to The Black Bear to get the photos Sam had unearthed of my dad. Sam had been my father's best friend and even though I had Peter, who was my dad in every way, Sam also played a fatherly role in my life. I found him in his office, dollar store reading glasses on the end of his nose while he worked on the staff schedules.

"Hi, kiddo," he said, coming around the desk to hug me. His shaggy hair was a mix of gray and blond and he was wearing it a bit shorter. "Do you have time for a cup of coffee?"

"I always have time for coffee, especially with you," I said.

Sam gestured at the sofa. "Have a seat. I'll be right back." As he passed his desk he grabbed an envelope and held it out to me.

"The pictures?" I asked, taking it from him.

He nodded. "They're from back when we started the band. Back when we were young and foolish." He smiled and gave his head a little shake. "I'll just be a minute."

I sat down on the sofa and opened the envelope.

There were half a dozen photos inside, and for me it was like having a time machine. There was my dad, so young—barely in his twenties—and Sam standing beside an old van that was more primer than paint. I studied my father's face. Gram always said that I had his eyes and smile and I could see that was true in the two pictures where he was holding baby me in his arms.

Sam came back with a couple of coffee mugs. He sat down beside me, leaning sideways to see what photo I was looking at. He rolled his eyes. "That was Gertie," he said. "The van," he added in response to my quizzical look. "The muffler made a god-awful rattle and the springs were shot but your dad said that we had to have a way to move our gear other than trying to take it on the bus." He laughed. "Man, was I ever that young?"

"I think both of you were very cute," I teased. "Look at that hair." In the photo both Sam and Dad wore their hair almost to their shoulders, layered and waved back from their faces.

"Don't make fun of my hair," Sam warned. "That used to take me a half an hour with a blow-dryer and a can of mousse. I'm probably personally responsible for any hole in the ozone layer."

We looked through the rest of the photos. Seeing my father so young and happy made me smile and gave me a lump in my throat all at the same time. I had a sense that Sam was feeling the same way.

He looked around the office. "I wonder sometimes what he'd think of this place."

"I think he'd love it," I said. "According to Mom and Gram he loved anything that had to do with music."

Sam nodded, thumb and finger stroking his beard.

"That he did. Something special happened when he was performing. The only thing that made him happier was you." He studied me for a long moment. "He would have been proud of the woman you turned into."

I felt the prickle of tears and had to blink hard a couple of times. I reached over and picked up the small brass monkey he kept on his desk to distract myself. The monkey, which had both hands over its mouth, had been given to him by my dad, a reminder Sam said, to think before he spoke. I'd always suspected there was a bit more to the story but Sam had never been forthcoming on the subject. The metal warmed in my hands and after a moment I set the monkey back on the desk.

"Some days I wish I could just sit and talk to him for a few minutes," I said.

Sam nodded. "Me, too, kiddo."

We talked for a few more minutes and then I looked at my watch. "I should get back to the shop," I said.

"I'm glad you came," he said. He indicated the photos. "You can keep those. I made copies."

I hugged him again.

On the way out through the restaurant I noticed Jackson Montgomery just being seated. "I see someone I need to speak to," I said.

"And I better get to the kitchen," Sam said. "I'll see you next Thursday at the jam if I don't see you sooner."

I nodded. "My favorite night of the week."

I walked over to Jackson's table. He looked up from his menu and smiled. "Hi, Sarah," he said. "Are you here for lunch, too?"

I shook my head. "I just came to see Sam." I gestured in the direction of the kitchen. "He's the owner."

Jackson indicated the other chair at the table. "Do you have time to join me?" he asked.

I hesitated. I hadn't said what time I'd be back and Charlotte had urged me to take my time. "All right," I said. "Thank you." I took the chair across from him, setting my purse and the envelope with the photos on the floor at my feet.

"So what's good here?" Jackson asked, tapping the menu with one finger.

"Everything," I said, "but I think you'd like the house burger."

"All right," he said with a smile. He looked around and a waiter started in our direction. Jackson reminded me of Jess, who could look up no matter what restaurant we were in and have a server immediately at the table.

"Slaw and rings?" the waiter, whose name was Caleb, asked. "Or fries?"

Jackson's gaze darted to me.

"Slaw and rings," I said. "I promise you won't be sorry."

"For both of us, please," he said to our waiter.

Once the young man had collected our menus and headed for the kitchen, Jackson leaned back in his chair. "Mac called me earlier. We didn't talk very long but it's a start."

"It is," I agreed. I'd hoped that Mac might call his friend after what he'd said earlier about Jackson's insight into Davis Abbott.

"I offered to take his case again. He turned me down but if you think he needs my help will you call, please, Sarah?" He pulled a business card out of his pocket, took out a pen and scrawled something on the back. "That's my cell."

"Mac already has a very good lawyer."

"I wasn't trying to imply he didn't. It's just that . . ." He made a helpless gesture with one hand. "I'd like to help if I can."

I took the card and tucked it in my purse.

The waiter returned with a large china mug and the coffeepot. I smiled a thank-you and added cream and sugar to my coffee. "You and Mac have been friends for a long time," I said.

Jackson nodded. "Since we were kids. Ever see him play baseball?"

"A couple of times in a charity game for the animal shelter."

"Can he still hit it out to left field?"

"And then some," I said. "How long has he been making those killer buffalo wings?"

"He still makes those?" Jackson asked.

"As often as we can talk him into it."

Now it was Jackson's turn to smile. "He perfected them back when we were in college. You've heard of the freshman fifteen?"

I nodded. He was talking about the weight gain a lot of first-year university students experience.

"Mac's ribs were the main cause of mine. It's good to know he hasn't lost his touch."

Caleb came back with our burgers then, along with more coffee. Jackson took a bite of his burger while I took the top of the bun off mine and added about half of my vinegary coleslaw.

"Oh man, this is good!" Jackson exclaimed, wiping a bit of ketchup from the corner of his mouth.

I'd just taken a bite of my own burger so all I could do was nod.

We'd eaten about half of our meal when Jackson set down his fork and reached for his coffee. "What's Mac like now?" he asked. "We only talked for a minute but he seemed . . . I don't know, quieter, guarded."

I wasn't sure how to answer. If Liz had been sitting next to me she would have said, *Tell the truth.* So that's what I did.

"The two of you haven't spoken in close to two years. It's going to take time for him to let down his guard with you."

Jackson sighed. "You're right." He made a face. "The stupidest thing I ever did was believe Leila's parents over Mac. He was—he *is*—my best friend. I'm ashamed of myself."

"So why did you?" I asked.

"That's the million-dollar question, isn't it?" He shook his head. "If you want to say Mac and I were like brothers—and we were—then you'd have to say Leila was like a sister to me. I thought Mac was crazy to buy that old house and then live in it while trying to do a bunch of the renovations. Ask him. He'll tell you I told him he was out of his mind."

He played with his fork, turning it over on the paper place mat. "For the record, I never thought Mac had deliberately tried to hurt Leila. But I did think what happened was his fault. I blamed him for the two of them living in that house in that state and I thought it was asinine for him to think he could go to his office all day and then spend half the night working on the house." He sighed. "I should have listened to him. I should have remembered that no one—not even Mac—made Leila do something she didn't want to do. I was a judgmental jerk. In the end it's as simple as that."

"Yeah, you were," I said. "But you're here now. That counts for something."

"I hope so," he said.

"What were Mac and Leila like as a couple?" I asked, reaching for an onion ring.

The smile returned to Jackson's face. "They were like something out of a romance novel. I used to rag on him because once he met Leila it was like every other woman ceased to exist." He looked around for Caleb and gestured to his cup when he caught the waiter's eye. "You've probably heard that Leila's great-aunt played matchmaker."

"She got them both to come to the same fund-raiser."

He nodded. "I was there and they literally did lock eyes across the room. No one else had a chance with either of them after that."

There were sides to Mac I hadn't realized existed.

Jackson got a faraway look on his face. "I admit at one time I was a little smitten with Leila. I think every man who was friends with her was a little bit in love with her." He looked away for a moment then his eyes found my face again. "I'm not trying to make excuses for how I treated Mac. I'm trying to explain why . . . why it was possible for me to believe what her parents were saying, that she was better off in their care."

I nodded without speaking. I was even more curious about Leila. What had she been like to inspire the kind of feelings both Mac and Jackson still clearly had for her? And what had it been like to be her sister, to be the dirty little secret to a perfect sibling? We really didn't know anything about Leila's sister, Natalie. Was I just grasping at straws now? Or could she be our killer? Was Leila's accident nothing more than a case of sibling rivalry? Was that what Erin Fellowes had discovered? Was that what had changed her mind about Mac?

Questions. More and more questions and again, no answers.

"Give Mac some time," I said.

"I'm trying," Jackson said. "It just drives me a little crazy that I could be helping him and he won't let me." He gave me a sheepish grin. "I'm a bit of a control freak in case that isn't obvious."

"I never would have guessed," I said solemnly.

He laughed and snared an onion ring. "These are really good."

"I told you, everything is good here."

He nodded. "I can see why Mac decided to stay in town." His gaze stayed on my face for just a bit longer than was appropriate.

"There is something you could do that might help," I said, pushing the last bit of my coleslaw onto the last bite of my burger.

"Name it," Jackson immediately said.

"Tell me about Natalie Welland."

He frowned. "Wait a minute. You don't think *she* killed Erin, do you? Why would Natalie want her sister's best friend dead?"

I set my fork down. "I'm not saying she did. I just . . . I don't know anything about her."

Jackson let out a breath. "Well, it was hard for her at first, seventeen years old and walking into a family she didn't know, but Leila was happy to have a sister after being an only child and in time they really did become sisters." He reached for his coffee again. "I thought she was trying too hard sometimes—Leila, I mean—but she seemed determined to let Natalie know they *were* family. I've thought more than once that Leila only started du Mer so they could work together." His mouth twisted to one side. "I just don't see how Natalie could have had anything to do with Erin's death. There was just no reason."

I glanced at my watch. I'd been gone long enough. I needed to get back to the shop. I looked around for Caleb. "If you're thinking about paying for lunch I'd like to remind you that I invited you, which means you're my guest." Jackson smiled. "You already know how persistent I can be."

"Thank you," I said as I got to my feet.

He stood up as well. "I enjoyed this. If you don't have any plans, would you have dinner with me tomorrow evening?"

I hesitated.

"Am I overstepping?" he asked. "Are you seeing someone?"

Was I seeing someone? Lord knows I had three would-be fairy godmothers who kept trying to push me in that direction. "It's not that," I said. "I have to go out of town tomorrow morning and I'm not sure what time I'll be back."

He gave me that dazzling smile again. "How about you call me when you get back and if you've already had dinner we can at least have dessert. I've talked way too much about my life. I'd like to learn more about yours."

He was charming and easy to look at. And there were more questions I wanted to ask him. I nodded. "All right."

It was a quiet afternoon at the shop. I got a coat of primer on my table and Mac and I debated whether we wanted to drive to Rockport a week from this upcoming one to prowl a neighborhood-wide yard sale. Based on last year's success we decided it was worth the time and gas.

When I went back inside I found Charlotte had come and set up the ironing board by the workbench.

She smiled as I came level with her. "How about coming for supper tonight?" she said.

I hesitated. Was this another attempt to get Nick and me together?

"Nicolas isn't going to be there," she said as though I'd somehow transmitted my thoughts.

I didn't want her to think I was still fighting with Nick. "I just don't want to talk about the case with—"

She put a hand on my arm. "I understand," she said. "It's all right."

"I would like to come," I said. "I just need to take Elvis home first."

As if he knew we were talking about him, the subject of our conversation came walking across the top of the workbench. He tilted his head to one side, doing his cute thing, and Charlotte reached over to pet him.

"Bring him along."

Elvis started to purr and looked in my direction, almost seeming to smile.

"Thank you," I said. "We both accept your invitation."

Charlotte smiled and went back to ironing the lace curtains she wanted to add to the front window display.

I gave Elvis a scratch behind his ear, leaning in close to his furry face. "You're such a suck-up," I said.

He licked my chin, his way of saying "If it ain't broke, don't fix it."

Charlotte had also invited Mac to dinner but he was going sailing so he took a rain check. Charlotte, Elvis and I drove over to her little yellow house after work. I'd spent a lot of time in that house growing up and I knew my way around it and the entire tree-lined court as well as I had my grandmother's house.

I set the little table in the kitchen as Charlotte put water on to boil for our spaghetti. She pulled out lettuce, an English cucumber, a couple of radishes and some tiny red tomatoes. I washed the lettuce as Charlotte chopped the vegetables for the salad. While we worked I told her that I'd shared her idea for offering classes at Legacy Place with Mr. P. and Mac.

"They liked the idea," I said. I reached for one of the tiny tomatoes in the colander and popped it into my mouth. They were sweet and delicious from ripening in the August sunshine in Charlotte's backyard.

"I have the rental agent's business card," she said. "That's probably who you'd want to talk to."

"Are you thinking about selling this house?" I immediately asked.

"Of course not," she said, putting a hand over the strainer as I tried to swipe another tomato. "I have a business card for Coleridge's Funeral Home as well. It doesn't mean I'm planning to avail myself of their services anytime soon. I just like to be prepared."

Something caught her eye on the stove behind us and she turned to check the spaghetti pot. I took advantage of her momentary distraction to pop a tomato in my mouth. I did my best to look innocent when Charlotte eyed me, a hint of suspicion in her gaze but in the end I gave myself away when I couldn't figure out how to talk around a mouthful of tomato.

We were just starting to eat when the back door opened and Nick stepped into the kitchen.

Charlotte immediately turned to me. "I didn't know he was coming," she said.

Nick caught sight of me as she spoke and the smile faded from his face. "I can go," he said.

I shook my head. "That's silly. This is your mother's house. You shouldn't have to leave."

"Well, I don't want to make you leave," he said, fingering the dark stubble on his chin.

I twirled my fork in my spaghetti and managed to spear a tiny meatball along with the pasta. "I'm not going anywhere," I said, putting the whole thing in my mouth and making a mental note that the next thing Rose and Charlotte were teaching me to make was Charlotte's spaghetti sauce.

I took my time chewing my food. Having a little fun at Nick's expense was probably going to come back to bite me. I finally looked at him. "We've disagreed in the past and we'll disagree again. I'm certain of that."

Nick laughed. "I can't argue with that logic," he said.

"Have you eaten?" Charlotte asked.

"You don't have to feed me, Mom," he said.

"So it's just a coincidence you stopped in at supper-time?" I asked, raising an eyebrow.

Color flooded Nick's cheeks. He dropped his gaze for a moment. "Busted," he said. "Please feed me." He reminded me of a mischievous little boy.

Charlotte got to her feet.

I stood up as well. "Sit," I said, waving her back to her chair. "Your supper's getting cold." I got a pot from one of the bottom kitchen cupboards.

"So is yours," she said.

I handed Nick the pot and sat back down.

Nick laughed. "Sarah's right," he said. "She's not subtle, but she's right. I can make spaghetti." He put water in the pot and set it on the stove, then he brought a place mat and utensils to the table.

I slid over to make room for him.

Once he'd set his place he sat down, folded his hands on his place mat and turned to look at me. "Have you found out who killed Erin Fellowes yet?"

"Nicolas!" Charlotte exclaimed.

He leaned toward me. "It's okay. She didn't use my middle name. I'm not really in any trouble." His dark eyes danced with humor.

I wanted to be mad at him, but I couldn't help but be charmed, at least a little.

I shook my head. "No," I said, "but we do have a couple of leads."

"You went to see Stevie Carleton."

I wasn't surprised he knew. I was certain he was keeping fairly close tabs on what the Angels were doing. "We did," I said, wiping a bit of sauce from my chin.

"You know it wasn't her." He said the words as a statement of fact, not a question.

"What makes you so sure?" I asked.

Nick glanced over at the pot of water on the stove. "She must have told you about the flat tire she had the day Erin Fellowes was killed. By the time it was fixed it was too late in the day for her to have made it here. Even if she drives like you do."

"I take it Michelle verified that?" I said.

Nick nodded. "I take it Alfred did the same," he said. I nodded.

Charlotte picked up her plate and got to her feet. "Decaf?" she asked.

"That sounds good," I said. "You sit. I'll make it."

Nick put a hand on my arm. "No, I'll get it," he said. He got to his feet. "Let me make the coffee, Mom," he said. "I'm trying to show Sarah that I have more than my boyish good looks to offer."

Charlotte looked at me. "This whole helpful act isn't actually working, is it?"

I held out my hand, palm down, and waggled it from side to side. "It's iffy," I said, "but he is cute trying, so why don't we let him keep going?"

Nick made coffee for us, cooked his spaghetti and warmed up some sauce and even got his mother and me each a slice of her apple coffee cake. We continued to talk about the case.

"You know about the fraud investigation into du Mer." Again, a statement of fact.

"Mac doesn't think Leila knew about the substitution of the cheap ingredients," I said. I didn't see the harm in sharing that small piece of information.

"I think he's probably right," Nick said, managing to spear two tiny meatballs with his fork.

I gestured at him with my coffee cup. "No, no, no. This is where you're supposed to disagree."

He threw up his hands in mock dismay. "Crap! I forgot my lines."

"I like it when the two of you get along," Charlotte said as she got up to refill her cup.

Once her back was turned I leaned over and socked Nick on the arm.

"Ow!" he mouthed.

"What have you done with the real Nick?" I wrinkled my nose at him.

He smiled. "It's not a big deal. I reviewed the details of Leila McKenzie's accident and for what it's worth I don't think Mac had anything to do with it."

"It's worth a lot," I said quietly. I noticed he didn't say anything about believing that Mac wasn't hiding anything. "What about Stevie's partner?"

Nick got to his feet, picking up his own plate and collecting my empty cake plate as well.

"Davis Abbott? He was in Canada."

I stood up as well and took Charlotte's plate out of her hand. "We have this," I said. "Sit."

"I can do a few dishes," she protested.

"So can Nick and I," I said. "Gram always said it builds character."

Charlotte smiled then. "Well, you two certainly are characters."

She sat back down and I looked over at Elvis, who was watching Nick just in case there were any meatballs that had been missed. The cat looked in my direction. "Keep an eye on Charlotte," I said. To my surprise he came right across the floor and launched himself onto her lap, where he quickly settled, his green eyes locked on her face.

I reached over to stroke his fur. "Good job," I said.

Nick was already running water in the sink for the pots. "Wanna do them all this way?" he asked.

I nodded. "Davis Abbott wasn't in Nova Scotia," I told him as I scraped the plates. "At least not when Erin Fellowes was killed."

Nick frowned, suds forming around his wrists. "Are you sure?"

"Absolutely," I said. I told him what Mr. P. had discovered.

"Will you get him to call me in the morning, please?"

"I will," I said. I grabbed a couple of forks and a spoon from the table and dropped them into the sink. "Do you know anything about Natalie Welland?"

"Leila's sister?" Nick asked. He hunched a shoulder.

I nodded. He was hedging.

He opened his mouth but didn't say anything, just exhaled softly.

I waited, drying a bowl and setting it beside me on the clean countertop.

Finally Nick spoke. "All I can say is that she hasn't been that forthcoming." And that's all he did say.

Nick and I finished the dishes and cleaned up the kitchen.

"Thank you, sweetie," Charlotte said, wrapping me in a hug. "When I invited you for supper I didn't intend for you to have to work for it."

"I don't mind," I said. "You make the best meatballs in the world." At my feet Elvis gave an enthusiastic meow and licked his whiskers just in case there was any doubt about his love for meatballs.

"Rose and I will teach you how to make them," Charlotte said. "They're easy."

"I was hoping you'd say that," I said with a smile. I turned to Nick. "It was good to see you."

"I'll walk you out," he offered. "I'll be right back," he said to his mother.

My SUV was in Charlotte's driveway. Nick had parked at the curb. I fished my keys out, unlocked the driver's door and set Elvis on the seat. Then I turned to face Nick, who was standing just a bit closer than personal boundary space would dictate.

"Are you coming to the jam next week?" I asked. "You missed half the fun last night."

"Do you want me to?"

"Yes," I said. "C'mon. We have fun and I don't want to be on the outs with you over a case, even this case."

"Are you sure Jess won't pour a bowl of salsa over my head?"

"I'm making no promises. But I am pretty sure the acid in the tomatoes would be good for your scalp." I grinned at him.

"I'll chance it, then," he said. He hesitated and then gave me a hug.

I slid in behind the wheel and started the car. Nick raised a hand in good-bye as I backed out of the driveway. We headed down the street and Elvis looked back over his shoulder, making a muttering sound low in his throat.

"I know," I said. "He drives me crazy, too."

Chapter 18

Mr. P., his messenger bag slung across his body, was waiting in the hallway when Elvis and I came out of the apartment in the morning. "Could I trouble you for a drive to the shop, Sarah?" he asked.

"It's no trouble and you're welcome to come with us anytime," I said. Elvis meowed loudly, seconding my words.

"I talked to Nick last night," I said as we waited for Rose.

"Did you learn anything?" he asked.

"Possibly." I told him what Nick had said about Natalie. "Do you think the police could somehow know something we don't?"

"Detective Andrews has likely spoken to the Boston police. I don't have any contacts there at the moment, but I'll see what I can find out from this end. All aboveboard, of course."

"Could you call Nick, please?" I said. I explained Nick's surprise when I'd told him Davis Abbott hadn't been in Nova Scotia. "Maybe he'll tell you something he wouldn't share with me," I added.

Mr. P. smiled. "I suspect if Nicolas were going to be susceptible to anyone's wiles it would be yours and not mine."

I felt my cheeks get warm.

Rose came out then, carrying a small, red and white cooler. "Just a few snacks for the road," she said.

We left for the salt works about eight thirty. The drive along the coast was beautiful. The sky was an endless arc of blue overhead and the sun sparkled on the ocean water.

"Do you know where you're going?" Liz had asked as I backed out of her driveway.

"I figured you'd tell me where to go," I said innocently.

"Sometimes you're really funny," she said. "This isn't one of those times." One of her perfectly manicured nails flicked the back of my head.

I laughed. "Yes, I know where I'm going. I checked the map before we left, Charlotte gave me directions and I have GPS on my phone." I knew the last comment would get a rise out of her.

"We are not using that disembodied robot voice. Do I need to remind you about the time we almost ended up in the ditch thanks to that thing?"

"You most decidedly do not!" Rose said emphatically. "We've all heard that story plenty of times, thank you very much."

I raised a hand as though I were back in grade school.

"What is it, dear?" Rose asked. "Do you need a washroom break?"

"No, I don't need a washroom break," I said. "I need a change of conversation. Tell me a little more about this salt works."

"It's quite simple, really," Rose said, shifting into teacher mode. "You know that they collect water from the ocean."

"Even in the wintertime?" I asked.

"No," Liz commented from the backseat.

"The sun isn't strong enough for the evaporation process during the winter. The salt houses are in operation from about the middle of March through October. They don't use any anticaking chemicals and they don't remove any of the trace minerals."

"In other words, the salt is just the way Mother Nature made it."

Rose turned to look at Liz and nodded. "That's right."

"Okay, I get that part," I said. "I'm guessing the sea salt is more expensive because of the quality and because the entire process is pretty labor intensive."

"That's likely why Natalie was looking for a less expensive alternative," Rose said.

"So what did she find? Table salt?"

A cynical snort came from the seat behind me. "More like road salt," Liz said.

My gaze darted to Rose again. "Seriously? The same stuff they put on the roads when it's icy?"

"Essentially."

"No wonder she was being investigated."

"In her defense, Alfred thinks that Natalie didn't realize she was buying road salt. She may have believed she'd just been getting a slightly lesser quality salt without out the trace minerals."

"So what prompted the investigation?" I asked. I had my window cracked just a little and I could smell the ocean air.

"Customer complaints," Liz said. "People were developing rashes and hives. Whatever the products had been doing for people's skin in the past they weren't having the same effect."

"And you're certain Natalie is going to show up today?" I asked.

"One hundred percent," Liz replied. "You might say Charlie Carroll made her an offer she can't refuse."

"Charlie Carroll is the supplier Natalie has been using." The road curved inland and we started up a long hill.

"That's right," Rose said.

"So what's the payoff? Why help us?"

"Maybe Carroll got an offer too good to refuse," Liz said.

I looked at her in the rearview mirror again. "What did you do this time?"

Her chin came up and she squared her shoulders. "I didn't *do* anything. I simply pointed out that it made a lot more sense to help us than it would to get the police tangled up in that business."

"Which is true," Rose added helpfully. Sitting there with her back straight and her hands folded in her lap she looked just like someone's doting grandmother, which meant people who didn't know her tended to underestimate Rose. Most didn't do it twice.

"So you blackmailed the owner?" I was directing my comment to Liz.

"I did not blackmail anyone. All I did was point out

that it was in Carroll's best interests—as well as ours—not to involve the police *at this point in time.*" She stressed the last part of the sentence.

I took one hand off the steering wheel for a moment and rubbed the space between my eyebrows.

"Do you have a headache, dear?" Rose asked.

I shook my head. "No," I said. "But I do have a bit of a pain in the neck."

"I'll bring you my magic bag after supper. You can heat it in the microwave. It's very good for things like that."

Behind me I heard Liz laugh.

Carroll Salt Works was just off the road in Marshfield. I could see the salt houses in the field beyond the parking lot, their rounded tops stretching long and low in the cleared space surrounded by trees. There was a bit of a breeze and I could smell the bite of salt in the warm summer air. "But this looks like the same kind of organic salt works that you described," I said to Rose as we got out of the SUV in the gravel parking lot.

"Oh, it is," she said. "The product Natalie has been buying is trucked down from a salt mine in Quebec."

Liz climbed out of the backseat and smoothed the front of her blue and white tunic. Instead of her usual high heels she'd made a concession to the uneven terrain and was wearing a pair of canvas platform shoes with a peep toe and a rope wedge heel—the equivalent, for her, of flats.

"Are you sure this is going to work?" I asked.

She tipped her head to one side and squinted at me, wrinkling her nose. "Such a cynic," she said. She turned and looked toward a gray-shingled building at the far

end of the gravel lot. The story-and-a-half structure had
a roll-up garage door just right of center and a window
to the right of that. Left of the garage door was what I
was guessing was the entrance to the business office.
The inner door was open and I could see what looked
like a desk through the wooden screen door. Someone
was walking across the parking lot toward us.

"There's Charlie," Liz said, starting toward the salt
works owner.

Charlie Carroll wasn't what I'd been expecting. I'd
been expecting someone older and harder both in phys-
icality and in bearing.

I'd been expecting a man.

"Charlie Carroll is a woman," I said softly to Rose.

"Oh, didn't you realize that?" she said.

"Neither you nor Liz said she was a woman."

Rose stopped and frowned. "Didn't we? Oh my goodness." She put one hand to her chest. "Did you ask?"

"No," I said slowly. "I just assumed."

She patted my arm, a gesture all three of them used
when they were trying to humor me as though I were
a child. "You shouldn't make assumptions, dear," she
said. "It's a much better idea to get the facts."

"Yes, I can see that," I said. I could see what they'd
done, too. When I'd insisted on joining them for this . . .
caper . . . they'd both taken a bit of offense at the impli-
cation that I didn't think they could handle things themselves. This bit of subterfuge was a way of pointing out
that I didn't know everything. I turned to look at Rose.
I could feel a smile pulling at my mouth. I'd been bested.
I wasn't quite sure what to say.

As if she could read my mind—and I'd had the un-

comfortable feeling more than once that she could—
Rose leaned toward me. "I think the word you're
looking for is 'touché,'" she said with a smile.

Charlie Carroll was maybe five foot five, an inch or
so shorter than me. I was guessing she was somewhere
in her late thirties to early forties. Her strawberry blond
hair was cut short and her smooth skin suggested she
was pretty diligent about wearing sunscreen. She wore
knee-length khaki shorts, green rubber boots that rose
almost to her knees and a gray T-shirt. She looked strong
and solid with the kind of muscled arms that suggested
many hard days of work as opposed to hard workouts.

"Sarah Grayson, meet Charlie Carroll," Liz said.

Charlie offered her hand and we shook. The calluses
I felt told me that she was hands-on in the business.

"Natalie is pretty good about time," she said. "That
means we have about half an hour until she gets here."
She looked at me. "Would you like a bit of a tour?"

I nodded. "Thank you. I would."

She started across the parking lot to the domed buildings Rose had said were the salt houses, and the three
of us followed. "These buildings are essentially greenhouses," Charlie explained. "We use the sun and the
wind to evaporate the water."

Closer to the buildings what I thought of as the smell
of the ocean was even stronger.

"Like any farmer, we're dependent on the weather."

As we walked from one building to the next Charlie
explained the process in a little more detail. "The water
goes into the first set of houses where anything that
might have been in it can settle out. At fifty percent
salinity it's pumped into a second set of houses where

the water is reduced to even greater salinity. Finally it ends up in the finishing house where the rest of the water is evaporated and what's left is just pure sea salt." She smiled. "Some processors use heat to extract the salt. We let Mother Nature do the work for us."

She went on to explain how the salt was ground, with about half of it ending up flavored for the restaurants that made up a large portion of the company's business.

"You started doing business with Natalie Welland what, close to two years ago?" I asked.

Charlie nodded. "That's right." She suddenly stopped walking. Hands in her pockets, feet apart she faced me, squinting in the sun. "Look, you know this is only part of my business. I also bring product in from Canada for nonfood, commercial applications."

There were a lot of euphemisms in that last sentence.

"You bring salt in from a mine in Quebec, which you sell to several snow-removal companies here and in New Hampshire for use on parking lots and driveways," Liz said. There was a challenge in her gaze. "For the most part," she added.

Charlie nodded. "Since we're being so plainspoken, yes. I sell to a number of small companies both here and in New Hampshire and I don't check up on any of them. I had no idea what Natalie Welland was doing. And if I had, I would have been the first person to turn her in."

I believed her. There was nothing evasive in her voice or her body language. She looked us right in the eye. She didn't mumble or shuffle and she wasn't making excuses.

"All we want to do is talk to Natalie," Rose said. "We don't want to jam you up."

I bit the inside of my cheek so I wouldn't laugh at her use of an expression I was certain had come from some crime drama on TV.

"Why don't we wait inside?" Charlie said. She checked her watch. "She should be here soon."

"Jam you up?" I said to Rose as we followed Charlie to the gray-shingled office building.

"You're not the only one who watches *Law & Order*," she said with a sly grin.

Natalie Welland arrived about ten minutes later. Charlie went out to the parking lot to meet her.

My first thought was that I would have known that Leila and Natalie were sisters. They had the same gorgeous cheekbones, the same smooth brown skin and long neck. Based on the photo I'd seen, Natalie was taller. Like her sister, she wore her black hair in corkscrew curls, in Natalie's case just past her shoulders. She wore a casual white and silver short-sleeved cotton dress and flat sandals.

She looked confused when she stepped inside the office. "Am I interrupting something?" she asked.

I was leaning against Charlie's desk. Rose and Liz had the two chairs in front of it.

Rose smiled and got to her feet. "You're not interrupting anything," she said, her tone warm and reassuring. The fact that she looked like—and was—the sweet, grandmotherly type didn't just cause people to underestimate her, it also tended to put people at ease at least a little. She handed Natalie a business card.

The younger woman studied it for a moment and then looked up at Rose. "You're private investigators?" She pulled at the corner of her bottom lip with her teeth.

Technically only Mr. P. was licensed at the moment, but Rose was about to be. I wasn't really sure what Liz and I were, but it didn't seem like a good time to quibble about semantics.

"Yes," Rose said. "We'd like to ask you a few questions."

Natalie immediately held up her hands. "I'm not talking to you. I'm taking the deal and there isn't anything left to say. I can't give people money I don't have."

Liz and I exchanged a look. I had a feeling the wheels were turning in her head the same way they were in mine. Natalie and the Federal Trade Commission had come to some kind of settlement agreement. She thought we were working on behalf of some of du Mer's customers.

"This has nothing to do with your company," Liz said. "We're investigating the murder of Erin Fellowes."

"Wait a minute, you're investigating a murder?" Charlie said from the doorway. "You didn't say anything about that."

"No, we didn't," Liz said. "We didn't say anything about a lot of things."

Charlie didn't speak again. She'd clearly gotten the message.

"We just want to ask you a few questions," Rose said. "Please. It'll only take a few minutes."

Natalie shook her head. "No. I can't help you." Her body had tensed when Erin's name had been mentioned.

She was about to leave, I realized. "We're investigating Erin's death because Mac is our friend," I said. I pulled out my phone, swiped a finger across the screen and found a photo. I turned the phone sideways and held it out to her. It was all of us, jammed around the table in Rose's apartment eating pulled pork sandwiches.

Natalie studied the screen for a moment. She didn't say anything but I saw the muscles in her jaw tighten as she clenched her teeth.

"We're here because we all care a lot about Mac and I think at one time you did, too."

"I still do," she said, in a voice so soft I almost missed the words.

"Erin came from Boston to see him," I said. "Do you know why?"

"No." She shook her head. "I didn't even know she was coming to Maine. All I know is she changed her mind, about him, I mean. Everyone . . ." She cleared her throat. "Everyone in the family thought that my sister's accident was Mac's fault. I didn't . . . I didn't know what to believe. Erin was always so positive about it and then, all of a sudden she wasn't. Something changed, I could tell, but I don't know what." Her expression hardened then. "There isn't anything more I can tell you."

Or maybe there wasn't anything more she *wanted* to tell us.

"You mentioned you'd taken a deal," I said. "Did you mean with respect to the investigation into du Mer?"

The nod was so slight I wasn't actually sure she'd acknowledged my question. She turned to look at Charlie. "That's why I'm here. I made a deal with the FTC. You're not in any trouble. I told them you had no idea what I was doing."

She turned to face us again. "Leila didn't know that

I was . . . changing some of our ingredients to get our costs down." She tipped her head in Charlie's direction. "She didn't know, either. So the company is going out of business, but no one will go to jail, customers will get some money and staff will get severance." She took a deep breath and let it out. "I'll get probation and community service and Leila's name will be cleared."

"That must have been a very difficult decision," Rose said kindly.

Natalie pressed a hand to her mouth for a moment. "I never meant for things to turn out the way they did," she said. "Jackson said sometimes things just go in a direction you didn't mean for them to go and you just do the best you can to fix things and go forward."

"Jackson Montgomery?" I asked.

She nodded. "He's helped a lot with du Mer. Erin, too."

Interesting that Jackson hadn't mentioned any of this when I'd asked about Natalie. I suspected he still felt a degree of loyalty to the family. Then I remembered the tiny carved wooden bird that had been in Erin Fellowes's pocket. Mac had said he thought it was Leila's.

"Natalie, did you give Erin anything from your sister's office? Some kind of remembrance maybe?" I asked.

"I let her take a couple of things, a photograph of the two of them, a needlepoint pillow and a couple of weeks ago she asked if she could have a little bird that Leila had in her desk drawer." She kept tapping her leg with two fingers.

I felt my heart begin to pound. That tiny bird did mean something. "Did anyone else take anything from Leila's office?" I asked. "Anyone else in the family?"

"No," she said. "Just Erin." Her gaze went from me to Rose to Liz. "You haven't asked where I was when Erin was killed."

"No, we haven't," Liz said. "Where were you?"

"At a meeting with the FTC and my lawyer."

I wasn't surprised. Natalie wouldn't have raised the question if she hadn't had an answer. "Jackson was with you?" I asked.

She shook her head. "No. He was in court. Someone else from his office was with me."

I remembered Jackson telling me the first time we'd met that he'd been in court. So I wouldn't be able to ask him about the meeting. But it wouldn't be that hard for Mr. P. to check.

That was pretty much the end of our conversation. Rose thanked Natalie for answering our questions. Liz took Charlie Carroll aside for a moment. I had no idea what they talked about but they both seemed satisfied with the conversation. Rose and I walked back to the SUV.

"Natalie Welland has mixed emotions about her sister," I said.

I knew Leila only from what little Mac and Jackson had shared and from the photos Mac had showed me, but even on the small screen of his cell phone I'd been able to see that there was something special about the woman, some spark that had made people want to know her. It was the same quality that Liz had. More than charm or personality, it was some undefinable quality that pulled people in. My grandmother called it "presence." It was as good a word as any. Whatever that elusive spark was, Natalie didn't have it.

"I think it must have been difficult to be Leila's little sister," Rose said. "She was smart, beautiful and successful."

I wondered what it had been like after so many years of being the family's dirty little secret to finally join it and find oneself in the shadow of the perfect big sister. Natalie had said she was trying to keep costs down but had sibling rivalry caused her to sabotage Leila's company? We kept coming back to du Mer. I couldn't shake the feeling that Leila's business was tied to what had happened. I just didn't know how.

Chapter 19

We headed home.

"Now what?" Liz asked from the backseat.

Rose sighed softly. "We must have missed something."

"Maybe it *was* just some random attack," Liz said.

"It wasn't," I said.

I could see Rose studying me from the corner of my eye. "I don't disagree, but why are you so sure?"

"It's like you said before." I glanced over at her for a moment. "Leila's accident, Erin believing Mac had something to do with that and then doing a complete one-eighty. Her showing up here saying she needed to talk to him and then a few hours later she's dead." I blew my bangs off my face. "C'mon, even a bad movie of the week couldn't get away with that many coincidences." I couldn't keep the frustration out of my voice.

"So we go over everything again," Rose said. "And again if we have to. Maybe we missed something, something so small that we didn't realize its significance. We'll figure it out."

I nodded, but I kept my eyes on the road. I had an idea about what that something small might be.

We stopped for lunch at a little diner about halfway between the salt works and North Harbor. Liz gave me directions and I could tell she was getting a kick out of telling me where to go.

"This place better be good," I said as we got out of the SUV.

"Would I steer you wrong, child?" she asked.

"You steered us down a one-way street," Rose said from in front of us.

"And we were only going one way so I don't see the problem," Liz replied.

Rose looked over her shoulder and sent a withering look Liz's way.

Liz linked her arms through mine. "We'll have lunch. We'll regroup and we will figure this out," she said, her voice low. "We're not going to leave this cloud over Mac's head. That's a promise."

The restaurant she had steered us to was a tiny building with a back patio overlooking the water. A young woman wearing denim shorts and a Red Sox T-shirt greeted us at the door. She leaned around Rose and her smile got wider when she saw Liz. "Hello, Mrs. French," she said.

"Hello, Kelsey," Liz said. "Could we have a table outside, please?"

The young woman nodded. Her blond hair was piled on top of her head in a loose knot that bobbed when she moved. She led us through a screen door to the wooden deck and took us to a table near the railing, where we could look out at the water but still be sheltered by a trellis entwined with purple clematis. "Your favorite table," she said.

"Thank you." Liz gave her a warm smile.

"Iced tea?"

Liz nodded and held up three fingers.

"I'll be right back."

"I'm not sure I wanted iced tea," Rose said.

"Iced tea, lemonade, water. Those are your choices." Liz ticked them off on the fingers she was still holding up.

"We don't have menus," Rose continued.

Liz leaned back in her chair and closed her eyes. "There are no menus. Your choices are fried clams, fish and chips or lobster roll. We're having lobster rolls." She opened her eyes.

"That's fine," Rose said. Her chin had come up a little. "I was just asking."

Liz closed her eyes again and Rose rolled hers at me.

"I saw that," Liz said.

"Well, now, it would have been pointless for me to do it if you hadn't seen it, now, wouldn't it?" Rose said. She tipped her face up to the sky like a sunflower.

"You know her," I said, pointing toward the building.

Liz nodded. "She's studying business. She won the Jack French scholarship." Jack French was Liz's second husband.

Kelsey came back with three tall glasses of iced tea that I knew from the first sip hadn't been made from powder in a can.

"This is lovely," Rose exclaimed.

Kelsey smiled at her. "Thank you. It's Mrs. French's favorite."

The lobster rolls came about five minutes later with roasted corn salad and kettle chips and I actually moaned as I took the first bite—and the second and the third.

"Why didn't I know about this place?" I finally asked Liz when there was one lone potato chip and a few stray kernels of corn left on my plate. I couldn't remember ever having a lobster roll that tasted so good and I've been eating them every summer since I was a kid.

"That's a very good question," Rose said, adjusting her glasses on her nose, the lenses darkened because of the sun.

"I have to have a few secrets," Liz said. Her gaze didn't quite meet mine so I knew she was hedging for a reason.

Kelsey came back then, smiling as she collected our plates.

"How were the lobster rolls?" she asked. The smile on her face told me she knew the answer.

"Absolutely delicious," Rose said.

The young woman's smile got a bit wider. "You'll have to come back and try our clams." She looked at Liz. "You and your friend are coming back for one more feed before I head back to class, right?"

Rose and I exchanged a look.

"When do your classes start?" Liz asked.

Kelsey named a date less than three weeks away. They talked for a minute about what courses she was taking and then she said, "I'll get your check."

"Who's your *friend*?" I asked, putting a little extra emphasis on the word "friend."

"I already told you Kelsey won Jack's scholarship," Liz said. "Were you not listening?"

"Yes, we heard that," Rose said, lacing her fingers and resting her hands on the table. "We mean the friend you had clams and chips with."

"Nobody said I had clams and chips with anyone," Liz said. "Kelsey asked if we were coming for clams and chips before the prime season is over."

I folded my own hands, tenting my index fingers like a church steeple and leaning my chin lightly against them. "No. Not we, meaning us. She asked if you and your friend were coming. *Friend.* Singular. Kelsey strikes me as a very smart young woman. I'm sure she can count." I raised an eyebrow. "Who is it?"

"None of your damn business," Liz said.

Rose and I just looked at her without speaking. I knew it would drive her crazy.

"Channing Caulfield," she snapped. "Are you happy?"

Rose and I tipped our heads together. "Ooo," we cooed like a pair of giggly teenagers.

"It was foundation business," Liz said. "There were documents I wanted him to look at." Her gaze darted to me for a moment and it occurred to me that those documents probably had something to do with Michelle's father.

Rose and I continued to smile at her. She leaned back in her chair again and crossed her arms over her chest. "This is exactly why I didn't tell you," she said. "There is nothing going on between Channing and me."

I believed her, but I knew the former bank manager had carried a torch for Liz for a long time. He'd helped on a couple of the Angels' recent cases and I suspected no matter how much she protested, Liz liked him a little more than she was admitting.

I straightened up and reached for the last of my iced tea. "You wouldn't tell us if there were," I said.

"No, I would not," she agreed. "I don't need my business discussed all over town."

"So how come you're allowed to meddle in my love life?"

Liz made a snort of contempt. "You don't have a love life."

"We don't meddle," Rose said. She actually looked aghast at the suggestion that they did. "We simply give you the benefit of our experience from time to time."

"Well, Liz always says a woman without a man is like a fish without a bicycle," I said.

"No one is disputing that, dear," Rose said. "It's just that sometimes you get tired of swimming around by yourself and when that happens it's nice to have a bicycle."

Across the table Liz gave me a triumphant smile. The topic had been successfully changed from her private life to mine and I had no clue how to answer Rose's comment.

I glared at her and resisted the urge to stick out my tongue. "We should get back on the road," I said.

"Do you have plans tonight?" Rose asked. She held up her hands. "I'm not meddling. I'm just asking. It is Saturday night."

"I have plans to get back to the shop," I said. I reached for the check but Liz beat me to it. She had surprisingly fast reflexes.

"This is my treat," she said. She held up one hand. "Don't waste your time arguing."

"We should have a barbecue tonight," Rose said as

we headed inside to pay the bill. "Do you think it would be too short notice for everyone?"

"Yes," I said. I knew "everyone" for the most part meant Nick.

Liz went to move past me and as she did she put a hand on my shoulder. "Don't screw with the master," she said softly.

The rest of our trip was uneventful. Liz asked to be dropped at her house, saying she had things to do. I didn't ask what. When we pulled into the lot at the shop I noticed that Mac was out in the old garage and I headed over to him while Rose went to brief Mr. P.

Mac was on his knees working on the leg of a low wooden rocking chair. He smiled when he caught sight of me and got to his feet, wiping his hands on the front of his jeans. "How did it go?" he asked.

"Natalie has an alibi," I said. "Unless Mr. P. can poke holes in it, we're back to square one."

He shrugged. "I didn't see how it could have been her. She would never have hurt Leila and if she wanted to hurt Erin she didn't have to come here to do it."

"We must have missed something. Rose and Mr. P. are going to go through everything again. Maybe they'll see something we didn't see before."

His mouth twisted to one side. "Maybe we aren't going to find any answers."

I was shaking my head before he finished speaking. "The answers are out there. We just have to ask the right questions."

Mac took a couple of steps closer to me. "Sarah, this isn't your fight."

"You ever watch *Bonanza*?" I asked.

Mac's eyes darted from side to side in confusion. It occurred to me that Rose was rubbing off on me, at least conversationally. "I don't think so," he said slowly.

"Gram and I used to watch it in reruns when I was a kid. It's a western from the 1960s set in the 1860s—the adventures of the Cartwright family, who lived on the Ponderosa ranch." I grinned at the memory. "After watching a few episodes I tried to rope Maddie Hamilton's garden gnome with a piece of Gram's clothesline."

Mac started to smile.

"Don't laugh," I warned, waggling a finger at him. "I got pretty good at it, especially considering I couldn't convince Gram to buy me a horse so I had to do my roping from my bike."

Mac was grinning by now. "Not that this insight into your childhood isn't fascinating but I'm guessing this somehow ties in to everything that's been happening."

I nodded. "Yes, it does. To be specific, the *Bonanza* theme song does, which Gram taught me and which I used to sing as I was practicing my cowboy skills." And then I sang a bit of the song to him. "If anyone fights any one of us, he's gotta fight with me!"

I put a hand on his arm. "Seriously, that's how I feel. That's how all of us feel. We're going to figure this out. And if I have to lasso the bad guy with a length of clothesline I will." I gave his arm a squeeze and headed for the shop. I'd meant every word I'd said, now all I had to do was make it happen.

About an hour later I headed down to the sunporch from my office. I had a cup of tea and a couple of questions for Mr. P. He looked up and smiled when I appeared in the doorway. "Is that for me?" he asked, indicating the cup and saucer in my hand.

"It is," I said, setting it down on the table far enough away from his computer that it wouldn't get knocked over and cause a problem.

"Thank you," he said. "Your timing is impeccable. I've been checking Natalie Welland's alibi and I'm ready for a break."

"It checks out, doesn't it?" I said.

"Yes, my dear, it does." He took a sip of the tea.

I shifted from one foot to the other, suddenly wondering if what I was about to ask him was silly.

"You have something on your mind," he said, his eyes kind behind his wire-frame glasses.

I nodded. "I do, but now I'm second-guessing myself."

"Why don't you tell me what it is, instead?"

"Remember that little carving that Erin Fellowes was carrying in her pocket?"

"I do," he said.

"If I described it to you do you think you could possibly figure out where it came from?"

"I can certainly try." He studied my face. "Do you think it's important?"

I raked a hand back through my hair. "Maybe. Mac thinks it was the same carved figure that Leila kept in her desk. He didn't know where it came from but he said Leila said it was to remind her of the kind of person she wanted to be." I blew out a breath and walked over to the window to stare outside for a moment. "I went to see Sam the other day. He has this little brass monkey—about two inches high—on his desk. My father gave it to him a long time ago after . . . after Sam said something that pretty much destroyed the band they were in together. I don't know what it was but I do know they didn't speak for a while over it. They patched things up because, well, Gram said they were as close as brothers, but Sam has always kept that little monkey because he says it's a reminder to choose his words carefully."

"Sammy is a very wise man," Mr. P. said.

I turned away from the window. "Natalie told us that Erin helped her pack up Leila's office and she asked for a photo of herself and Leila, a pillow and that little carved bird."

"Maybe Erin gave it to Leila." He reached for his tea again.

I shook my head. "I don't think so. If her best friend gave that little carving to her she would have told Mac. It means something."

"Do you have any idea what?"

I closed my eyes for a moment. When I looked at Mr. P. again there was no indication in his expression that he thought I was off on some wild-goose chase. "I don't know," I said. "It meant something to Leila and it meant something to Erin. Of all the things she could have asked Natalie for, aside from that photo, the only thing she wanted was a pillow and that little bird. And it was important enough that she brought it with her. Why? If we can figure that out, maybe we can figure out everything else."

Mr. P. nodded. "How can I help?"

I moved back over to his desk. "I thought if we could find out where it came from maybe we'd be able to find out when Leila bought it and then we could work backward and try to figure out what was happening in her life at the time." I made a face. "That made a lot more sense in my head than it does when I say it out loud."

He smiled. "It makes sense to me, my dear. Tell me everything you remember about that carving."

I described the tiny bird as carefully as I could. Mr. P. set to work on his laptop and I went back up to my office. Less than half an hour later he knocked at my door. He was carrying his computer.

"You found something?" I asked.

"You tell me," he said. He set the laptop on my desk, and I came around to look at the screen. "Is this the carving Erin Fellowes had with her?"

"That's it!" I exclaimed. "Mr. P., you're a genius."

He smiled. "Thank you, Sarah. I wouldn't say I'm a genius." He glanced briefly at the screen again. "It occurred to me from your description that what we might be looking for was a netsuke."

I frowned. "I've heard the word but I don't exactly know what that is."

Mr. P. took off his glasses, pulled a small cloth from the pocket of his gold shirt and began to clean them. "Netsuke originated in seventeenth-century Japan. Traditional kimono had no pockets, which meant men had to carry their belongings—tobacco, money—in containers, which were fastened to the sash of the kimono by a cord. The cord was held at the top of the sash by a netsuke, like a toggle."

"That's why the holes," I said, remembering Erin turning the tiny carving over in her fingers.

"Exactly." He touched the screen with a finger. "Your bird is actually a mandarin duck, *oshidori*. See the tiny carved feathers?"

The detail on the tiny creature was incredible. Both Mac and Stevie had said Leila had been interested in Asian art. It made sense that she'd had the *oshidori*.

"The mandarin is a symbol of fidelity," Mr. P. continued. "Ironic because like most ducks they only mate for a season and then move on to a new pairing." He gestured at the computer screen. "This one is part of a collection at the Metropolitan Museum of Art. I think it's possible that it and the netsuke we believe was Leila's were originally part of the same set. It and of course Leila's, if I'm correct about it, date from the late nineteenth century."

"Wait a minute. Are you saying it's not a replica?"

"From what I can tell, no."

"It's valuable."

He nodded. "There's no question about that. You said Leila always kept it in her desk?"

"Yes. Both Natalie and Mac said she kept it in one of the drawers."

The old man's eyes narrowed. "It seems unlikely she didn't know what she had. She studied art history at college for two years."

"Which Erin would have also known." I exhaled loudly in frustration. "This means something. It has to. I just wish I could figure out what."

Mr. P. rested his hand on my arm for a moment. "I'm going to see what I can find out about the piece in the museum's collection. Maybe we can figure out how Leila ended up with her netsuke." He picked up his laptop and headed back to his sunporch office.

I was too restless to go back to paperwork. I called Jackson to accept his dinner invitation and checked the

Web site for orders. It seemed far-fetched to think a tiny little carving, no more than an inch by an inch and a half, could hold the key to the accident that had put Leila in a coma and to the murder of her best friend, but it was all we had right now. I headed downstairs to the shop.

In the following couple of hours I sold a Martin guitar, two quilts and four of Avery's map-covered lampshades and I polished every mirrored or glass surface in the shop. It was close to closing time when Rose appeared in the doorway to the workroom and smiled at me. I walked over to her. I felt certain Mr. P. had brought her up to date.

"Alfred has something he'd like to show you," she said. "I'll stay here and help Avery." Avery was in the middle of showing the grandparents of a nine-year-old a dressing table I'd refinished about a month ago. Based on the couple's body language I didn't think she needed any help making the sale.

Mr. P. was at his desk, making notes on a lined yellow pad with a fine-tipped black pen.

"Rose said you had something to show me?" I said, poking my head around the doorframe.

"I think I've traced Leila's netsuke," he said. "Elizabeth has a connection to someone on the board of the Metropolitan Museum."

It really didn't surprise me that Liz had that kind of connection.

"She put me together with one of the curators at the museum. It turns out they had tried to buy the other ducks when they went up for sale about two and a half years ago."

I sat on the edge of his desk. "They didn't succeed."

He shook his head.

Then it hit me what he'd said. "Ducks." *Plural.* "Wait a minute," I said. "There was more than one duck?"

Mr. P. beamed like he was the teacher and I was his star pupil. "Yes, my dear. Both of them"—he looked down at his notes—"were purchased by a private collector somewhere in New England. It seems that for a time netsuke were popular as a token between lovers and it cut into the museum's ability to expand their collection. So far I've had no luck getting the collector's name." He paused for a moment. "There are still a couple of techniques I haven't tried yet."

I nodded. I had a feeling I wouldn't be too crazy about those techniques so it was probably better I didn't ask about them. I glanced at the computer screen. Mr. P. had several photos open on the computer, one overlapping the other. In one of them I spotted Davis Abbott holding up a beer. "What are those?" I asked.

"The photos that young Mr. Abbott said he would send. He finally did." He brought the image of Davis holding his beer—and obviously intoxicated—to the forefront. "I have to say I don't understand some people's propensity for documenting everything they do with a photograph, but it does make my work much easier sometimes." He minimized the image and brought up the remaining half dozen one at a time. Davis's one-night stand was visible in three of them. In one she appeared to be on his lap.

The last photo looked to have been taken in a lawyer's office.

"What's this?" I asked.

"Remember Davis admitted he got a copy of the trust

agreement?" Mr. P. said. "He took it with him when he went to see Leila about challenging the trust."

I frowned at him. "I remember. How did he do that, by the way? No lawyer would just hand that document over to him."

"I wondered the same thing. It turns out Stevie asked Marguerite's lawyer for a copy of the document. Davis picked it up." He raised an eyebrow.

"So Stevie knew a little more about what Davis was up to than either one of them has been letting on."

Mr. P. smiled. "I think Stephanie and her young man have a very flexible definition of the truth."

I studied the image. "Is this Jackson Montgomery's office?" I asked, squinting at a diploma on the wall behind the office desk."

"Yes, it is," Mr. P. said. "He was Marguerite Thompson-Davis's lawyer."

I was having dinner with Jackson later. I could ask him more about the trust, if there actually had been any way to break it.

I took another look at Davis Abbott's selfie. He was sitting on the edge of Jackson's desk, one hand on a long, brown envelope lying on the polished wood surface, which I guessed held the trust papers. Jackson's desk was much tidier than mine—a laptop on what would be Jackson's left, a lamp, a yellow pad of paper, two photos in matte black frames and what seemed to be a couple of paperweights. Something was written on the envelope, I realized. I leaned in for a better look.

My heart began to pound and the sound of rushing water seemed to fill my ears. Something must have shown in my face.

"Sarah, are you all right?" Mr. P. asked.

I pointed to the screen. "You're uh . . . you're going to think I'm crazy but I know who killed Erin Fellowes and put Leila McKenzie in a coma," I said.

Mr. P. studied the computer for a long moment. Then he looked at me.

"Yes?" I asked.

He nodded. "Yes."

We spent the next twenty minutes going back over what we knew, looking for holes in my theory. Everything held together. By the time it was time to close up shop we had a plan.

Rose was folding a crocheted tablecloth when I stepped back into the shop. "I think I may have a sale for this," she said. "A young woman was looking at it and she asked me for the measurements. I wouldn't be surprised if she comes back tomorrow."

"It's pretty," I said, moving to grab one end. "But it's a lot of work to starch and block the thing."

"My mother used to starch my father's shirts," Rose said. "I remember how scandalized her mother was when Mama bought a can of spray starch." She laughed. "My mother really embraced aerosol cans—spray starch, spray whipped cream, spray cheese. Even hair in a can for my father."

We folded the lacy tablecloth and Rose put it over the back of a wooden chair. She looked around the room for anything else out of place but between the two of them, she and Avery seemed to have tidied up the space. Avery already had the vacuum going.

"Are you still going to Charlotte's for dinner?" I asked.

Rose nodded.

"Are you going to be there for a while?"

She reached past me to straighten a place setting on the table behind me.

"As a matter of fact, I am. Charlotte and I are going to go through a box of old photos. Liz is looking for pictures from the summer fair the foundation used to host. I don't know why she wants them."

I had a pretty good idea why but that wasn't my story to tell.

"Don't you have a date, dear?" Rose asked.

Was dinner with Jackson a date? I'd thought of it more as a fact-finding mission. Of course now I was certain I knew what the facts were so I wasn't sure what this was. I nodded. "I'm having dinner with Mac's friend Jackson. But I won't be that long. I'll stop by Charlotte's afterward."

"Did you and Alfred confirm Natalie's alibi?" Rose asked as we moved out of Avery's way. The teen was single-minded with a vacuum cleaner.

"We did. I'll tell you all about it when I see you."

"All right," she said. She gave me a teasing smile and winked. "Don't worry if you get held up."

Jackson and I had dinner at The Black Bear. He talked a little bit about his and Mac's college years, but then he steered the conversation to the shop, asking how I'd ended up owning and running a repurpose store. I explained about losing my radio job and ending up at Gram's to sulk. He laughed when I said sulking got boring pretty quickly.

We didn't talk about Erin's murder or the case against Mac and I was just as pleased that we hadn't. In the back of my mind I was still sorting through what I'd figured out and what came next.

"It's a beautiful night," I said after dinner. "How about a walk along the harbor front?" I thought of Rose, telling me not to worry if I got held up.

"Sounds good," Jackson said. He didn't seem to be in any hurry to end the evening.

The sun was low, and streaks of orange and gold looked like they'd been painted across the sky. There were very few people out enjoying the end of the day. "This really is a beautiful place," he said. "I can see why you like it here."

"I admit I do have my moments in January where I sometimes second-guess myself," I said lightly.

We moved around a couple who had stopped to take a photo of the view across the harbor and a small man with a cane and a straw fedora with a striped hatband bumped into Jackson. Even as I was realizing it was Mr. P., he was excusing himself and moving past us, pretending not to know me. What the heck was he doing prowling around down here? Why wasn't he on his way over to Charlotte's to help me explain to everyone else what he and I had figured out?

I needed to get going. I smiled at Jackson. "How long are you staying?" I asked.

"I have to head back to Boston on Monday." He raised an eyebrow. "Will you have dinner with me again before I go?" Before I could answer he gave me his charming smile. "Or lunch? Or breakfast?"

"I'll have to check my schedule," I said. "I have a lot going on right now."

"You mean with everything that's happened with Mac."

I nodded. "Yes."

"It was good to talk to him," Jackson said. "It wasn't a very long conversation, but still . . ." He let the end of the sentence trail off.

I let the silence settle between us. We were almost at the far end of the walkway along the harbor.

"What's his lawyer like?" Jackson abruptly asked.

"Josh. Josh Evans," I said. "He's a good lawyer and a good guy."

"You know him?"

I turned a bit so I could see his face as we walked. "I've known Josh since we were kids."

"So you trust him?"

I nodded. "I trust him with my life, with Mac's life."

Jackson fingered his beard. "I'm sorry. I know how that must have sounded."

"I know what you mean," I said. We were just about past the area where the windjammers that took people out on day cruises were anchored. There was no one else around.

"Mac is like my brother," he said. "I know I haven't acted like that recently. I care about him. I want him to have the best representation."

"You cared about Leila, too, didn't you?" I said. I put my hands in my pockets because suddenly they were trembling.

He nodded, taking a deep breath and exhaling slowly. "Yes, I did. I still do."

I stopped walking. "So why did you try to kill her?"

Mac stepped out of the shadows then, stopping in

front of Jackson. "Yeah, Jackie," he said. "I'd like to know the same thing."

Jackson was good, I had to give him that. His gaze went from me to Mac. "Teaming up to ambush me," he said. "I can't fault you for that." He cocked his head to one side and studied me. "Let me guess. You read Sherlock Holmes when you were a kid."

He'd been charming me only to find out what we knew. It made me squirm to think I'd almost been taken in by that charm.

"You were in love with Leila," I said, ignoring his comment. I watched Mac from the corner of my eye. He was totally focused on Jackson. "That didn't change when she picked your best friend."

"Maybe—a *long* time ago—I had feelings for Leila, but I was happy when she and Mac got married."

He said the words so smoothly I almost believed him. Almost.

I pulled my hand out of my pocket and held it out. The tiny carved duck lay in the palm of my hand. "You had an affair."

I hated saying the words out loud just as much as I had when I'd told Mac about the affair a few hours earlier.

"This belonged to Leila. You gave it to her. You knew she loved Japanese art. It's an *oshidori*—a mandarin duck—a symbol of fidelity, oddly enough. Your fidelity to her, maybe? It was part of a set. You kept the other one. When you saw those two netsuke come up for auction did you think it was a sign from the universe?"

He didn't answer. Not that I'd really expected him to.

My heart was pounding so hard in my chest the sound seemed to echo in my ears. "Leila kept this as a reminder of what she almost lost because of your affair. But I think you told yourself that somehow she kept it because she loved you, even if she didn't admit it to herself. Then Erin figured it all out. She was coming to show this to Mac and tell him that what happened to Leila wasn't an accident. That it was you."

Something flashed briefly across his face and I knew I was right.

"You slept with my wife," Mac said. Rage flashed in his dark eyes, and pain as well.

"Don't make it sound like something cheap," Jackson said in a voice edged with anger. "She's not that kind of person. We had one perfect night. One, and Leila was consumed with guilt about it because you had her brainwashed. She felt obligated to you."

Mac swallowed hard. The muscles in his neck stood out like thick twists of rope. "She loved me and I loved her," he said.

"I loved her!" Jackson shouted. "We could have had a life together—we would have but you ruined it. You can pretend all you want that she didn't care about me but it doesn't make it true." He all but spit the words at Mac. "Who did she come to when she found out that her company was being investigated by the FTC? Who? Me, not you."

Mac said nothing.

"I told her I would fix it all. I knew people and I could make the whole thing go away. And I gave her that carving to show her that she could always count on me."

Something in his body language, in his words, twigged for me. "You knew what Natalie had been doing," I said.

Jackson's gaze slid sideways. "Natalie and I had gotten . . . close. I figured it out." He turned his attention back to Mac again. "And I was helping her fix things. I could have fixed everything but Leila had been living with you, Mr. Moral High Ground."

It seemed as though I could feel the animosity toward Mac coming off Jackson. One hand clenched and flexed at his side and my stomach rolled as I thought of that large hand clamped over Erin Fellowes's mouth and nose.

I took a breath. I needed to keep Jackson talking. "But Leila was angry that you hadn't told her how Natalie was cutting corners. She wasn't grateful. All she had to do was just let you take care of everything. But she said she was going to talk to Natalie and then she was going to go to the authorities." I was very aware of the fact that it was only the three of us standing there by the water and Jackson Montgomery was a big man.

He pressed his lips together and didn't say anything.

"You went to the house," I continued. "You wanted to talk to her away from the office. You borrowed the spare key from Natalie. All you were going to do was wait inside and talk to Leila when she got home." I was guessing at the last part but a tiny twitch under his left eye told me I'd guessed correctly.

I nodded like I understood and in a way, I did. I understood that Jackson had a very warped idea of what love was. My mom would have said, *Someone worked on him.*

Jackson gave a snort of disgust then. "It was an old, run-down house. Leila deserved better. Natalie told me she was sleeping in a downstairs room because of the work that was being done upstairs."

"You wanted her to see how much she needed you," I said. It was a struggle to keep my voice steady and even. "I get that."

"I didn't want to hurt her," he said.

I nodded. "I know." That much I did believe. "You realized that you could make a small adjustment to a vent pipe and carbon monoxide would seep into Leila's room. Just a bit."

I didn't take my eyes off his face but out of the corner of my eye I could see Mac, his entire body rigid with anger. "Then you could rescue her and she'd see that you were the one she could count on, she'd see just how much she needed you."

"I would never hurt Leila," Jackson said. It wasn't really a denial.

I moved a step closer and laid my hand on his arm, hoping he wouldn't somehow feel how much my legs were shaking. "You didn't get there in time."

He closed his eyes for a moment and swallowed. "I had an accident, just a minor one. Once again, Mac was the hero."

He seemed to have forgotten that Mac was standing right in front of him. I needed to keep the focus on me so he'd keep talking. "How did you know that Erin was onto you?"

"Erin was at my office. She saw my duck. They were a set. She started nosing around. She'd seen the mate in Leila's desk drawer. That's how I know Leila cared about me because she wouldn't have kept it if she hadn't."

It would have been better if Leila hadn't kept the tiny carving, but I didn't think she'd done so because she cared about Jackson. She'd done it because she loved

Mac. Every time she looked at the tiny bird she would have been reminded of what it represented, what she'd put in jeopardy when she slept with Jackson.

He swiped a hand over his mouth.

"When Erin helped Natalie clear out Leila's office she found her duck," I said.

Jackson seemed to need to get things off his chest now. "She wouldn't leave it alone," he said. "She told me she remembered Leila telling her that she was looking for a new lawyer because it was better if friendship and business didn't mix. She said Leila had told her no one, not me and especially not Leila herself, was as perfect as they seemed." He sighed. "She asked me about the birds. I told her I'd given Leila hers for her birthday because she'd liked the one I had in my office."

I dropped my hand, resisting the urge to wipe it on my dress. "She didn't believe you."

"She told Natalie that she was coming to see Mac. I had a pretty good idea why."

When I saw the mate to Leila's bird on Jackson's desk I knew there had been some kind of connection between them. I remembered how he had told me that every man who knew Leila fell a little bit in love with her. Mr. P. had made a phone call to Stevie Carleton, who told us that she'd seen the tiny carved bird in Leila's desk drawer and when she'd asked her cousin about it Leila had explained what it represented and said she kept it to remind herself how lucky she was to have Mac.

From there it wasn't much of a leap to figure out that it was Jackson, not Davis Abbott—or Mac—that Nick had seen arguing with Erin. And when I'd told Mr. P. what Nick had heard Erin say he had quickly pointed out that the reason she'd said Mac's name was likely because she was talking *about* Mac not *to* him.

I remembered the gray car Glenn had seen across the street from McNamara's, that he thought might have followed Erin after she stopped there looking for directions to Second Chance. "You followed Erin," I said.

"She was going to ruin everything," Jackson said. "Do you think I like what she made me do?"

I shook my head because there was no way I could say anything.

"Leila is going to get better, wake up and we'd have a future now that Mac was out of the picture." He looked baffled that I didn't seem to get what he was talking about. "Erin was going to ruin that, so she left me with no choice. I had to kill her. I'm sorry. I'm going to have to kill you, too."

Chapter 20

Mac lunged for his old friend but Jackson grabbed my arm, pulling me in front of his body like a shield.

"Let her go," Mac growled, his voice laced with menace.

"I'm done letting you ruin my life," Jackson said. He was oddly unemotional. One arm held me tight against his body while the other felt for something in his pocket. A gun?

Whatever it was it wasn't there. I flashed to Mr. P. bumping into us earlier. What had he done?

Jackson swore and shifted the arm that was holding me so he could look at his pocket. I turned my head to the side and bit down on his arm. At the same time Mac came at us. Jackson's hand came up and punched the side of my head. Hard. The boardwalk seemed to ripple under my feet. Everything happened so fast after that. It wasn't until later that Mr. P. filled in the details for me.

Jackson caught my shoulder and threw me off the dock into the water. Mac's fist connected with Jackson's chin, sending the lawyer sprawling down onto the boardwalk. Nick came seemingly out of nowhere, sprinting across the wooden decking in just a couple of long strides. He kicked off his shoes and dove in after me, and Michelle and Cal Barnes came running down the boardwalk, guns drawn. It was over.

I came up sputtering, the side of my head throbbing and a high-pitched ringing sound in my ears. Nick was just a few feet away. "You all right?" he called.

"I'm okay," I said, coughing and spitting out water. I kicked my feet out of my cute canvas shoes and let them sink to the bottom of the harbor. Then I swam toward Nick. A police officer helped pull me out of the water and wrapped a gray blanket around my shoulders.

"I think I ruined the mic," I said to Nick, who stood dripping beside me.

He reached over and pushed the wet hair back off my face. "You sure you're all right?" he asked, dark eyes scanning my face.

I started to cough and he made a move toward me. I held up my hand until the coughing jag passed. "I'm fine," I said. "I just swallowed a little water, that's all."

"Don't worry about the mic," he said. "We got what we needed."

"Thank you for jumping in after me," I said, squeezing some of the water out of the ends of my hair. "How did you know I was here?" Before he could speak I answered my own question. "Mr. P."

Nick nodded.

"He picked Jackson's pocket."

Nick rolled his eyes. "Yes. And that wasn't my idea, believe me."

I looked past him to see that Jackson was in handcuffs and Michelle was reading him his rights.

Nick followed my gaze. "I need to talk to Michelle," he said. "You sure you'll be all right for a few minutes?"

I nodded. "I'm fine. Go."

He leaned over and kissed my cheek and walked away.

Mac had been standing a few feet away. Now he came over to me. "I'm sorry," he said.

I shook my head. "No. You don't have anything to be sorry about. But I'm sorry that Jackson . . . that he wasn't . . ." I didn't know how to finish the sentence.

"I should have known."

"Don't do that," I said.

He made a move to touch me and then, maybe thinking better of it, yanked his hand back.

I pulled the blanket a little tighter over my shoulders. "Mr. P. and I talked to Stevie. Leila loved you. She did. I can promise you that." I believed it and I wanted Mac to as well.

"She wasn't the person I thought she was," he said. "And maybe part of that is because I put her up way too high on a pedestal." He was clenching his teeth, the muscles tight along his jaw.

"I have to go see her," he went on. "And I have to talk to her parents. I'm leaving tonight. Michelle said the charges against me will be dropped."

I nodded. My chest hurt all of a sudden. Mr. P. had joined Nick and Michelle but mostly he was watching Mac and me.

Mac looked away for a moment. "I . . . I'm resigning,

Sarah. Please thank everyone for their help and for believing in me."

"Tell them yourself when you come back. Take as much time as you need but I'm not taking your resignation." I swallowed down the lump in my throat, leaned over and kissed his cheek. "We'll all be here when you're ready." I hesitated. "Me included."

I turned then and headed across the weathered wooden walkway. Mr. P. came to meet me. A uniformed officer was leading Jackson away.

"Trixie Belden," I said to Mr. P.

He frowned. "I'm sorry, my dear. I'm not following you."

"I read Trixie Belden when I was a kid. Not Sherlock Holmes. They were my mom's books from when she was young." It suddenly seemed important that I get that out there.

He nodded. "Good to know," he said. He offered his arm and I took it and I didn't look back.

I gave Michelle a brief statement. The microphone I'd been wearing had captured all my conversation with Jackson. I peeled it off my skin and handed it to her. "I'm sorry it got wet," I said.

She smiled. "I'm sorry you did."

Mr. P. and I headed for Charlotte's. "Once again I owe you," I said.

"You owe me nothing, my dear," he said. "I'm just glad you're all right and Mac has been exonerated."

"You called Nick." I shot him a quick glance.

He shook his head. "No. Mac called Nicolas when he figured out why you had gone to meet Mr. Montgomery for dinner. I just tagged along for the ride."

"Where did you learn to pick pockets?" I asked. "Or is that something I'd be happier not knowing?"

I saw him smile from the corner of my eyes. "Did I ever tell you that I spent some time working in a carnival?"

I shook my head, not even trying to hide a smile. "Alfred Peterson, you never cease to amaze me," I said.

We drove in silence for a couple of minutes. "I could teach you," he offered.

"I was beginning to think you weren't going to offer," I said.

"So that's yes?"

"That's yes."

I walked into Charlotte's kitchen still wrapped in the soggy gray blanket, wearing a pair of flip-flops that had been in the backseat of my SUV. Avery was leaning against the counter feeding a bit of cheese to Elvis. Liz, Charlotte and Rose were sitting at the table having tea—with my grandmother. She turned and smiled at me. "Hello, sweetie," she said.

Keep reading for an excerpt from

A WHISKER OF TROUBLE

Available now!

Elvis regarded breakfast with disdain. "Oh, c'mon," I said, leaning my elbows on the countertop. "It's not that bad."

He narrowed his eyes at me and I think he would have raised a skeptical eyebrow if he'd had real eyebrows instead of just whiskers—which he didn't, since he wasn't the King of Rock and Roll or even a person. He was just a small black cat who *thought* he was a person and as such should be treated like royalty.

"We could make a fried peanut butter and banana sandwich," I said. "That was the real Elvis's favorite."

The cat meowed sharply, his way of reminding me that as far as he was concerned he was the real Elvis and peanut butter and banana sandwiches were not his favorite breakfast food.

I looked at the food I'd pulled out of the cupboard: two dry ends of bread, a banana that was more brown than it was yellow and a container of peanut butter that I knew didn't actually have so much as a spoonful left inside, because I'd eaten it all the previous evening, *with* a spoon, while watching *Jeopardy!* with the cat. It wasn't my idea of a great breakfast, either, but there wasn't anything else to eat in the house.

"I forgot to go to the store," I said, feeling somewhat compelled to explain myself to the cat, who continued to stare unblinkingly at me from his perch on a stool at the counter.

Elvis knew that it wouldn't have mattered if I had bought groceries. I couldn't cook. My mother had tried to teach me. So had my brother and my grandmother. My grandmother's friend Rose was the most recent person to take on the challenge of teaching me how to cook. We weren't getting very far. Rose kept having to simplify things for me as she discovered I had very few basic skills.

"How did you pass the Family Living unit in school?" Charlotte, another of Gram's friends, had asked after my last lesson in Rose's small sunny kitchen. Charlotte had been a school principal, so she knew I'd had to take a basic cooking class in middle school. She'd been eyeing my attempt at meat loaf, which I'd just set on an oval stoneware platter and which I'd been pretty sure I'd be able to use as a paving stone out in the garden once the backyard dried up.

I'd wiped my hands on my apron and blown a stray piece of hair off my face. "The school decided to give me a pass, after the second fire."

"Second fire?" Charlotte had said.

"It wasn't my fault." I couldn't help the defensive edge to my voice. "Well, the sprinklers going off wasn't my fault."

"Of course it wasn't, darling girl," Rose had commented, her voice muffled because her head had been in the oven. She was cleaning remnants of exploded potatoes off the inside.

"They weren't calibrated properly," I told Charlotte, feeling the color rise in my cheeks.

"I'm sure they weren't." The corners of her mouth twitched and I could tell she was struggling not to smile.

Tired now of waiting for breakfast, Elvis jumped down from the stool, made his way purposefully across the kitchen and stopped in front of the cupboard where I kept his cat food. He put one paw on the door and turned and looked at me.

I pushed away from the counter and went over to him. I grabbed a can of Tasty Tenders from the cupboard. "Okay, you can have Tasty Tenders and I'll have the peanut butter and banana sandwich." I reached down to stroke the top of his head.

He licked his lips and pushed his head against my hand.

I got Elvis his breakfast and a dish of fresh water. He started eating and I eyed the two dry crusts and brown banana. The cat's food looked better than mine.

I reached for the peanut butter jar, hoping that maybe there was somehow enough stuck to the bottom to at least spread on one of the ends of bread, and there was a knock on my door.

Elvis lifted his head and looked at me. "Mrrr," he said.

"I heard," I said, heading for the living room. It wasn't seven o'clock, but I was pretty sure I knew who it was at the door.

And I was right. Rose was standing there, holding a plate with a bowl upside down like a cover. "Good morning, Sarah," she said. She held out the plate. "I'm afraid my eyes were a little bit bigger than my stomach this morning. Would you be a dear and finish this for me? I hate to waste food." She smiled at me, her gray eyes the picture of guilelessness.

I folded my arms over my chest. "You know, if you don't tell the truth, your nose is going to grow."

Rose lifted one hand and smoothed her index finger across the bridge of her nose. "I have my mother's nose," she said. "Not to sound vain, but it is perfectly proportioned." She paused. "And petite." She offered the plate again.

"You're spoiling me," I said.

"No, I'm not," she retorted. "Spoiling implies that your character has been somehow weakened, and that's not at all true."

I shook my head and took the plate from her. It was still warm. I could smell cinnamon and maybe cheese?

There was no point in ever arguing with Rose. It was like arguing with an alligator. There was no way it was going to end well for you.

"Come in," I said, heading back to the kitchen with my food. I set the plate on the counter and lifted the bowl. Underneath I found a mound of fluffy scrambled eggs, tomatoes that had been fried with onions and some herbs I couldn't identify and a bran muffin studded with raisins. Rose was a big believer in a daily dose of fiber.

It all looked even better than it smelled, and it smelled wonderful.

Rose was leaning forward, talking to Elvis. She was

small but mighty, barely five feet tall in her sensible shoes, with her white hair in an equally sensible short cut.

I bent down and kissed the top of her head as I moved around her to get a knife and fork. "I love you," I said. "Thank you."

"I love you, too, dear," she said. "And thank you for helping me out."

Okay, so we were going to continue with the fiction that Rose had cooked too much food for breakfast. "Could I get you a cup of . . ." I looked around the kitchen. I was out of coffee and tea. And milk. "Water?" I finished.

"No, thank you," Rose said. "I already had my tea."

I speared some egg and a little of the tomatoes and onions with my fork. "Ummm, that's good," I said, putting a hand to my mouth because I was talking around a mouthful of food. Elvis was at my feet looking expectantly up at me. I picked up a tiny bit of the scrambled egg with my fingers and offered it to him.

He took it from me, ate and then cocked his head at Rose and meowed softly.

"You're very welcome, Elvis," she said.

"Why don't my eggs taste like this?" I asked, reaching for the muffin. Scrambled eggs were one of the few things I could make more or less successfully.

"I don't know." Rose looked around my kitchen. Aside from the two crusts of bread, the empty peanut butter jar and the mushy banana on the counter, it was clean and neat. Since I rarely cooked, it never got messy. "How do you cook your eggs?"

I shrugged and broke the muffin in half. "In a bowl in the microwave."

She gave her head a dismissive shake. "You need a cast-iron skillet if you want to make decent eggs." She smiled at me. "Alfred and I will take you shopping this weekend."

I nodded, glad that my mouth was full so I didn't have to commit to a shopping trip with Rose and her gentleman friend Alfred Peterson.

It wasn't that I didn't like Mr. P. I did. When Rose had been evicted from Legacy Place, the seniors' building she derisively referred to as Shady Pines, I let her move into the small apartment at the back of my old Victorian. Mr. P. had generously made a beautiful cat tower for Elvis as a thank-you to me. He was kind and smart and he adored Rose. I didn't even mind—that much—that Alfred had the sort of computer-hacking skills that were usually seen in a George Clooney movie and he was usually using them over my Wi-Fi.

It was just that I knew if I went shopping with the two of them, I was apt to come home with one of every kitchen gadget that could be found in North Harbor, Maine. Rose had made it her mission in life to teach me to cook, no matter how impossible I was starting to think that was. And Mr. P. had already—gently, because he was unfailingly polite—expressed his dismay over the fact that I didn't have a French press in my kitchen.

Rose smiled at me again. "Enjoy your breakfast," she said. "I need to go clean up my kitchen."

"Do you want to drive to the shop with me?" I asked. "Or Mac and I can come and get you when we're ready to head out to Edison Hall's place."

Rose worked part-time for me at my shop, Second Chance. Second Chance was a repurpose shop. It was part antiques store and part thrift shop. We sold furniture, dishes, quilts—many things repurposed from their original use, like the teacups we'd turned into planters and the tub chair that in its previous life had actually been a bathtub.

Our stock came from a lot of different places: flea markets, yard sales, people looking to downsize. I bought fairly regularly from a couple of trash pickers. Several times in the past year that the store had been open, we'd been hired to go through and handle the sale of the contents of someone's home—usually someone who was going from a house to an apartment. This time we were going to clean out the property of Edison Hall. He had died over the winter and clearing out the house had turned out to be too much for his son and his sister.

Calling the old man a pack rat was putting it nicely. Rose and Mac were going with me to get started on the house, along with Elvis, because I'd heard rustling in several of the rooms in the old place and I was certain it wasn't the wind in the eaves.

"Why don't I just come with you?" Rose said. "That will save you having to come back and get me."

"All right," I said, picking up a piece of the muffin and wishing I had coffee. "Does half an hour give you enough time?"

She smiled at me. "It does."

I put down my fork to walk her to the door, but she waved one hand at me. "Eat," she ordered, already heading for the living room. "I can see myself out."

I stuffed the bite of muffin in my mouth and waved over my shoulder as the door closed behind her.

I finished my breakfast, sharing another bite of the scrambled eggs with Elvis. He followed me into the bathroom, washing his face while I brushed my teeth. When we came out of the apartment, Rose was just coming out of hers.

"Perfect timing," she said, bustling over to us, as usual carrying one of her oversize tote bags.

Ever since I'd seen the movie *Mary Poppins*, I'd thought that Rose's bags were like the magical nanny's carpetbag. You just never knew what was going to be inside. This one looked as if it had been made from the same blue-striped canvas as a train engineer's hat.

"I have coffee just in case we're out," Rose said, patting the side of the carryall with one hand.

"Just coffee?" I asked as I picked up the canvas tote at my own feet. Mine was filled with a stack of thrift store sweaters that I'd brought home and felted for my friend Jess.

"And some tea bags." Rose held the door so Elvis could go out first.

I looked at her, raising one eyebrow.

"And a coffee cake." She followed Elvis outside. "Don't make that face, Sarah. We all work better after a cup of tea and a little taste of something."

"If I keep on having a 'little taste of something,' I'm going to turn into a big something," I said, pulling out my keys and pushing the button to unlock the SUV.

"Nonsense," Rose said, making a dismissive gesture with one hand. "All that running you do, you'd be skin and bones if I didn't feed you." She set her bag on the floor of the passenger side of the vehicle and climbed inside. Elvis had already jumped in and settled himself in the middle of the backseat. I set my bag and my brief-case next to him.

"Are those more tablecloths?" Rose asked, half turning in her seat and pointing at the canvas tote.

I slammed the passenger door and slid in behind the wheel. "No. It's a bunch of sweaters I felted for Jess."

Rose's gray eyes lit up. "Is she going to make more slippers?"

I nodded as I stuck the key in the ignition.

Jess was a master at recycling and upcycling clothes. Her latest project was making slippers out of felted wool sweaters. We were going to sell them at Second Chance. She'd made me a red pair of slipper "boots" that I'd worn at the shop most of the winter. So many customers had asked about them that Jess and I had scoured area thrift stores over the weekend looking for sweaters that would felt well. I had done the actual process in my washer and dryer, and Jess was coming by the store to pick up the soft, shrunken sweaters.

"Do you think she'd make a pair for me?" Rose asked. "And for Alfred? They'd be lovely to wear around the apartment."

"I'm sure she would," I said. I concentrated on backing out of the driveway and tried to push away the image of Alfred Peterson, who generally wore his pants up under his armpits, in a pair of bright felted boots halfway up his calves.

Second Chance was in a brick building from the late eighteen hundreds located on Mill Street, where it curved and began to climb uphill. We were about twenty minutes by foot from the downtown, and easily accessed from the highway—the best of both worlds for catching the tourists. We had a decent side parking lot and an old garage, which we were working on turning into work and storage space.

Tourists came to North Harbor during the spring and summer for the beautiful Maine seacoast. In the fall and winter it was the nearby hills with the autumn colors and skiing that drew them in.

I parked close to the back door because we'd need to load some empty boxes and garbage bags in the back of the SUV. I'd already arranged to have a Dumpster for the garbage and a bin for everything that could be recycled delivered to Edison Hall's house.

It looked as though spring was going to be a busy time for us between the influx of tourists eager to get away from the city after a cold winter that had stretched all the way from the Atlantic Canadian provinces down to Virginia, and the work I was planning on the old garage. I wouldn't have said yes to clearing out Edison Hall's house if it hadn't been for my grandmother. She'd known Edison's sister, Stella, since they were, as she put it, captains of opposing Red Rover teams on the playground.

"Please, do this for me," Gram had asked when she called from South Carolina. She and her new husband, John, were working their way back to Maine after almost nine months of an extended honeymoon traveling around the country and working on several housing projects for the charity Home for Good. "I know what I'm asking, believe me. I was in that house a couple of years ago and it could only have gotten worse."

I'd pictured her shaking her head, lips pressed together.

"I'll call Stella," I'd told Gram. I couldn't say no to her, which was why both Rose and Charlotte were working for me. And how bad could Edison Hall's old house really be? I'd reasoned. Very bad, I'd discovered. The man was a pack rat.

I followed Rose and Elvis into the workroom at the back of the store. I could smell coffee. The morning was getting better and better. I set the bag of felted sweaters on the workbench that ran along one wall of the work space and headed into the shop. Mac had just come downstairs. He was carrying a heavy pottery mug and he held it out to me. His title, on paper at least, was store manager, but he was a lot more than that. He was my colleague, a second set of eyes and sometimes the voice of reason I needed to hear. And more and more he was the person I turned to when I needed someone to talk to. It had started the past winter when I was almost killed in my own house. It was Mac I'd called, Mac who I'd shared with how scared I'd really been. Our friendship had only deepened in the following months.

"You read my mind," I said, dropping my briefcase at my feet and taking the cup from him. "Thank you."

As good as Rose's breakfast had been, this was one of those mornings when I needed a nudge of caffeine.

Mac smiled. "You're welcome."

This past winter the building where he had rented an apartment had been sold. So we'd renovated part of the second-floor space above the shop and now Mac had a small self-contained apartment up there and I worried a lot less about security for the store. Not to mention that most mornings the coffee was on when I arrived. It seemed to be working out well for both of us.

Rose and her furry sidekick, Elvis, were disappearing up the steps to the second-floor staff room. I knew she'd be back in a couple of minutes with a slice of coffee cake for both Mac and me.

Mac walked over to the cash desk where he'd set his own coffee mug. He was tall and lean and the long-sleeved gray T-shirt he wore showed off his muscles very nicely. He had light brown skin and kept his black hair cropped close to his scalp.

I took a sip of my coffee and pushed a stray piece of hair back off my face. Usually I wore my brown shoulder-length hair down, but I'd pulled it back into a ponytail, since we were going to be working for most of the day on the old house. "I saw the boxes you left by the back door," I said. "Thank you."

"There's more under the stairs if you think we need them," he said, walking back over to me. He studied my face. "Are you having second thoughts about taking the Hall estate on?"

I shook my head. "No. The numbers are good. We both checked them. We'll make a nice little profit and I think the price is reasonable as far as what Stella Hall will have to pay. The house just makes me a little sad, piled full of . . . well, boxes of junk that no one else wants." I ducked my head over my cup and gave him a sidelong glance. "If I tell you something, do you promise not to laugh?"

His brown eyes met mine. He put a hand over his heart. "I promise."

"The first time we went out to look the place over—when we were trying to decide what to charge Stella—when I got home that night I cleaned out two closets."

Mac smiled. "Just between you and me, I came back here and put two boxes of old parts in the scrap-metal recycling bin."

"And how much did you pick back out the next day?" I teased.

"No comment," he said, taking another sip from his cup.

I laughed.

Mac could fix just about anything. About eighteen months ago he'd left his high-powered job as a financial planner to come to Maine and sail. I had no idea what had prompted him to make such a dramatic change in his life. I'd asked him once and he'd very skillfully evaded the question.

I hadn't asked again.

During the sailing season he spent every spare minute crewing for pretty much anyone who needed an extra set of hands on deck. Wooden boats were Mac's passion. There were generally eight windjammers tied up at the North Harbor dock during the season, along with plenty of other boats, so there were lots of opportunities to get out on the water.

I knew eventually Mac wanted to build his own boat. He worked for me because, he said, he liked the satisfaction of having something tangible to show for his efforts at the end of the day. There wasn't anything he couldn't fix, as far as I'd seen. Second Chance was successful as much from his efforts as from mine.

"It probably wouldn't hurt to take a few extra boxes," I said, walking over to the front window to straighten two quilts that were hanging on a wooden rack. "According to Gram, Edison was a collector of—well, a lot of things. Maybe some of his collections will turn out to be something we can sell here or in the online store."

"We have some of those plastic bins out in the garage," Mac said. "Do you want to take maybe half a dozen?"

I nodded. Rose came down the stairs then, still trailed by Elvis. She handed me a slice of coffee cake on a blue-flowered napkin.

I smiled. "Thank you."

"You're very welcome." She smiled back at me.

Elvis looked up at me and blinked his green eyes.

"No," I said, breaking off a chunk of coffee cake. "Don't think I don't know Rose already fed you a piece."

The cat made a huffy sound and headed for the workroom.

Rose handed a piece of coffee cake to Mac. "I left half of the cake for you upstairs in the blue tin," she said.

"Thank you," he said. "I fixed your iron. It was just a loose connection. It's on the workbench."

Rose clapped her hands together. "Aren't you wonderful?" she exclaimed.

Rose's steam iron was probably as old as I was. It gave off copious amounts of steam, surrounding her in a cloud as if she were standing in a fogbank. And it was as heavy as an anvil. But she liked using it and when it had stopped blasting steam a few days ago, Mac offered to see what he could do. I wasn't surprised he'd been able to fix it.

"I may as well go do those last two lace tablecloths," Rose said. "I can probably get them done before Charlotte gets here."

"Thank you," I said. "I think we'll put the bigger one on that table." I pointed to a long farmhouse kitchen table that sat about three feet from the back wall of the shop. Mac had sanded it for me and I'd whitewashed the top and painted the legs black. It had turned out even better than I'd hoped. With the lace tablecloth and several place settings of vintage china, I knew it would make customers think of happy meals shared with family and friends.

Charlotte arrived about five minutes to nine. Her cheeks were rosy and her white hair was a little mussed.

"Did you walk?" I asked. "I could have picked you up."

"Yes, I did," she said. "It was a lovely morning for a walk." She pushed her glasses up her nose and looked down at me. Even in flats Charlotte was at least an inch taller than I was. She had perfect posture—it seemed she was incapable of slouching. And she still had the steely glare of the high school principal she'd been before she retired.

"I'll just go put my things upstairs and you can head out to Edison's." She hesitated for a moment and then reached out and gave my arm a squeeze. "Thank you for taking this on, Sarah," she said. "I've been in that house." She shook her head. "I know Stella tried to get Edison to keep the place up, but he acted like running a vacuum cleaner around would kill him. The dust bunnies have probably taken over."

"I have Mac and Rose *and* Elvis in case there's anything with more than two legs," I said. "We'll be fine."

"Nicolas is using this against me, you know," she said, pulling the soft cotton scarf from her neck and tucking it into the pocket of her jacket. "He says my garage is in danger of looking like Edison's."

Nicolas Elliot—Nick—was Charlotte's son, a former EMT who now worked as an investigator for the medical examiner's office.

"Did you suggest that maybe he should come and clean it out?" I asked. I'd known Nick since we were kids. In fact, when we were teenagers I'd had a huge crush on him. I'd seen him butt heads with his mother over the years. I'd never seen him win.

Charlotte shrugged. "No. Although I did point out that about ninety percent of the boxes in there belong to him." A smile played at the corners of her mouth. "That was the last I heard about the garage." The almost smile turned into a grin as she started for the stairs. "I'll be right back," she said over her shoulder.

By quarter after nine we were on the road, with Mac riding shotgun and Rose and Elvis in the backseat. I'd been serious when I told Charlotte that I was taking the cat along to deal with anything that had more than two feet. While I believed that all living creatures had the right to life, liberty and the pursuit of the animal equivalent of happiness, I didn't really want most of the four-legged ones sharing my space while they were doing it—Elvis excluded, of course.

Before I'd acquired Elvis, or maybe more accurately, before he'd acquired me, the cat had spent some time living on the streets around the harbor front. I wasn't sure if that was where he'd honed his skill as a rodent wrangler, or if that particular ability came from his previous life, whatever that had been.

Edison Hall's house was a small white bungalow on the outskirts of town. It was usually a short trip over to Beech Hill Road, but a water main had broken on the street a few days earlier. Now it was being repaved, down to one lane for traffic. When it was our turn to go, I tried not to wince as the tires threw bits of pavement up against the undercarriage of the SUV. Elvis sneezed at the sharp smell of tar and when I looked in the rearview mirror he was making a sour face, despite Rose stroking his black fur.

There was a single-car garage at the end of the short driveway at the Hall house. I was happy to see the Dumpster I'd ordered sitting on a patch of gravel to the left of the garage. As I backed in, I caught a glimpse of the smaller recycling bins against the long right wall of the garage, on the old stone patio by the path to the back door, exactly where I'd asked Aaron Ellison to put them.

"Do you want to leave everything here and take another look around, maybe make a plan of attack?" Mac asked as he undid his seat belt.

I nodded. "Remember all those wine bottles that were in the basement?"

"Uh-huh."

"Apparently Ethan moved them up to the kitchen. Stella left me a message saying they were supposed to all be moved out yesterday, but I want to make sure."

I had told Stella that we didn't have the expertise to handle her brother's wine collection. She'd said that Edison's son, Ethan, was planning on hiring someone to put a dollar value on the bottles so they could be sold.

Rose had already picked up Elvis and was getting out of the SUV.

I pulled the keys Ethan had given me out of the pocket of my jeans and climbed out as well.

I noticed the smell the moment we stepped in

the front door. Mac looked at me and frowned. "Rat?" he asked.

I made a face. "Maybe." It wouldn't be the first time we'd shown up at an empty house and found a dead animal. A couple of times it had been mice, once a raccoon and once a seagull that appeared to have fallen down the chimney.

Elvis squirmed in Rose's arms. She looked at me and raised an inquiring eyebrow.

"Let him go," I said. "It's the fastest way to find whatever it is that crawled in here and died."

The cat was already making his way to the kitchen. There seemed to be a path more or less through the stacks of boxes. One thing I could say about Edison Hall: The house wasn't dirty. Charlotte was right about there being dust bunnies everywhere, but there were no bags of garbage, no muddy footprints or bits of spilled food. The place was piled, but I had the same thought I'd had the first time I was in the house with Edison's sister, Stella: The old man had had some kind of system for the boxes that were piled everywhere. The problem was, I had no idea what that system was.

Elvis meowed loudly. I couldn't see him, but from the sound he was in the vicinity of the kitchen.

"I'll go," Mac said.

I shook my head and stuffed the keys back in my pocket. "It's okay. I'll go."

The cat gave another insistent meow. "I'm coming," I called. I made my way in the direction of the kitchen. There was a path through the boxes, although it was a bit like being in a tunnel made of cardboard.

"I'll get the shovel and a couple of garbage bags," Mac said.

The path widened at the kitchen doorway. Elvis had somehow climbed up onto a stack of cartons about shoulder height. He was looking down at the floor, but he turned his head and his focus to me as I reached the doorway.

"Mac, forget about the shovel," I said, raising my voice so he'd be sure to hear me.

"What do you need?" he asked.

I hesitated and after a moment he appeared behind me.

"What do you need?" he asked again.

I moved sideways so he could see that the body lying on the kitchen floor didn't belong to a mouse or a raccoon.

"I think we need nine-one-one," I said.

ABOUT THE AUTHOR

Sofie Ryan is the author of the *New York Times* bestselling Second Chance Cat Mysteries. She also writes the *New York Times* bestselling Magical Cats Mystery series under the name Sofie Kelly.